CW01082674

Love Sport

THE CRICKET CLUB
BOOK 3

MARGAUX THORNE

© Copyright 2024 by Margaux Thorne
Text by Margaux Thorne
Cover by Dar Albert

Dragonblade Publishing, Inc. is an imprint of Kathryn Le Veque Novels, Inc.
P.O. Box 23
Moreno Valley, CA 92556
ceo@dragonbladepublishing.com

Produced in the United States of America

First Edition October 2024
Trade Paperback Edition

Reproduction of any kind except where it pertains to short quotes in relation to advertising or promotion is strictly prohibited.

All Rights Reserved.

The characters and events portrayed in this book are fictitious. Any similarity to real persons, living or dead, is purely coincidental and not intended by the author.

ARE YOU SIGNED UP FOR DRAGONBLADE'S BLOG?

You'll get the latest news and information on exclusive giveaways, exclusive excerpts, coming releases, sales, free books, cover reveals and more.

Check out our complete list of authors, too!

No spam, no junk. That's a promise!

Sign Up Here

www.dragonbladepublishing.com

Dearest Reader;

Thank you for your support of a small press. At Dragonblade Publishing, we strive to bring you the highest quality Historical Romance from some of the best authors in the business. Without your support, there is no 'us', so we sincerely hope you adore these stories and find some new favorite authors along the way.

Happy Reading!

CEO, Dragonblade Publishing

Additional Dragonblade books by Author Margaux Thorne

The Cricket Club Series
A Perfect Match (Book 1)
The Play's the Thing (Book 2)
Love Sport (Book 3)

The Eglinton Knight Series
Knight of the Jaded Heart (Book 1)
Knight of the Broken Heart (Book 2)
Knight of the Wicked Heart (Book 3)
Knight of the Bleeding Heart (Book 4)

Prologue

AS A LITTLE girl, Miss Ruthie Waitrose heard much talk of destiny. It was her father's destiny to be a baron, just as much as it was for him to die falling out of a carriage and smashing his soft head against a paver stone, undeniably drunk.

As such, it was Ruthie's older brother's destiny to inherit the barony at a young age and, naturally, using his father's hedonistic lifestyle as a source guide, continue to run up debts and run it into the ground.

That was when Ruth's mother's gimlet eye finally turned to her. At ten, Ruthie showed no signs of being a great beauty or mind. But she would one day, God willing, become a woman—a blue-blooded one—and her practical mother understood that those types of women were always in demand.

Before sending her off to the nursery one late afternoon, Ruthie's mother declared that she would marry brilliantly. No debate was to be had. It simply must happen for the sake of the family. For the sake of her brother's destiny.

There was that word again. It was then that Ruthie learned that her mother had a plan for her—an ambitious one. But Ruthie didn't have a destiny. Apparently, only men had those. Women had something infinitely more practical.

They had *purpose*.

They served as the social fabric that kept society proper and warm. They were the form and not the function.

Listening to her mother explain this important role before bed was disconcerting, to say the least. And rather disheartening.

Ruthie fashioned her dolls into knights. She'd read *Ivanhoe* and *Rob Roy* more times than she could count. She dreamed of a great love that rivaled her parents' storied romance. Despite the fact that her father had sold all their horses to pay his creditors, in Ruthie's mind, she always galloped, never cantered. Yet her mother was ordering her to amble.

That night, her pillow was soaked through with tears. But in her discomfort, a revelation was born. Desperate times tended to create desperate thoughts. Perhaps a destiny wasn't what Ruthie wanted in life after all. What was so romantic about having one's life planned out before it even began?

That willful thought had felt positively profane...and freeing.

Ruthie was a good girl (as her mother routinely told her). A God-fearing, good girl. And from the crib, she was taught of God's divine plan. Who was she to rebel against that sacrosanct idea?

Well...she was a girl who read too many books. A girl who craved adventure. A girl who didn't desire such an ordinary *purpose*.

Ruthie wanted a chance. A chance to change her fate. A chance to create the life that *she* wanted.

By the time her pillow had dried, Ruthie was asleep in her bed, a tiny smile on her face as she dreamed about all the chances she would take when she grew older and how those little chances might make the biggest differences. She would be fearless and carefree. Like a pirate casting out into uncharted waters, she would throw caution to the wind and see where her fortune and her long legs would carry her.

The world would be her playground. Her imagination and courage would guide her.

Yes, her sleep was blissful that night. And deep.

And mischievous.

Because as sleep tends to do, it worked so well that the next morning Ruthie woke with little memory of those far-off dreams or the positivity they'd conjured, and her confidence faltered. She could only recount her mother's steely strategy along with the uncomfortable pain it had left in her chest.

As yellow light leached into the nursery, it carried with it the haunting realization that brandishing a sword against the giants in her fantasies was one thing, but rebelling against her formidable flesh and blood mother was another. Daytime was not a place for flights of whimsy, nor a welcoming hall for chance.

Which was why from that moment on, Ruthie always looked forward to the night. There she could find belief in herself. Under darkness she could be whoever she wanted. In the shadows, Ruthie could see herself clearly.

In the moon's blue glow, anything was possible. Clouds always flooded the sky. If her future was written in the stars, Ruthie didn't have to see it.

Chapter One

London, England, April 1849

THE MAN HAD a superb arse.

Ordinarily, that thought would have alarmed Harry Holmes.

He chuckled to himself as he focused on the enigmatic figure across the room. Harry wasn't in the custom of admiring the curvy figures of the upper-crust men who lost their fortunes night after night in his little slice of iniquity. But, then again, this peer—this lad with the trim waist and slender neck—wasn't an ordinary customer. Nor was he ne'er-do-well voyeur. This young buck had turned up at the Lucky Fish every night for the past week, and—though he kept his head down, though he kept his voice low, though he never met anyone's eye—he'd managed to catch hold of Harry's full and undiluted attention each and every time. The superb arse was only the half of it. The more pertinent fact was that the man was clearly a woman. And for some ridiculous reason, Harry was the only one who knew it.

"Who the hell is she, Vine?" Harry muttered around the signature cigar clenched between his teeth.

Thomas Vine glanced up from the open ledger in his hands and sighed when he noticed that his boss had not bothered to listen to him as he'd carped on. Shoving his glasses higher on his nose, the factotum followed Harry's sights to the young man standing ramrod straight next to a chum as they played at one of the club's packed card tables.

"Holmes? Harry?" Vine said curtly. He cleared his throat, which, because of his love for the pipe, sounded like broken glass being swept up by a thick broom. "Did you want to have a talk with Spector?"

Harry blinked, eventually tearing his eyes from the long, nubile legs of the young woman that were tastefully hidden behind a pair of badly tailored trousers. The *gentleman* appeared to love the game vingt-en-un. It was all she ever played. Once she found the table, she never left until her night was over. She won more than she lost, but that wasn't much in any case. Harry always made it a point to ask.

Vine's grainy voice scratched at his periphery again. What was he asking? Something about Spector?

Harry rolled the cigar around in his mouth, skimming it lazily along his teeth. Five times. The act was comforting, serving to always bring him back to the matter at hand, which unfortunately meant dealing with his nervous right-hand man's never-ceasing questions. Usually, they didn't bother Harry to this degree. Creating lists, creating order, was what he excelled at. It was one of the few things that helped him relax at the end of a long day. Only now, as he watched his club, the rich degenerates and poor lords mingling together like a busy ant colony, Harry's mind continued to wander. All he wanted was a brandy and a comfortable seat...and an answer to this woman's foolishness.

"Spector?" Harry asked, finally turning to one of the only people he trusted in the entire world. And even then, not much.

Small and thin-boned, Thomas Vine was an unfortunate-looking man with one wandering eye and a circle of dusty hair around his head better suited for a monk. Because there was nothing remotely religious about Thomas Vine. Harry once saw him rip off a man's ear with his bare teeth when the man deigned to cut in front of him in line at the pub. Vine had been thirteen at the time. Harry hadn't been much older, and he learned an important lesson that day—never mistake size for strength. Never get in the way of Thomas Vine and his ale, either.

"Yes, Spector," Vine replied, not hiding his impatience. "There's been some talk. Too much. I hear he's unhappy that Dugan and his men are muscling in on your old territory."

"Dugan's not *muscling in*," Harry answered tersely. "I gave him my blessing. Dugan knows those light-handed days are behind me."

Vine sighed. "Yes, and as we discussed before, Spector and many of your men continue to be confused by this...about-face."

About-face? Harry managed to keep his expression blank, though he did betray his annoyance and sucked hard on his cigar, launching a thick plume of smoke into the air to join the clouds of others that clotted along the scrolling plasterwork on the high ceiling.

There was nothing slapdash about his current business decisions. Going legitimate, leaving his unlawful roots behind, was always the plan. A man couldn't build a future on criminality...Well, Harry could, but he just didn't want to anymore. It was that simple. He was tired of the perfidy, exhausted with always keeping one eye open at night. His gambling den was the most successful in town, and it was one hundred percent clean. That was what made it so successful. The precious dukes and earls searching for entertainment always wanted to believe they were in control, that the house wasn't taking their money, they were losing it fair and square—so Harry created a place that did just that. He wasn't square with those blue-blooded bastards—but he was fair...enough. And in the ten years since he'd opened the Lucky Fish, he'd made more money than God, more money than the queen herself, no doubt. And he'd shared it liberally with all those who had stuck with him from the beginning. The men who'd believed in him during his lying and thieving days. The men who'd slept in alleys and gone hungry all because of his far-flung plans.

And now they were upset with him? Now they were threatening mutiny because Harry no longer had the desire to steal in the dead of night and risk getting his hand chopped off?

What was so damned horrible about sleeping on your stomach in your nice, cozy bed without worrying about getting stabbed in the back?

Harry shouldn't have been confused. He'd seen it before. Some men lived for the chase, the adrenaline of never knowing what could happen from one day to the next. But Harry had too much responsibility, too many men eating at his table. He couldn't afford to be cavalier anymore. He'd turned into a family man without knowing it, with a gaggle of children to feed but no wife to cook the food.

Harry paused, waiting for his anger to subside. "Tell Spector or anyone else that if they're confused, then they can move on."

"Move on?" Vine chirped.

Harry lifted an elegant eyebrow. "Fuck off," he clarified. "If they don't want to make decent money with me, they can make a name on their own...or try their hand with Dugan. He's always looking for good men, since half of them end up dying from one thing or the other. Hazard of the trade."

Vine rubbed his eye. It was the one that could never look a man straight on. The eye that he would stab a man for mentioning. "With all due respect," he said, the words stumbling out of him. "I think we should use a gentler approach. The last thing anyone needs is a disgruntled gang—"

"But you already told me they're disgruntled, so tell them they can fuck off. I'm tired of ungrateful hangers-on. I'm tired of people asking and not giving. I'm tired..." Harry's words trailed off. His focus snapped back to the lovely lady in disguise at the table. The friend she always came with whispered something in her ear, only to lean back and bray at his own joke. The younger women didn't laugh. True to form, she stared studiously at her cards.

"You're tired…?" Vine prompted, waiting for Harry to finish his sentence, but Harry didn't have the heart to tell him that he couldn't. That was the end. He couldn't believe it himself, but Harry Holmes was tired. Of everything. All of it. Though if someone had asked him at the precise second what he was tired of, he wouldn't have been able to explain it. He had everything he could possibly want, and yet he wanted more. That fact didn't surprise him. A man who grew up with an empty belly would always be hungry, no matter how much food you gave him.

But as Harry continued to stare across the crowded room where laughter and tears, smoke and gin, lost dreams and childish greed competed jovially like perfumes in a whorehouse, an answer to his restless spirit almost knocked him to his knees.

Vine tried again. "You're tired…" he repeated.

With a flick of his head, Harry stopped a servant walking by with a tray of champagne and grabbed a flute. He downed it instantly before returning the flute, along with the end of his cigar, to the tray. All the while his gaze never wavered. "I'm tired of not knowing," he finished, surging into the crowd.

Vine's protestations thinned out as Harry escaped from him. Harry didn't worry. Vine would handle the men; he always did. No doubt he was worrying over nothing. Harry paid him an exorbitant amount of money to do so. Nevertheless, in the morning, he would increase the factotum's pay. It was the only reasonable thing to do. It wasn't Vine's fault that Harry had been so…unsettled of late. A transition was taking place. A new normal was being created. It was only natural that growing pains would occur—for Harry as well as the men.

He just had to solve this little mystery first. Then he could work out how to calm the rising tide of his ennui. Females weren't new to his club. Women of the night regularly bumped shoulders with high-class mistresses; however, ladies pretending to be gentlemen was something he didn't see every day.

And at forty-two, Harry had thought he'd seen everything.

A path opened for him. He was grateful, since the thought of touching anyone—however slightly—made every hair on his body stand on end. Harry's club was popular, but that didn't mean he was. Even with his fine clothes and silky manner of speech, he still recognized fear whenever his patrons dared to catch his eye. Which was how Harry preferred it. Whoever had said it was better to be feared than loved was right. From his limited experience on the subject, love didn't make money—it spent it. The men who ventured through his door lost just as much on cards as they did on love. Like all things, it was a gamble. And Harry's gambling days were long over.

Though he did dabble from time to time. When the mood was right. And his curiosity was piqued. And he had nothing to lose because there was nothing to risk.

That was how he separated himself from the men who came to the Lucky Fish.

Hearts were like fortunes—once lost, they were lost forever. Harry Holmes never played with his own money, only other people's. The same went for hearts.

The dealer at the vingt-en-un table noticed Harry before anyone else, his well-trained eyes bobbing up from the deck of cards in his hands. *Arthur.* A ruddy flush crept up to the tips of his cheekbones. He was a good lad, employed at the Lucky Fish for six years now. Nimble with his fingers. Harry had found him as he had most others, on the streets, fleecing old men and women left and right and separating them from their pearls and pocket watches.

A look passed between them. A fleeting glance. A question going back and forth between employer and employee. It happened every blue moon when Harry gave a signal to fix a game, and make sure the right (or wrong) cards were given to the right player. The Lucky Fish *was* a clean gaming hall, but there were times that merited interference. But not tonight. Harry answered with a barely there shake of his head, and Arthur set his attention back on the game.

Harry slid against the high table next to the *gentleman* with the long, shapely legs. She didn't acknowledge him, though Harry knew his appearance had caused a stir. Conversations lowered to a murmur; the air sparked with anticipation.

He waited for the surrounding noise to regather steam before he started his own little game. He leaned close to the woman, smirking as his lungs inflated with distinct notes of orange and rosemary. Normally, Harry couldn't stand perfumes—they made his head pound and his stomach threaten to turn—but this combination was different. Soft and thin, the smell reminded Harry of a woman's silk nightgown, barely there...a wisp of an idea.

Harry closed his eyes, suppressing a groan. It was a weakness in him—one that he kept to himself. Women that smelled clean and fresh like they'd rolled around in the grass, weaving intoxicating flowers in their hair like May Day queens. Women that reminded him of days when everything was exciting and new to him.

"I don't know you," Harry said lightly, canting his body to capture the mysterious lady with his full attention.

She kept her gaze down, swallowing. A thin muscle flexed along the side of her smooth and whisker-free throat. Harry smiled. Was everyone daft or just ignoring the obvious? This close, there was no way the girl could be mistaken for a man, no matter how far down she shoved her hat. She wore a finely starched collar, but there was no Adam's apple bobbing over it.

Harry was no stranger to subterfuge. People attempted to pull the wool over his eyes every day. Membership to his club was by invitation only, meaning everyone in town wanted to be a part of it. However, Harry allowed one sweet reprieve. Any member could bring a guest, and most of Harry's nights were filled with learning who the newcomers were and how best to accommodate their particular vice. But for some strange, bewildering reason, Harry had let this mystery person slide. He'd let his curiosity fester to a gargantuan level. Was he a masochist? Or did he realize that the reveal would inevitably be less intriguing than the riddle? Was he so bored with life that he was creating games for himself? Christ, that was what he had cricket for!

"I asked you a question," Harry said.

She had long, slender fingers, and she held her card close to her chest. Slowly, she lifted it to her chin as her eyes flickered down.

"You didn't ask a question," she returned in a comically deep and scratchy voice. Harry choked back a laugh. He wondered if it hurt her throat to make that wretched sound.

"It was implied," he lobbed back, crowding her with his body without touching her, noticing that they were almost the same height. Men always yearned for short, petite women; Harry couldn't understand it. Her mouth—her lips—matched his perfectly. There would be no crick in his neck when he kissed her.

Harry frowned at the bizarre thought. He couldn't remember the last time he'd kissed a woman. Years. But here he was, quite certain that he would do it tonight, and he wasn't even unsettled by the idea. Why the hell not? He could do it; he didn't have to feel her entire body—only her lips. He just had to steal her away from her friend first. That shouldn't be too difficult. The silly oaf was so enamored by the game that he hadn't even looked at Harry. They couldn't be *together*…Could they?

Harry watched as she rolled her tongue over her front two teeth, her eyes still stuck on her cards. Was that a tell? Hell yes, it was. Harry could spot one a mile away. His little minx had a winning hand. It would be gentlemanly to let her reveal it. But the curtness of her behavior was leaching all the gentlemanliness from him. And besides…Harry Holmes was no gentleman.

The dealer was busy sliding a card to the oaf. The lady was next. Harry couldn't wait that long.

"I want to speak with you. *Now*."

Her fingers tightened around her card, and she hugged it against her heart. Still, she did not look at him, her pointy chin directed down, her body guarded. "After this hand," she answered, her voice somehow ridiculously deeper.

"I think not," Harry said, a shiver of irritation running through him. Clenching his jaw, he reached out and covered her card with his gloved hand, using more force than he'd intended to break it from her grasp.

She gasped, finally raising her face to his.

Blue. Lovely blue eyes. Clear as day. And—*Lord above*—freckles? The sweet, light brown spots dotted her skin like tiny stars. Harry was certain if he stared long enough, he would find patterns to answer all the questions of the universe.

For now, though, he would settle for one.

But his mystery lady beat him to it.

"Who do you think you are?" she spat, ripping herself away from his grasp. He settled his hand on her upper arm, herding her away from the game, never so grateful for the layers of fabric between them. It always made touching others so much more tolerable.

"Why don't *you* answer that question first?"

Fear made the lady turn to stone under his touch, and all the ridiculous affection was lost in her voice as he led her away from the table. "I didn't do anything wrong."

"I didn't say you did."

"Then why won't you let me keep playing?"

"I told you," Harry replied, weaving her through the parting crowd, avoiding the eyes of all the onlookers who were salivating at the notion of him ostensibly throwing a customer out of the club. Usually, he had men perform that honor for him.

He held his prisoner close as they moved into the foyer and her earthy scent knocked him in the chest once more. "I don't know you, and I'm tired of being ignorant," he said through gritted teeth. "So, you either help me with that or you leave."

The lady squared her shoulders, yanking her elbow from his hand. She backed away, maintaining a dignified distance, allowing Harry to once more admire the femininity that she tried so hard to hide. Despite the smattering of freckles, her cheeks were pale and creamy. Harry didn't have to run his fingers along her sharp jaw to know that it would feel as soft as a rose petal, and even more delicate.

That didn't prohibit the willful woman from jutting it toward him now though in abject—*annoying*—defiance. "I'm Charles Waitrose," she said, forgetting or just not caring to answer in her fake voice. "I'm in town visiting my cousin, Sir Reginald Coffer, who is a member here," she added imperiously. "And he suggested we come tonight and have a bit of fun. No harm in that."

Harry squinted. Who the hell did she think she was fooling? A better question was—who the hell did she think she was speaking to? Even now, the chit's wig was sagging precipitously over her right eyebrow. Her top hat was doing its damnedest, but it wouldn't hold for much longer. Her game was over—in more ways than one.

Harry crossed his arms. Throwing a lady out on her arse was not what he had in mind for the night, but hard people always benefited from hard lessons. He was a testament to that.

"All right, then," he said, feigning heavy regret. Before she could dodge him, he struck out quickly, handling her upper arm once more. She struggled, but apparently, *Charles Waitrose* wasn't the bulky, strong type of country gentleman and was simply no match. "Out you go."

She tripped as he dragged her toward the door. "What?" she exclaimed, panic rising quickly and uncontrolled. "You can't. I have to stay. You don't understand."

Harry nodded to his man at the door to get out of the way so he could haul it open himself. They stopped at the threshold; Harry gave the excited woman more than enough time to rethink her answer before he took a step onto the porch. "Oh, I understand, believe me," he replied icily as he led her down the three steps to the footpath. The moon was covered by dusty, fat clouds, and their only audience was a few drunken stragglers stumbling out of the club, despondent that their pockets were much lighter than when they'd entered.

He yanked the hellcat down the footpath, only releasing her once he knew she wasn't going to run back to the door. He put his hands in his pockets like this was just an ordinary occurrence, one that happened so often that it had lost its curious appeal. The lady's eyes blazed at his nonchalant, bored behavior.

"You understand nothing," she rasped. "My brother lost badly here. He *always* loses here." She wrapped her arms around her frame, warding off the cold.

Harry chided himself. He probably should have asked if she'd left an overcoat inside. Before he could rethink his decision, a sliver of yellow snagged his attention. A lock of wheat-colored hair escaped from under the brown wig and landed against the side of her straight nose. The asymmetry made him want to itch.

With a puff of breath, the woman blew the hair off her face, and a sob escaped her lovely throat.

"I need the money," she said softly.

"No, my lady, you need excitement." Pretending she was a man had lost its allure *and* its fun.

The woman seemed to agree. Those cornflower-blue eyes flew back to his, but she didn't bother correcting him.

"No. I need money. And I need it now. And this was my only way of getting it…until you came along."

Harry wasn't sure how to respond to that. He dug into his jacket pocket, taking out a cigar. He lit it and took a few contemplative puffs. "I can't allow nonsense in my club."

She crossed her arms. "Your entire club is nonsense. Do you know what the men do in there? The ridiculous bets they make with one another? Wait—" She clenched her fists at her sides. "*Your* club. You mean…"

Harry smiled broadly around his cigar. "Harry Holmes, at your service. And you, Miss Charles Waitrose, need to go home to your nice, warm bed before I call your father."

"He's dead."

Fuck. "Well, then your mother."

She shrugged. "If you can rouse her at this hour then you're a better man than I."

Harry growled. "You're not a man."

"That's beside the point," she replied with a flippant wave of her hand.

"That's the whole point—"

"I need money and it's in your club. So if you would just kindly forget this entire conversation and step aside?" She began to walk around him, and Harry was so dumbfounded by her bravado that he almost let her go. She was two steps past him before he collected himself and snaked out a hand to her upper arm again, this time without tensing every muscle to do it. Harry couldn't remember ever touching a person this much. That fact alarmed him more than her attitude. "You're going home," he insisted, hauling her into his chest.

Her eyes widened as they focused on his cigar. "You can't make me," she seethed. "However, if you're going to be difficult, then I will find someplace else to win my fortune. I hear there are some good games to be had down by the docks."

Harry's heart jumped, and he yanked the cigar out of his mouth. "You will stay away from there, you hear? The docks are no place for a lady."

The side of her mouth curled slightly. Harry hadn't appreciated her lips enough, more fixated on her freckles and arse and her long, lithe figure, but that little movement, that elfish curl, would, no doubt, haunt him in his dreams tonight. "How do you know I'm a lady?"

Harry's laughter was stilted and pained. So many people had tried to murder him in his eventful life, and this conversation might be the one thing that finally did him in. "Well, you're not a gentleman."

The indentation deepened in her cheek. "But why do you assume I'm a lady?"

Slowly, Harry released her, pleased that she didn't move away. He lifted his hand to her face, pausing for a daunting second before placing the tips of his gloved fingers along the sloping line of her jaw. How was he doing this? Why was his body not revolting in terror? He shook his head wistfully, his rampant thoughts choking his mind so thickly, all he could do was let them out. "Ordinary women don't feel like this."

Her eyelashes fluttered at his husky tone. Harry should have been ashamed of his behavior. He was like a lovestruck lad enamored with the first woman who gave him a smidge of attention, but he couldn't bring himself to dwell on the embarrassment…not when she looked at him like that, like he was a normal man doing normal things to woo a woman in the middle of the night.

"I'm young," she replied. "All young women have skin like this."

"And you think I'm too old to remember that?" Harry chuckled.

She blushed prettily. "I didn't say that. And you're not old."

"Older than you. Old enough to know a lady when I feel one."

"So, you've felt many ladies?"

"Enough," he grunted. But that was a lie. A very large one.

Her expression clouded, though she kept her tone light. "And if I tell you that I'm a lady, will you let me back in your club?"

Harry smiled. "Nice try, but no. How much is your brother in the hole for?"

"The hole?"

"Debt."

She nodded. "More than I care to say."

Yes. That sounded about right. "You should let him fix his own problems."

The lady shrugged his fingers from her face. The world had inserted itself back in their conversation. "I would do that, but my brother has a fondness for gambling, it seems. Only, he's not very good at it."

Harry's fingers still tingled as they fell to his side. He replaced his cigar in his mouth, feeling more like himself again, allowing the smoke to choke away her feminine smell. "And you thought that you would save the family farm, huh? With a little vingt-en-un? Tell me something, Miss Charles. I've seen you here every night this week and haven't heard of any great success...Are *you* any good at gambling?"

She backed up another foot, her lips losing all trace of a smile, screwing up in distaste. "I'm learning. Besides, how hard can it be?"

"Hard."

Her eyes rolled so dramatically, Harry thought they would roll right off her perturbed face. "It's just cards."

"Just cards?" he scoffed. Harry spun the cigar around in his mouth, not stopping until he reached five rotations. "If you believe that, then you are destined to be as bad at it as your brother—"

"Charlie! Oh—" Behind them, a shrill voice stopped short at the entrance. Harry turned to find the lady's pudgy cousin standing outside the door. Even with the paltry street lights, Harry could make out the man's sweaty, ruddy complexion. He had the look that Harry saw night in and night out. Winning and losing money in quick succession presented like a rash on these young men. Their faces were always red and sickly when they eventually left the club.

Sir Reginald Coffer locked his hands behind his back, his eyes darting nervously to Harry. "Charlie! Where have you been? I'm in desperate need of your good luck." He cleared the panic from his throat. "Hello, Mr. Holmes. We haven't formally met, but I'm—"

Harry threw up his hand. "I know who you are, Sir Coffer. And I just met your charming"—he fixed a wry smile on the woman—"cousin. And now, it's time for both of you to leave."

Coffer's mouth drooped. "Leave?" he squeaked.

The woman stepped forward. "No worries, cousin. We're going to the docks."

"You're going home," Harry growled. "Don't make me drag you there, because I will. If you don't think I will find out the location, you sadly underestimate me."

She rounded on him. "And if you think I'm going to let you stop me from saving my family, then you sadly underestimate *me*."

"Um…cousin," Coffer said. "Perhaps we should listen to the man—"

"Stay out of this, Reggie."

"Come get your cousin, *Reggie*," Harry said, holding the woman's death stare. His anger and exasperation had dug themselves so deep that he had lost his bearings on what was going on around them. More people swept past, coming and going to the club, but he paid them no mind. This woman—this infuriating woman, this *Charlie Waitrose*—was going toe to toe with him, and she was barely out of the nursery. Her youth was the only answer to this madness. Only the incredibly young were foolish enough to believe they could do what they wanted—that they could bend the world to their whim. Well, Harry was one of the best to ever do it, and even he had his limitations. So fucking many of them.

That was why he didn't pay attention to the lone man stumbling down the street. That was why he didn't register that although the man was acting like he was drunk, he didn't have the telltale stink of alcohol on him. That was why Harry's instincts didn't kick in until it was too late, when the gun was already in the air and pointed right at him.

The last thing Harry Holmes remembered was Ruthie's mouth. It had opened into a giant circle, so perfectly round, to unleash a mighty scream. But he didn't hear it.

The gun went off, and the earth crumbled under his feet. His head hit the pavement. Later he would be grateful that it wasn't a knife. Harry detested being stabbed. All the touching…all the tousling…It was such a disgusting, intimate thing.

Chapter Two

BLOOD. SO MUCH blood. Over him. Over *her*.

Everything was happening…moving…throwing Ruthie off her axis. Reggie was shrieking as he scrambled to her. But Ruthie couldn't hear anything. It was as if the world had shut off all sound, knowing that there was only so much she could take.

Her mind and her hands were full.

Because after the gun had fired, Mr. Holmes had collapsed into her, dragging her to the ground.

Ruthie landed hard on her behind, tensing just enough to keep her head from banging onto the ground. Mr. Holmes had no such luck. Her body clumsily caught his, but his head knocked on the pavement, gruesomely bouncing up from the hard ground like a child's ball. He was dead. He had to be. The man's life was lazily draining out in puddles on top of her like red ink spilling out of its pot.

Someone tugged at her arm, attempting to lift her to her feet; however, Ruthie was as lifeless as the man draped over her. All her energy, all her senses, focused on Mr. Holmes as she cradled his head in her hands, smoothing the jet-black hair off his high forehead. How peaceful he looked, she thought whimsically. *How…lovely.* She'd never seen a dead body before—not even her father's. If this was death, was it truly something to be feared?

"What the bloody fuck!"

The dead man was alive.

Ruthie jolted back to reality as Mr. Holmes's arms flailed out into the night air, eliciting another strangle of colorful curses and a harsh intake of breath.

The unsavory man jostled in her arms, but Ruthie's hold was strong, not allowing him to escape.

Someone was back to tugging. "Ruthie! Let him go, love. Let him go!"

Ruthie shook her head, feeling a moment of clarity shake through her bones. Her mind opened enough to allow the outer world to swarm back in, and she realized that she was not alone with Mr. Holmes. Far from it. Raising her head, she found a crowd beginning to seep out of the club and swarm around her. Reggie positioned himself above her, shielding her from the majority of the madness, though nothing could keep one gentleman away.

With an agility that belied his silver hair and rough-hewn face, the man dropped to his knees at Mr. Holmes's side, covering the wound with both palms.

The older man's countenance betrayed nothing. His breathing remained mild and even as he took in the bloody damage. "What did you get yourself into this time, Harry?" he asked under his breath. He twisted away from the body, snapping his crimson fingers at a couple of boys that looked like they should have been tucked away in a nursery at this time of night. "Go get Dr. Cameron," he yelled, leaving no room for questions or arguments. At once, the boys hurried down the street.

Mr. Holmes's head grew heavier in Ruthie's hands, drawing her attention back to the man in her lap. His sigh was laced with pain and...resignation? "Don't bother, Ernest," he replied lazily, even while his chest rose and fell quicker, his breathing more labored. Ruthie had never been shot before, but she understood pain, and this man was in an excruciating amount of it.

"Miss..." Ernest coughed, staring at the top of her head. Her wig! It must have flown off when she hit the ground. "I apologize…my lord? May I?" He leaned closer, slowly wedging his hands in between Mr. Holmes's body and her lap. "He doesn't like to be touched."

Ruthie's mind was still working at half pace. She hadn't the faintest clue what this *Ernest* was doing. What did he mean that Mr. Holmes didn't like to be touched? Who didn't like to be touched? And why was he trying to take Mr. Holmes away from her? She had him. He was safe in her arms.

Mr. Holmes seemed to agree with her, because even with his depleting strength, he resisted the older man's intentions. "You're the only one trying to touch me, dammit. And I said stop. You're my butler, not a miracle worker," he muttered, slapping Ernest's hands away. "This is the end. I knew it. *She* knew it. She…she fucking told me." His words dropped suddenly like they'd been thrown off a cliff. Ruthie had to lean over the poor man to hear them out.

"I…I didn't say anything," she stammered, throwing beseeching eyes to the butler. She shook her head frantically as the words tumbled out. Suddenly, everything that had just happened hit her like a brick to the chest. A sob choked her throat. "I never said he was going to die. I didn't tell him that. I wouldn't. I *thought* he was going to die. Actually, I thought he was already dead, but I didn't…I didn't…"

The butler patted her arm. "Shh…shh, lass. You did nothing wrong. He wasn't talking about you."

The dam broke and tears fell quick and fast down Ruthie's face. "Then…What…I don't understand…"

The butler's smile was kind as he, again, tried to wedge his hands under Mr. Holmes's heavy body. "I'll tell you when we get him inside. He's out of his mind right now, and losing a lot of blood. Do you see that?" Ernest's words were slow and measured, as if he were speaking to a child—but they worked.

Ruthie blinked away her tears and stared at the picture the butler was trying to show her. The pool of Mr. Holmes's blood was growing larger by the second. What had she been thinking? He wasn't safe in her hands. She would be the death of him if something wasn't done soon.

She inhaled deeply, and the thick, cloying smell of the blood curdled her stomach. "Yes...yes," she said, raising her head to find her cousin. Poor Reggie appeared as tragic as Mr. Holmes. His face was as green as the grass in Hyde Park after an afternoon rain shower. "Reggie...I can't get out from underneath. Help me, please."

Ruthie reached out her arm, but Mr. Holmes smacked it back down with a painful groan. Why did the man continue to move when it hurt him so much?

"I said no," he muttered through clenched teeth. His eyes were closed now, his jaw willfully set. "If I'm going to die...I'm going to die right here...just like she...just like she told me I would. Cold and alone. Like I deserve. I'm ready to meet my maker."

Good Lord! And men said women were maudlin.

The butler rolled his eyes, thwarted once again, and sat back on his ankles. He ran a hand over his face, which was quickly losing its composure. His studied veneer was cracking, and Ruthie could finally see the worry. Luckily, she remembered that she was quite adept at dealing with maudlin, overly dramatic people.

"But you're not alone, Mr. Holmes," she stated reasonably. Her words didn't prod his eyes back open, although she noticed his pale lips twitch. "You're surrounded by people and creating quite a spectacle, actually. So why don't you let us get you inside? We'll put you in your bed, and if you want us to leave you alone then, we will so you can die in peace. We won't even throw a cover over you, so you can meet your maker as cold and miserable as you like."

Ruthie could feel his resistance thaw. She nodded to the butler. This time when Ernest wedged his hands under Mr. Holmes's body, there was no struggle.

"Help me get him up, sir," Ernest said over his shoulder. Reggie jumped into action, sliding into place on Mr. Holmes's other side. He held his mouth in a stiff line and looked close to losing all his dinner, but he managed to do as the butler asked, and together they lifted Holmes off Ruthie and carried him to the club entrance.

A freezing chill whipped over her as she was freed. The wet blood had soaked through her clothes so deeply it felt like it had leached into her bones. It was sloppy and cumbersome, but she dragged herself to her feet. Loneliness and a vague, uncomfortable, bereft feeling overwhelmed Ruthie as she was left behind. She'd done her job; her part was over in this odd, gruesome play. Reggie would come back for her soon, and they would leave. It was as simple as that. It felt like hours since the shooting, but it had only been minutes. She still had time. She would bathe and change her clothing at Freddie's townhouse then slip back into her home before her mother woke. It would be like this never happened. The event would fade into a dream, and one day, when she was old and safe, she would wonder if it had ever happened.

Ruthie was abandoned by the crowd who followed Mr. Holmes back toward the gaming hall, all interest in her forgotten. The night was young for them as well. There was still more gambling and debauchery to be had. This was London, after all. If there was any interest in her botched disguise, it was long gone. Her secret was safe.

But why did it feel like her heart was breaking? Why did it feel like something was dying inside of her? Like she was somehow…incomplete?

A murmur of commotion caught her attention. The crowd had stopped moving. Tall enough to see over it, Ruthie noticed Ernest duck his head to Mr. Holmes.

The butler motioned for her to come to them, and something indescribable—unmistakable—leapt in her stomach. The swarm of people divided, allowing Ruthie easy passage, and she was back to Mr. Holmes in seconds. His eyes remained closed, and his pallor was dangerously gray.

Ernest's mouth twisted in annoyance. "He won't go in without you," he said pitifully.

Without saying anything, Mr. Holmes lifted his hand slowly off his chest. It waited in the air.

For her. To take.

Ruthie didn't waste any time. It was too precious. She clasped his hand. He flinched at her touch but didn't pull away. A sheen of sweat hung at the top of his forehead, and his skin appeared clammy and waxy, but his hand was warm and sure inside hers.

Ernest shrugged. "It seems like he doesn't want to die alone after all."

MR. HOLMES DIDN'T want to die cold, either.

After making it up three flights of stairs and countless dark, forbidding corridors, the unlikely trio eventually situated the man in his room on the biggest bed Ruthie had ever seen. It took monumental maneuvering, but with the help of Mr. Holmes's blue silk sheets, they managed to slide him to the center of the mattress and cover his shivering frame without adding to his distress. Not that he would have cried out. Mr. Holmes had mercifully passed out as they were climbing past the second floor.

"Jesus," Reggie remarked in a hushed tone, stepping away from the bed to admire the curious splendor surrounding them. "Would you look at this place?"

Only then did Ruthie allow herself to gawk at the most unusual room she'd ever stepped into. The space was fastidiously clean and organized—but she couldn't begin to understand the items Mr. Holmes surrounded himself with. Most of them should have been in a vault somewhere, or in a pirate's treasure chest deep in the ocean. For instance, who needed ten ancient-looking swords lined up like sentries along the wall? And why were tiaras stacked like a pyramid on top of a massive bureau?

She scrunched her nose. "It's a bit eccentric…and cold."

Reggie chuckled. With a quick look at the sleeping patient, he wandered over to the bureau, skimming a finger lightly over a tiara that held so many emeralds that Ruthie figured she'd need both hands to lift it.

Reggie whistled. "This could keep anyone warm at night. But…it can't possibly be real…Could it?"

Ernest huffed from the bed, prodding at his master's clothing, unbuttoning and rearranging as much as he could in an effort to make the ailing man as comfortable as possible. "Of course they're real. Everything Mr. Holmes owns is real."

Reggie's brow reached up to his thinning hairline, and he shared a pointed look with Ruthie. "One of these would solve your problem easily enough…"

"Reggie!" she exclaimed. "We're not thieves!"

"Don't even think about it," Ernest snapped. "I took you for a gentleman. I must have been mistaken."

Reggie shrugged, giving the tiara one more hangdog glance before reluctantly meandering back to the bed. "I am a gentleman, just a decidedly light-in-the-pocket one. But aren't we all?" His laughter was brittle. "Oh, come now. It was just a joke…I think." He shoved his hands in his pockets, frowning at the invalid. "It's not like he'd know, anyway. Besides, what are the odds that he'll make it? Not good, I'd wager."

A thin cough sounded from the bed. "And that's why you're shit at cards, and you'll always be shit at cards," Mr. Holmes rasped. "You don't know anything about odds, and you never will."

Ruthie was so relieved he was still alive that she frowned. She hurried to Mr. Holmes's side, hands on her hips. "Stop doing that!" she ordered him.

Slowly, his gaze lifted to hers. Even at death's door, his eyes were green and striking, maybe even more so because of it. "Do what?"

Taken aback by the gentleness in his voice, Ruthie had to fight to remember just what had made her so incensed in the first place. She bit her bottom lip, thankful her mother wasn't here to scold her for it. "Pretending to be asleep and listening to our conversations!"

Mr. Holmes stretched against the sheets, wincing at what the small action cost him. "I wasn't pretending. I *was* asleep, and planned to stay that way until I heard your cousin's asinine comments. Usually, it's customary to wait until a person's dead before looting his belongings."

Ruthie's gaze dropped to the floor, embarrassment flooding her cheeks. "We had no intention of looting. He was only playing."

Mr. Holmes answered her with a wry expression. "Sure he was," he said, closing his eyes again. The man had lovely eyelashes. Dark as night, sooty and full, just like his hair.

For goodness' sakes, Ruthie! Contain yourself. Now is not the time!

"We really should be going," she said.

Reggie nodded, casting one last wistful look at the tiaras. "Yes. We'll be off now," he added as if this had all been a lark, a friendly carriage ride in the country. "I trust you have this handled—"

A banging knock on the door cut him off. Ernest ran to it, throwing it open with little grace. The action pawed at Ruthie's conscience. The butler wouldn't behave that way if he wasn't worried. She didn't want to watch a man die, but leaving him during his last moments seemed wrong for so many reasons.

Reggie came to her side; however, she couldn't budge when he attempted to steer her toward the door, past the boys she recognized from the street earlier.

"He's here! We found Dr. Cameron, just like you told us to!" they cried, speaking over one another. Red-cheeked and out of breath, the boys reminded her of two dogs who'd just performed tricks for their owner, proud and hungry for praise.

But it wouldn't be forthcoming, not with Dr. Cameron stealing the show. He stumbled in after them, almost tripping twice until he found his footing before Ernest. He had a curly mop of hair and a nose as red as a ripe cherry, and smelled like he'd taken a bath in a vat of wine and something else Ruthie couldn't quite place.

Mr. Holmes sneered. "For fuck's sake, he smells like he's spent the last week drinking at a whorehouse!"

Yes. That. Mr. Holmes had hit the nail right on the head, Ruthie concluded.

The taller boy nodded eagerly. "You're exactly right, Mr. Holmes. Found him at Old Sarah's. She was only too happy for us to take him…Said he'd been there for long enough."

Ernest lifted his nose. "What's long enough? A month?"

"Oh, stop with the bloody nonsense," the doctor exclaimed. With righteous indignation, he punched his fists into his hips; however, the effect was lost when they kept slipping off. Not only did the man smell horrendous, but he looked like he'd been dipped in grease. What went on at Old Sarah's, Ruthie wondered? "I'm the best damn doctor in this blasted city," he continued, speaking slowly to prevent slurring. "Do you want my help, or do you plan on ridiculing me all night while you bleed out?"

Mr. Holmes's lips screwed up to the side. He was in between a rock and a hard place, and yet he was too stubborn to admit it.

"Yes please, doctor," Ruthie said, stepping away from Reggie. She returned to the bed, motioning to Mr. Holmes's stomach. "It was a gunshot. Here, you see. It struck him in the side. Can you do anything?"

"Will you get this fool out of here?" Mr. Holmes yelled, folding his arms across his chest. He sucked in a breath to combat the pain. The man was determined to cut off his nose to spite his face. "I'm going to die, and if that degenerate comes any closer, I might be sick. Just let me go peacefully and clean, without the smell of liquor and whores in my lungs."

"Some might consider that the perfect way to go," Reggie

piped in.

Ruthie covered her face with her palms. "That's not helping."

Dr. Cameron stumbled to the bed, flicking his head at Ernest. "Help me roll him to his side. I need to see the wound more closely."

Mr. Holmes scoffed. "You couldn't see a cannon in your face right now."

"But I bet I could see a dead man…which you will be if you keep this up," the doctor shot back, leaning over the bed as Ernest worked on doing as he asked.

She was so engrossed in the doctor's inspection, Ruthie didn't notice Reggie creep up behind her. "We need to go, now," he said firmly, tickling her ears with his furtive whisper. Ruthie swatted him away. His voice was heavy with warning, which told Ruthie everything. Reggie wasn't exactly known for his pragmatism, which was why she'd enlisted his help to begin with. But it seemed like even her cousin had a line he wouldn't step over…namely incurring her mother's wrath.

"I want to watch this," she said.

"Ruthieee," he whined. "They don't need you anymore. You're covered in blood. *I'm* covered in blood. We have to go. *Now.*"

Ruthie's brow wrinkled as she strained to hear Dr. Cameron. With Reggie's harping she could barely make out what the doctor was saying, something about the bullet going through. She definitely heard the word *clean*. That was positive, wasn't it? Unless the doctor was talking about cleanliness being next to godliness, and in that case, was he talking about washing the body before Mr. Holmes met his maker?

Why couldn't she leave? Ruthie had never considered herself a voyeur, but it wasn't like she'd ever had a chance to be. Her mother held too much control over her life to allow that.

Ruthie didn't notice until it was too late that Reggie was dragging her toward the door. On impulse, she grabbed at the handle, but her cousin caught her hand. "No," he said. "This has gone on long enough." Reggie leveled her with a weighted look that clogged her protestations in her throat. "The man is going to die, my dear," he went on. "It doesn't matter what the doctor does. You can't do anything either. But I can. I can get you away, safe in your home so you don't have to see it. Now, let's go."

"Um…sorry…Not so fast, if you please."

Ruthie twirled around to find Ernest, Dr. Cameron, and Mr. Holmes focused on her.

"No," Reggie said with greater conviction. He moved to block her from their sight, which didn't do much, since the top of his head only came up to her chin. "I'm taking her home. We've done our Good Samaritan bit. We can do no more."

"But we think you can," Ernest said.

Reggie lifted his arms at his sides. "There's nothing more I can offer."

"Not you." Mr. Holmes scowled. "Her."

"Me?" Ruthie squeaked, sidestepping her cousin.

Mr. Holmes nodded. "I need a woman," he said.

Dr. Cameron looked thoroughly confused. "There's no woman here. What the hell is he talking about?"

Ruthie ignored him. "There are plenty of women downstairs."

"They're not exactly the sewing types," Ernest interjected.

"Sewing?" Ruthie shook her head. "You want me to *sew*?"

"I said I could do it," Dr. Cameron muttered.

Mr. Holmes coughed himself into a fit. "You drunken, lecherous fool. With where your hands have been, I wouldn't let you sow seeds."

The poor doctor cowered away from the bed, folding into himself. "Honestly, Harry. There's no need for such vicious name-calling."

Ernest came back to her. "So will you do it?"

Ruthie couldn't hold a thought in her head. "Do what?"

"Sew the wound," he explained. "If he makes it through the night, the good doctor says he has a chance. We assume you can sew a straight line."

"Yes…I suppose I can."

Ernest slapped his hands together. "Then it's settled. I'll get everything you'll need."

All at once, everyone scurried around her like mice. Reggie paced the room, ripping his hands through what was left of his hair; the doctor retreated to a corner where he opened his black bag and took out a flask; Ernest flew to the door and screamed out for someone named Jessica.

Only Ruthie and Mr. Holmes remained motionless, each regarding the other curiously, comically, as if this were all a show performed for their benefit.

When she couldn't take it anymore, when it felt like she would jump out of her skin under his frank perusal, Ruthie blurted the first thing that came to mind.

"I thought you were ready to die."

A smile formed on Mr. Holmes' face. For the first time since the gunshot, Ruthie didn't detect an ounce of his pain. "I remembered that I'm much too busy to die."

"Can death be dictated to so easily?"

His smile broadened. "By me? You bet your arse it can."

Chapter Three

"OUCH. BLOODY HELL, woman!"

Ruthie jerked her hand away from the ragged gash, the needle trembling furiously in her fingers. "I'm so, so, sorry, Mr. Holmes!"

Mr. Holmes's head plopped onto the pillow. His breath was ragged and shallow, as if he were in the middle of a never-ending race. It certainly felt like that to Ruthie. She'd only been stitching half an hour, but the process seemed interminable. After cleaning the wound, the doctor had left her to it with very little direction. *Keep it straight* was all he'd told her. *Keep it straight!* From the man who couldn't walk a line if his life depended on it?

And how was Ruthie supposed to keep it straight when Mr. Holmes shuddered and jerked at the mere touch of the needle on his flesh? She'd hoped he would pass out again and leave her to her business, but that had been wishful thinking. The dastardly man was bright-eyed and cognizant.

It was beyond annoying. *And* unhelpful.

"Stop apologizing," Mr. Holmes grumbled toward the ceiling. "And stop calling me Mr. Holmes. You're stitching my skin; I think that allows using my Christian name, don't you?"

"I don't know," Ruthie said. "I suppose it does." She had never called a man who wasn't related to her by his first name before. The intimacy sent odd tremors up her spine. And she'd certainly never sat alone in a room with one. It was positively foreign and exotic, like traveling to Paris...which she'd never done. She bet that Parisian women were always doing things like this.

She stuck the needle into him again, once more amazed that performing this gruesome action wasn't making her dinner come up like it had Reggie's. The first moment she'd pierced Mr. Holmes—Harry—Reggie had bolted from the room, leaving disgusting noises in his wake. Still, she had to give her cousin credit. He'd refused to leave her. Instead, he'd taken up Ernest's offer and was playing downstairs with "house money," whatever that meant.

The doctor had also refused to retire entirely, wanting to be close in case the patient took a turn for the worse in the night. Harry wouldn't allow him to sleep on the couch against the wall...something about syphilis, whatever that was. So the doctor was currently passed out on the floor next to the door. Ernest had had the benevolence to shove a pillow under his sweaty head, though he'd had to promise Harry that he would burn it later.

"Now it's your turn."

Ruthie narrowed her eyes on her line, making her stitches small and neat. It was a shame her mother would never know about this night, because she'd be so proud of Ruthie's steady hand! "My turn?"

"To give me your name. Ow. Fuck!"

Ruthie cringed. "Sorry! That just...surprised me, that's all."

Harry's exhausted expression morphed into curiosity. "Why? We've already deduced you're not truly Charles Waitrose. So, what is it? Charlotte?" He squinted playfully. "No, you don't strike me as a Charlotte. Maybe Annabelle?"

Ruthie smirked, shaking her head.

"Beatrice?"

"Ugh, yuck." She stuck out of her tongue.

Harry clutched his chest. "Ow, fuck. Don't make me laugh."

"Oh, sorry!"

"Fuck, stop apologizing—"

"Ruth," she answered, swiftly cutting him off, afraid that he would utter another foul word. "Or Ruthie, as my friends call me."

The lines bracketing Harry's mouth softened. His voice turned equally as gentle. "Ah, Ruth. The symbol of loyalty and devotion."

Ruthie returned to her task, focusing on her stitches. Staring at him when he had that look on his face didn't seem like the best idea. Feelings bubbled up inside her, ones she didn't realize she had. "You know the Bible?" she scoffed.

"Don't sound so surprised. My mother was Irish. I was raised on the Bible, force-fed it along with my stirabout."

"You don't sound Irish."

A wicked grin formed on his face. "Are you hintin' you want some brogue, lass? Oh, weel, I can be accomodatin' when I need to be," he replied in a mellifluous wave of sound that instantly reminded Ruthie of music. The fluttering was back in her chest. The doctor was going to be so disappointed in her. There was no hope that this scar was going to be straight.

She placed her left hand on the side of his injury, steadying his skin as she tried another stitch. Harry still wore his shirt, but from the small patches of body Ruthie could see, he was pale and marble-like, the kind of creamy white that women in her social group would spend a fortune to achieve. His muscles twitched and rolled under her fingertips, making what she was doing all the more confusing. Harry Holmes couldn't be at death's door. He felt warm. He felt like life. And the more he spoke so casually to her—not *at* her, as she was so accustomed to—the more inconsequential his wound appeared, almost retreating right before her eyes.

"Why don't you always speak like that?" Ruthie cleared her throat, worrying that the deep hunger she heard was obvious to him. "With the accent, I mean."

"Ahh, well…Irish accents aren't good for business, lass. Tough but true. I threw that accent into the ocean the moment my mother dragged me on to the boat bound for this cursed country."

"So, you miss it, then? Ireland?" Ruthie asked. She caught him staring wistfully at the wall behind her, as if memories were playing out in front of him.

"Only in my dreams, when I can't help it."

Ruthie snorted before letting out a long, blustery breath. Just a few more stitches and she'd be done. Thank the dear Lord. She actually believed she'd done slightly more good than bad. With a terrifying—exhilarating—night like this, she honestly couldn't ask for more.

"Aren't you the man that said he could delay death? It seems odd that you can't battle dreams the same way. Bend them to your indomitable will."

"Point to you," Harry said thoughtfully, grimacing through a stiff chuckle. "But I've always thought of death as an adversary, you see, someone fighting *against* me, trying to take something from me. I grew up with nothing—less than nothing—and when that's ingrained in you, you learn to defend yourself rather quickly. But dreams"—he placed a hand on his forehead, holding it there for long seconds as he formulated his words—"dreams are a part of you. You can't fight anyone but yourself." He dropped his hand and gifted her with a tired, rakish grin. "And I'm the toughest bastard I know."

Ruthie returned the smile, finishing up her last stitch. She tied the thread and cut off the end with a decisive snap of the scissors that Dr. Cameron had left for her. "I think you might be right."

"Damn right I am."

Harry Holmes might be missing blood, but he hadn't dropped an ounce of ego this night. "Looks like my work is done here." Ruthie stood up from her knees and wiped her bloody hands on the front of her trousers. "I…suppose I should wake up the doctor and go find Reggie. I need to get home before my mother finds out I'm gone."

The smile stalled on his face. "Yes, Ruth, the decent and no-ble daughter, must never upset her mother."

"You don't know the half of it, Mr. Holmes."

Ruthie started to back away, but Harry's arm snapped out and caught her wrist, bringing her back to her knees.

"Mr. Holmes—!"

His eyes burned the words to a halt. They seared into her, shining into her soul with the unyielding force of a miracle come to life. His color was high, his hold strong. Sweat continued to pool on his forehead and above his lip. Ruthie was reminded of a trapped animal, in a corner and determined to claw and scratch his way out, no matter the consequences.

But she also saw fear. Unmistakable, unmitigated, pure, human fear.

The words rushed out of him. "I can't die tonight."

Ruthie placed a hand on top of his. He still wore his gloves. Ernest had attempted to take them off earlier, but Harry wouldn't let him. She'd always been embarrassed of her hands. Along with her height, everything about her always felt oafish and large. But now she appreciated the length of her fingers, the width of her palms. They covered him completely. "Shh. You won't. Don't think like that."

"You don't understand," he said. "I have too much to do. Too much to make right."

"Mr. Holmes…Harry," Ruthie said gently, attempting to ease his torso back on the bed. "You have all the time in the world. Don't worry. It's not good for you. Your body needs to heal. You should rest."

"I don't want to go to sleep." Harry's gaze bobbed around the room, almost like it was worried to rest on something, afraid that something was chasing him. "Please don't leave me. I feel better when you're here. I feel safe, and I haven't felt that way in a long, long time."

"Oh, Mr. Holmes—"

"*Harry.*"

Anguish overwhelmed her. He was asking too much. "*Harry.* I can't stay. But I wouldn't leave you if I thought you were going to die. I promise you. You're too strong—and stubborn—for that."

Harry released his hold and fell back to the mattress. "You don't know me," he said bitterly, locking his eyes on the ceiling once more. "I've done things..." He blew out a breath. "I've done...*things.*"

The comment was so vague, and yet Ruthie understood what he was trying to say. She sat on the bed, taking his hand once more. "You're not going to die."

"Oh, really?" he scoffed. "How much would you bet on it?"

Ruthie's neck straightened so quickly that she heard a pop in her spine. "Bet?"

"If you hadn't noticed, you're in a gambling hall. The finest one in the world," Harry murmured. "So, what would you bet? A pound? Two pounds? Five?"

How had their conversation taken this turn? Ruthie shrugged. "I don't know—a pound, I guess."

Harry tossed up his arms. "Oh, Jesus Christ. I'm bloody done for! A fucking pound."

"Oh, fine, then ten pounds! There. Are you happy? I bet you ten pounds that you will survive the night. Can I leave now?"

"No." He reached for her once more, clasping her hand and laying it on his chest. "You can't leave until I fall asleep."

Ruthie tried to tug her hand free, but it was no use. Even wounded, Harry was too strong for her. "That's absurd. I have to go—"

"Woman, I've worked since sunup *and* been shot. I'll be out in minutes. Just have a little patience, for fuck's sake."

Ruthie frowned at the surly patient. "You really shouldn't speak to me that way."

"Ha!" Despite his outburst, Harry's heartbeat slowed under her palm. Was it really because of her? Did she truly make him feel safe? It was the loveliest thing anyone had ever said to her—not that many lovely things had been said to her, but still…she'd treasure it forever. "I knew you were a lady." He caressed the top of her hand with his thumb. "I told you. It showed in your skin."

"You think you're so clever," Ruthie retorted dryly. "I'm not a lady. My father…" She paused. Was she saying too much? Should she tell him anything about her life? Instantly, she concluded that it was harmless. What did it matter? She'd never see Harry Holmes again after this night was over. Ruthie was sure of that. "My father was a baron. Not a very important one, but a baron all the same."

Harry's eyes were closed now, and his breath relaxed into an even rhythm. "A baron's daughter…" After a moment, he added, "Ruthie, the ever-loyal companion, is too *honorable* to let me die."

"You know your peerage *and* the Bible. Impressive."

"I'm a man of many surprises."

Ruthie desperately wanted to tell him to surprise her by staying alive through the night but held her tongue. Instead, she replied, "So, you think I won't let you die? I was always told I had no special skills, but, apparently, my mother was wrong. I can stop death. That'll show her."

She was expecting a polite chuckle, but nothing came from Harry, who lay placidly below her. She waited a few more minutes, but as she began sliding her hand out from under his, he finally spoke.

"What do you think it's like?"

Ruthie leaned over his chest to catch his thin, haunted words. "What is what like?"

"Death."

"I'm not sure," she answered slowly. "The church tells us that heaven—"

"I don't want to hear what those bastards at their pulpits have to say. I don't want silly stories. I asked what *you* think. Tell me."

No one had ever asked Ruthie what she thought about things. Her entire life she was taught to listen and obey, do as her family dictated. Now that someone finally wanted her opinion, she gave it proper consideration. She gave him her truth.

"When you were first shot and were lying on me, I remember thinking how calm you looked," Ruthie began, gaining confidence as the confession poured out of her. "I wondered why people could fear death so much when it didn't appear terrifying at all. It seemed...peaceful."

She tensed, ready for his laughter or scorn, but neither came. Instead, Harry squeezed her hand tighter. "Those are the words of a young person—a person with their whole life left in front of them."

Ruthie cocked her head. She didn't feel young. Most days she felt like the oldest person on the planet, full of worries. "You don't know me," she said, echoing his earlier statement.

He squeezed her hand once more. "I know you won't leave me tonight."

Ruthie's voice came out more bitter than she intended. "Because I'm like Ruth from the Bible?"

"No," he said, "because you're Ruthie. *My* Ruthie."

Chapter Four

*D*AMN THAT *ERNEST*. The man wouldn't stop rambling on—nor would he take his eagle eye off his employer, ready to pounce if he showed any signs of pain.

The noble and reserved butler had turned into a mother hen overnight. If he was being completely honest with himself, Harry hadn't expected to see the dawn. He'd witnessed his fair of bastards with gunshot wounds, and very few of them survived. Despite his lovely nursemaid's guarantees, he hadn't believed his eyes would ever open again. But Ruthie had been right. Which meant that Harry Holmes had lost their bet. That had never happened before, and he never expected it to happen again.

Which was why he was in a hurry to get out of that godforsaken room. The morning after the shooting—after the cursed doctor had inspected Ruthie's *rather* crooked stitches and deduced that an infection hadn't set in—Harry had attempted to put the whole episode behind him. There was no point wallowing, no point lazing about without his nursemaid there to entertain him.

However, when Harry had tried to get up, he was hit by two unfortunate, unyielding walls—one was his surly, stubborn butler, and the other was the bloody agony that struck him like a blunt axe to the chest. Every tiny movement caused his stomach muscles to tighten, which sent excruciating bolts of torment through every single pathway in his body. Begrudgingly, Harry had done what Ernest commanded and retired once more to his bed, but he refused to be complacent.

If he couldn't go to work, then work would have to go to him. For seven interminable days, Ernest and Vine reported to him. Five days was what he would have preferred, but his body would not be dictated to. He would have to settle for seven.

By necessity, Harry had always been a quick healer. His mother had never been one to pamper her only child—to say the least—and when he was ten he finally deserted his home to make a name for himself on the streets. he knew enough to understand that there was no one in that dirty city to catch him if he fell. Harry would have to catch himself or make sure he never lost his balance—he chose the latter.

At thirteen, he had already started his first gang, and by twenty, Harry's Boys were making a name for themselves as the roughest thieves and scoundrels in the rookery. He could have stopped there; however, the more the money had piled up, the more he craved. There could never be enough. So Harry changed course. He gave his fists a rest and focused on his mind. He was tired of stealing from the well-to-do behind their backs. It made more sense for them to just give him their money.

Enter gambling.

From as far back as he could remember, Harry had loved numbers. They comforted him. All that certainty—there was no ambiguity to waste your time with. For a child who never knew who his father was, that certitude was a godsend. His mother squandered most of her life on her knees praying to an elusive God for good luck. Harry's god was numbers. And unlike his mother's deity, they never let him down.

Formulating odds came easy to him. What took most hours took Harry seconds. He bet on everything: cards, boxing matches, races, cricket matches—everything except horses. Only fools who wanted to lose everything bet on horses. And he used his winnings wisely, combining his earnings to open the Lucky

Fish on St. James Street the day before his thirty-first birthday. He understood that in order to appeal to the blue-bloods, he had to play on their turf. His establishment wasn't another "hell" located in a foul-smelling, seedy hole in the wall. The Lucky Fish was elite, a place to be seen, a place where a gentleman could be a gentleman with a fine cigar in his hand and a sweet-smelling whore that paraded as a lady on his lap.

Now, ten years in, he had everything he wanted. More than he could ever want.

And he had a hole in his side to show for it. It was like he'd never left the rookery.

She'd almost been right about him. And Harry could never allow that. Dying alone was not an option. Not anymore. Nor could he die with a guilty conscience. It was true that he didn't give one flying fuck about his mother's God, but he was still Harry Holmes. A good gambler knew when to hedge his bets, and he was the best.

Which was why Harry didn't have a moment to lose.

"Last night was packed again, but uneventful," Ernest droned on, reading off a list in his hand. "Lord Chemly came in again… Lost so much he started crying at the table. He told me he was good for it, but I mentioned that when you're better you might be paying a house call." He gave his master a pointed look over the paper. "He assured me he had some pieces of jewelry you could explore when his wife is out of town next week."

Harry waved an irritable hand. "Fine, fine. What else?"

With a put-upon sigh, Ernest hid himself behind his paper once more. "I've been informed that Prince Auguste of Mecklen-burg-Schwerin will be in town next week. I hear that he's hoping we will be hospitable."

"Who?"

Ernest shrugged. "He's one of the Germanic princes."

"Fuck. There's too many of them to remember." Harry sighed. "Make sure the prince has everything he needs, but do not give him any of our girls. The last time a grand duke honored us with his presence, the girls almost mutinied because he was a walking case of syphilis."

Ernest made a note on his paper. "Indeed. I'll get right on it. Yes, I remember the smell as if it were yesterday."

Harry jabbed his fists down on the mattress to hold his weight and cautiously slid his legs off the side. He held his breath, waiting for a rush of pain to come, but only encountered a minor pinch.

"Now stop wasting my time, Ernest. Get to the point. Have they found the bastard who did it yet?"

Ernest raised his brow. "I thought Mr. Vine had told you?"

Harry muttered a curse, maneuvering his body until his feet were solid on the cold wooden floor. "Told me what?"

"Several men have come forward. They told Vine it was one of Dugan's men."

"Dugan? Did Vine really say that?"

Ernest shook his head. "He said he told you."

"Fuck, he probably did," Harry said. "I must have forgotten. I've been...distracted."

"By Miss Ruthie?"

Harry's head shot up. He didn't appreciate the cloying smile on Ernest's face—not at all. That was also a significant change since the shooting. The solid, no-nonsense, humorless Ernest was gone. It seemed that everything to do with Miss Ruthie Waitrose brought out the amused rascal in him. All at Harry's expense.

"Of course Miss Ruthie," Harry barked. "Now shut up and call for my valet. I'm going out."

Ernest stepped forward in a hurry. "Oh no you're not. Dr. Cameron said you still have another week of convalescence. Your wound is healing, but it is not healed, Mr. Holmes!"

"I don't give one goddamn," Harry retorted irritably. He sucked in a deep breath, ballooning his cheeks as he pushed into the mattress, putting more weight into his feet. He would walk out of this room today or he would die trying.

"Stop that," Ernest clucked. "Stop that right now. There's no reason for this. Everything is running smoothly. Vine is more than capable of watching over the hall while you rest. You're only going to make things worse."

Harry lifted his fingers from the bed as he straightened his legs to standing. *There. That wasn't so hard.* His muscles nagged all over, in places he wouldn't have assumed. He felt like Sleeping Beauty, though he doubted the young princess felt so tight and raw when she woke from her long sleep. Harry didn't make a habit of dwelling on his age, not finding it particularly helpful for his peace of mind; however, today his forty-two years on this earth were unavoidable. True, he'd been shot, but what was equally true was that he was a middle-aged man—with all the aches and pains that accompanied it.

"Call my valet," Harry growled, taking a few tiny steps. "I'm going out." He ran a palm over his bushy beard. Harry wasn't a one-shave-a-day man—he was a *two*-shaves-a-day man. "I need a shave and a bath and my best jacket."

Ernest returned a bewildered look. "Why? Are you off to see the queen?"

Harry chuckled despite himself. Giddiness filled him and he suddenly felt warm inside. Warm and incredibly right. He'd come up with the decision two days ago and hadn't wavered once. Harry's gut was never wrong. His gut was sacrosanct. Now, all he had to do was act.

"Someone more important than the queen," he replied easily. "Someone who is not going to make anything worse, only better. Someone who will fulfill all my needs."

The wrinkles of concern evaporated from the old butler's face. "Oh, I see. You need a woman. Yes, I suppose it's been long enough. I hadn't thought of that. But you don't need to get dressed up for that. And you certainly don't need a shave and a bath. Just lie back down and I'll send Arthur out to Sarah's. She'll be only too glad to help, I'm sure—"

"For fuck's sake, Ernest, I don't want a woman. I mean, I do… I mean, I am…" Harry raked a hand through his hair.

"Are you blushing, Mr. Holmes?" the butler asked. "And I've never known you to be tongue-tied before."

"I'm not bloody tongue-tied," Harry retorted, storming across the room. He passed Ernest with a glare and threw open the door, hollering for his poor valet to "get his arse in here immediately."

He threw the butler a smug smile. "There. That wasn't so difficult. Maybe I don't need you at all, Ernest."

The valet scurried into the room, his skinny arms full of the instruments needed for Harry's shave. As he set everything up on the dresser and began to sharpen the razor blade, the butler and his master squared off, both silent, each sizing the other up with ruthless contemplation.

"Where are you going?" Ernest asked quietly, his words slicing through the thick air.

Harry paused, torturing the inquisitive older man with silence. Then he *hmphed* and massaged a minty cream onto his face as the valet held up a mirror, now used to the fact that his employer never utilized his services, choosing to always shave himself. "That's none of your business."

Focused on his reflection, Harry didn't witness the scrutiny Ernest directed at him or the arrogant smile that eventually slid onto the butler's face as he retreated toward the door.

Harry concluded that the conversation was over, and was just about to run the blade down his cheek when Ernest's words stopped him.

"Say hello to Miss Ruthie for me," the butler said cheerfully before sailing out of the room. "I hope she says yes."

The blade dropped from Harry's hands. The valet hurried to pick it up. He wiped it off on a cloth and handed it back to his master.

"Ridiculous man," Harry muttered, placing the blade on his face once more. He studied his reflection for a long moment and then added, "Of course she's going to say yes."

Chapter Five

"LADIES, PLEASE, QUIET down now—please, we really need to get something done today," Mrs. Myfanwy Everett cried, clapping her hands together loudly. "I know everyone is excited to reconvene, but I absolutely must return home before Samuel realizes I'm gone. If he finds out, he won't let me out of his sight until the baby is born. I love my husband, but I'm beginning to realize there's something to that old saying, 'absence makes the heart grow fonder.'"

Lady Jennifer Bramble rolled her eyes playfully at her friend. Her equally growing belly added evidence that so much had changed since Ruthie first joined the London Ladies Cricket Club last season. "You shouldn't have come! I told you that we didn't need to meet at the clubhouse; we could have gone to your home instead."

Myfanwy pulled a face, swiping a few errant brown wisps of hair off her forehead. "No, I needed to get out of there. Samuel has taken to hovering. He's always next to me, asking if I'm all right or if I need anything. The second he told me he had to spend the day at the Flying Batsman, I knew that was my chance."

Ruthie lifted her eyebrows at her friend, Miss Anna Smythe— nay, now Lady Anna—and suppressed the smile on her lips.

Surprising no one, Myfanwy had married the team's surly coach, Samuel Everett, at the end of last season and was now abundantly with child. Along with his other numerous business ventures and a cricket career, Samuel owned the inn that sat next to the club's new field and clubhouse.

"I'm confused," a brown-haired woman replied, scrunching her nose in thought. Lady Maggie had joined the group around the same time as Ruthie, although they hadn't formed an easy friendship. Even though Maggie was the daughter of a marquis, Ruthie's mother ordered her to keep her distance from the lady during Society events. She referred to Maggie as a "tomboy," and not in a good way. "Aren't we all supposed to want husbands who lavish us with attention and care?" Maggie asked.

Myfanwy returned a wry grin that didn't reach her eyes. "Well, you know what they say about too much of anything…"

The group chuckled as the captain attempted to wrangle their attention. "Let me speak and get this over with. I can't sit for more than ten minutes without my lower back aching. Now I know why God chose women to carry the babies; men wouldn't have been able to handle it."

Jennifer patted Myfanwy's hand. "Get to the point, dearest. We don't want to scare the poor girls away from having children."

"Too late," Maggie quipped.

"All right… Where was I?" Myfanwy went on. "Honestly, I can't keep a thought in my head for more than a—"

Jennifer broke in. "Myfanwy!"

The captain's back straightened. "Yes, indeed. I know we have a few more months before the season begins, and I can't wait until we're once again training for our match with the matrons. I have no doubt we will clobber them this year and every year after."

A round of affirmations came from the ladies.

"Are they still calling themselves the Matrons Cricket Club?" Lady Anna asked. "Some of us are married now, which is why we changed our name. Why don't they?"

"They aren't exactly fans of change," Lady Everly replied wryly. She would know, thought Ruthie. The matrons had politely kicked Lady Everly out of their club after her late husband died. And just as the matrons refused to change, so did Lady Everly refuse to let that old wound heal. Even now at the mention of her old club, her lips puckered as if she'd just swallowed a lemon.

Ruthie would never breathe this confession to anyone, but Lady Everly tended to frighten her. Yes, the lady was a few years older than her, no doubt wiser and world-wearier, but it was more than that. The beautiful woman spoke with a confident forwardness that Ruthie was certain she would never obtain. Lady Everly's severity reminded Ruthie so much of her own mother, and she didn't appreciate those reminders whenever she was lucky enough to be out of the house.

"Ladies," Myfanwy cut in, "we're not here to discuss the matrons and their lack of creativity"—she lowered her voice—"or their lack of talent. The reason I've called you here today is to let you in on some great news! As you know, Lady Anna put on a clinic a few months ago to introduce our beloved sport to young girls. Well, I don't need to remind you that it was a resounding success. The turnout for the event was better than we could have imagined."

The group broke into an animated round of applause. Lady Anna lowered her chin, her cheeks blooming red. "It wasn't just me," she said bashfully. "I couldn't have done it without Lady Everly and Miss Ruthie."

The applause turned to Ruthie, and it was her turn to blush. Needless to say, accolades weren't something she experienced often—especially at the cricket club. Even she could admit that the sport didn't come naturally to her, and she was far from the best player on the team…maybe close to the worst. However, she had to give herself some credit. Mr. Everett's coaching style was ruthless yet effective, and she was making decent strides. By the end of last season, she'd stopped being considered an easy out whenever she was up to bat. She still had leagues to go before being as great as Myfanwy or Jennifer, but Rome wasn't built in a day, and neither would her cricket career be.

"You all did wonderfully," Jennifer announced through the cheers. "It was a monumental undertaking."

"It certainly was," Myfanwy agreed. "And it helped us gain some much-needed exposure that will allow us to take our little show on the road."

Anna paused in sipping her tea. "On the road?"

"Yes," Myfanwy replied excitedly. "I've been contacted by a few women's teams outside the city—not too far, but far enough. They've asked if we would put on clinics for them and also play in a few exhibition games for their towns. And they actually want to pay us to come! Isn't that wonderful?"

Ruthie scooted to the edge of her seat. She couldn't believe what she was hearing. Getting *paid* to play cricket? Putting on more clinics for women? It all sounded like a dream.

"How far is *far*?" Anna asked. Ruthie's excitement abated as she regarded her friend. Anna hadn't told the group that she, too, was with child. Speaking of dreams, having a child was Anna's, and she'd never thought that it would happen. Now that it was almost within her grasp, there was no way she would let anything jeopardize it.

"Not too far," Myfanwy replied, inspecting her nails despite the fact she was wearing lace gloves.

"Myfi," Lady Everly drawled. "How far?"

Myfanwy faced the group. "Just Exeter and Bath...and maybe Ipswich and Manchester."

"Exeter!" Lady Everly cried. "They've heard of us all the way in Cornwall?"

"It's Devon, not Cornwall," Maggie cut in.

"Close enough," Lady Everly muttered.

"I've never been to Manchester before," Jennifer said. "It sounds so exotic."

Maggie scoffed. "Manchester? Exotic?" She snorted, and Ruthie could practically hear her mother *tsking* in her ear. "It's full of factories and smells even worse than the Thames on a hot day. Also, it's full of Irish people."

"What's wrong with Irish people?" Ruthie asked tetchily.

Maggie shrugged, casting her a curious look. "Nothing," she said slowly. "It's just something my father always says. There's just a lot… That's all."

Ruthie sat back in her seat, squeezing her hands together. That was odd. Why had Maggie's comment made her so upset? She felt the entire group watching her and wished she could hide behind her chair.

"Anyway," Myfanwy went on, steering the focus back to her, "by my calculations, we could be on the road for three to four weeks. Since the season is winding down and everyone is retreating to the country for summer, I think it's perfect timing. I'm already negotiating houses for us to stay in, families that have the rooms to accommodate us—and who are perfectly respectable, so no one's parents should balk. Besides, Jennifer and I—and now Anna—are perfectly suitable married ladies and will make wonderful, *responsible*"—her smile turned malicious— "chaperones for all of you."

Ruthie's excitement plummeted. As Myfanwy's news created fresh rounds of animated chatter, she had an indescribable desire to melt into a puddle on the carpet. Three weeks? Away from home? Her mother would never allow it. It didn't matter that the season was winding down. Her mother's only goal this year was to see her eldest daughter *suitably engaged*—which meant to the richest man who would take her. So far, Ruthie's Season had been an unmitigated disappointment; however, the lack of suitors didn't make her mother more despondent, only more determined.

"I'll be making calls on all your mothers," Myfanwy continued, "to make sure that everyone is comfortable with the arrangement. In the meantime, brush up on your skills. I know we're probably rusty, since we've been lazing about all winter. Don't worry, though—I'll schedule some practices for us before we leave. Nothing too intimidating, maybe five or six…maybe ten or twenty. Let me think on it."

Ruthie slouched back in her chair as the whirlwind of conversations took off around her. She didn't have anything to think on. Her club was going to leave the city for a month, and she wouldn't be able to join them. And ever since Harry Holmes uncovered her ruse at the Lucky Fish, she'd been too timid to ask Reggie to take her to another gaming hall. Time was running out, as were her options. If Ruthie didn't recoup her brother's losses soon, her mother would throw her to the highest bidder in an effort to save the family in the short term.

It was all too much.

And it was all Ruthie's fault.

For a brief moment, she'd allowed herself to have high hopes in a different purpose. A different kind of future than the one mapped out for her.

She'd taken a chance on herself and was coming up short.

LADY CELESTE GLIDED into the foyer the moment Ruthie closed the front door. The epitome of femininity and gentle breeding, Ruthie's mother never rushed or gave the vulgar notion that she was any place other than exactly where she was supposed to be. And to Ruthie's disappointment, that place was usually right over her shoulder, watching her like a beautiful and ruthless hawk.

"Finally!" Lady Celeste exclaimed, helping Ruthie take off her lightweight shawl to hand to the maid. "I didn't expect your little club to run so long. Lord Dawkins dropped in. He mentioned that we all might take a walk in the park today. I told him you'd be delighted. Straighten your shoulders, dear. No one wants a warped wife."

Lady Celeste had been too focused on her daughter's shoulders to notice her expression. Ruthie was quite positive that men didn't desire wives who looked like they wanted to spit each time they were referenced.

"Do I have time for tea?" she asked, moving to the drawing room, her mother one elegant step behind. Her legs were half the length of Ruthie's, yet, still, she always managed to keep up with her daughter's long gait with minimal effort, as if she were floating instead of walking.

"Yes, but do it quickly, please," Lady Celeste replied before asking the maid to bring in a tray with tea *and only tea*—no biscuits. "And don't make a mess. We don't have time for you to change. He'll be here any minute."

Ruthie sighed, sinking into her seat. The last thing she wanted to do was spend the afternoon being judged and inspected by her mother *and* Lord Dawkins. The viscount had visited twice in two weeks, and Ruthie couldn't understand why he kept coming back. He only ever spoke with her mother and barely looked at her, which stood to reason, since he was closer to her mother's age, and Lady Celeste was undeniably lovely. It was the same for all of Ruthie's suitors—if one could even call them that. The men her mother foisted on her never *suited* her.

"Mind your dress, Ruthie," her mother ordered her. "Maybe you shouldn't be sitting. I'd hate for it to wrinkle more than it already has."

Ruthie's neck wilted, but she refused to stand. For some sad reason, this little form of disobedience felt like she'd won a small war.

"Ruthie, please," my mother said. "Your shoulders. I've told you—women of your height need to be aware of their poor posture. If you keep that up, you'll look like the Hunchback of Notre Dame."

Ruthie couldn't hide her exasperation at her mother's chuckle. Nor could she contain the sardonic bitterness in her voice when she replied, "Really, Mother? You believe that my poor posture might one day turn me into a hideous, reclusive monster that makes women weep and children cry?"

Lady Celeste swatted her daughter's knee playfully. "Not if Lord Dawkins has anything to say about it!" When Ruthie's countenance didn't change, her mother tried again. "I was only joking, love. There's no reason to stay so sour. I only want the best for you. I know you think I'm being hard on you, but it's for your own good. You'll understand when you have your own daughter one day."

Ruthie sulked. "When I have my own daughter, I won't force her to spend time with men who aren't interested in her or constantly harass her by pointing out her faults—"

She gasped, covering her mouth with her hand. Had she really just that? Out loud? In front of her mother?

What was the matter with her? Ruthie didn't have to think on that question too long. She knew the reason too well. A dismal cloud of pity had trailed her the entire way home from the cricket club meeting, and it had only swelled heavier and blacker with each step.

The maid entered the room with the tea, setting it up on the side table next to Ruthie. The light clinking noises sounded like the bells of Notre Dame as Ruthie waited for her mother to speak, which would happen the second the maid left. Lady Celeste's pale, lineless face was pinched, as if the words were trying to tear out of her mouth, but she wouldn't dare reproach her daughter in front of the servant.

"I'm sorry, Mother," Ruthie rushed out the moment the maid was gone. "I didn't mean it. I know you only want what's best for me." Her conscience was racked with guilt—not because of her rude comment, but because she wanted to say so much more but had, as ever, lost her nerve.

Lady Celeste took her time, wallowing in the apology. Slowly, methodically, she ran one finger along her temple like she was searching for a stray piece of her rich russet hair to put back in its place. It was an act. Nothing was ever out of place on Lady

Celeste. From the top of her hair to the tips of her shoes, the lady always looked the part. And would spend the majority of her life making sure her daughter did as well.

Whenever she was alone with her mother, Ruthie often thought of balance and how the world needed it to make sense. Heaven had its hell, men had their women, and the summer had its winter. Now, Lady Celeste had her daughter. One of the greatest beauties of the *ton* had a plain, gawky giantess for a child. The notion created some kind of order. Because who could have *everything*?

In her day, Lady Celeste had made a decent match. Her father had only been a baronet, and she'd married a baron—an incredibly handsome one. They had caused quite the stir in London. People would attend the same balls as the couple if only to stand in the periphery of their luminous selves. They were a lively pair, gay and fun, and always the last to leave an event.

But…balance.

The partying, the fun, had taken its toll. The marriage became tempestuous and volatile. Gossips gleefully filled Society papers with the marvelous rows the couple had. And after three children, the baronet refused to slow down. He continued to attend the same balls and soirees as before—only without his capricious wife. In the end, there was nothing original about the story. The fashionable crowd had heard it time and time before. Men tired of wives. Women tired of husbands and sought outside pleasures to hide the disappointment. The baron may have boasted a gorgeous figure, but he never had a head for money. And he quickly spent his own as well as his wife's.

Life was the one party that the baron left too early. When he died, Ruthie had just turned ten. Her brother, Mason, was barely twenty and would now be the head of the family, with an inconsequential title and very little in the coffers.

But…balance.

Lady Celeste had two daughters and, by God, she would make the most of them.

Ruthie tensed, sipping her tea silently, waiting for the tirade. But it didn't happen. Instead, Lady Celeste lowered into the chair next to her daughter. Ruthie watched her mother carefully, surprised at how tired she looked, how the bags under her eyes were more pronounced than usual, full of colors that juxtaposed with the woman's creamy, even visage.

When her mother finally spoke, her voice was haunted and grave, a figment of the real thing. "You know the money's gone. Been gone for years," she said, clasping her hands together primly in her lap.

Ruthie swallowed the lump in her throat. "I do," she croaked. It was something the entire household knew but never spoke about. Their situation must be dire if her mother had deigned to acknowledge it now.

Lady Celeste went on. "Your brother is doing his best, but we might… Well, we might have to leave town soon." She blinked slowly. "Perhaps live with my brother and his family in Berkshire. We would rent out this house to…make ends meet."

Doing his best? Doing his *best*? If by "doing his best," her mother meant that Mason was putting the family even more into debt, then yes, he was doing his best!

But Ruthie only had the heart for one outburst that day, and she curbed her ire.

"Where is Mason?" she asked instead.

"He's still sleeping. I was told he came in late last night."

Ruthie snorted. "Of course he did."

Lady Celeste's bright eyes narrowed. "Your brother is making contacts, doing all things a young lord needs to do in the city."

Ruthie's fingers whitened around her teacup. If she was the ever-devoted daughter from the Bible, then Mason was the prodigal son who was always welcomed back to his family's table and given a place of honor.

"You should only support your brother," Lady Celeste insisted. "He is trying to do what's best for this family."

"While I'm the sacrificial lamb being sent out to slaughter?"

Ruthie slapped her hand over her mouth once more.

Lady Celeste's eyes had turned into slits. "A bride is hardly a sacrificial lamb. I'm giving you a life, not taking one away."

Ruthie scoffed, all her willpower retreating. *So much for being the dutiful daughter.* "By selling me off to a man who is old enough to be my father?"

"Lord Dawkins is a viscount!"

"An *old* viscount who only looks at my chest!"

"Because his head only comes up to your chest. It's not his fault he's short!"

A knock banged on the front door.

"Oh, he's here!" Lady Celeste exclaimed, hopping to her feet. She glided over to a glass cabinet against the wall, pinching her cheeks while checking her reflection—an unnecessary action, since Ruthie's comments had already made her face and neck red.

Ruthie lumbered to the window that looked onto the street and peeked out the lace curtain. Indeed, a gentleman was waiting outside the front door, only it couldn't possibly be Lord Dawkins. For starters, he was much too tall and had too much hair. Too much black hair. Raven hair…

The gentleman turned around on the steps, glancing her way, and Ruthie stumbled back from the window, throwing the curtains from her fingers. She must be hallucinating. It couldn't be *him*. What was *he* doing here?

Although Ruthie was struck into a daze, the lies tumbled out of her mouth. "It's only Reggie, Mother," she said, running out of the room. "I'll tell him that we don't have time to talk now."

"Tell him to come back tomorrow," Lady Celeste called. "And don't scream like a hoyden. Don't run, either."

Ruthie beat the butler to the door, slamming her hand over the handle before him. "I'll open it, Baker. It's Reggie."

With a slight, disbelieving sniff, Baker stood down, giving Ruthie a curious glance before retreating from the foyer.

Ruthie closed her eyes and took a steadying breath before yanking the door open.

Mr. Harry Holmes faced her on the doorstep, his hand poised in the air to knock once more. Freshly shaven and smartly dressed, he was a different man from the last time she'd seen him. For starters, he wasn't covered in blood. A man in the prime of his life, he stood tall, healthy, and full of vitality. Lady Celeste would have approved of his posture.

"What. In the world. Are you. Doing. Here?"

Harry flashed his white teeth. "Well, it isn't the best greeting I've ever received, but certainly not the worst." His brow lowered as he sobered. "No matter. I came to tell you I owe you ten pounds." He ducked his head, his smile turning sheepish. "And that I'd like you to be my wife."

Chapter Six

R UTHIE SLAMMED THE door in his face.
Hard.

Fuck.

Maybe that hadn't been the best way to propose. But Harry had never proposed to anyone before. He figured it would be best to get it out of the way first. Why wait to the end of the conversation, putting his nerves through needless torment? And he *was* nervous. Harry hadn't expected to be. In fact, the entire ride over to Ruthie's home, he'd only felt confident—magnanimous, even.

However, the second she opened the door, all that confidence had vanished. Did she have to look so adorable? From the grumblings in his club, he'd learned that marriages based on respect and admiration were better than ones where attraction and passion ran high and fast. But he was attracted. *Very.*

He'd considered that his near-death experience had created a romantic view of the woman, but he was happy to be wrong. Ruthie was just as pretty and interesting as he'd remembered, even as she scowled at him with her rosy lips puckered in distaste. Her color was high and bright, reminding him of ripe peaches, her long brown hair falling sweetly down her back. Even the pale freckles covering her entire face were enchanting to Harry. She reminded him of the baby doe, satiny soft and innocent, in need of great care and attention. In need of him.

Harry blinked at the door, wondering if he should knock again or leave. He heard a commotion inside the house. Two women speaking about hats and...the sun? One was definitely Ruthie, but the other voice sounded strikingly similar. Was it her sister or mother? Harry had performed his due diligence. Over the week, he'd made it his business to know everything about his intended fiancée. However, in all his research, nowhere were there clues that she would be the kind of woman to slam the door in his face.

Dammit. Should he knock again? It had taken all his reserves to stop after the first time. Usually, his annoying affliction forced him to knock five times. Not completing the cycle was absolute torture for him, but Harry was out in public and knew better. It took monumental strength, but he could control his aberrations when he had to; unfortunately, he didn't know how much more he had to spare today. He was using most of it to battle the pain in his side, which had only got worse during the jostling of the carriage ride.

He could feel his temper rising, but he'd be damned if he went home without an answer—the one he wanted, and a door slammed in his face wasn't it. He'd come too far.

Reluctantly, he raised his fist to knock for a second time, but Ruthie emerged with the fire still in her eyes, this time wearing a thin yellow shawl and a bonnet that was so wide that it could shade both of them.

"Hurry," she cried, stepping lightly down the steps onto the footpath. "I don't have much time."

"Wait," Harry said, trailing behind her, grimacing as he held a hand against his side. "Where are you going?"

Ruthie flicked her head to his carriage. "Is this yours? Good. Get in."

She didn't wait for an answer, or for his driver to climb down from his perch to open the door or let out the stairs for her. Ruthie launched herself inside and frantically waved at him to do the same.

Dumbfounded, Harry shared a look with his driver. "Drive us around the park," he muttered. He waited for the driver to look away before he touched the handle five times and followed the lady into the carriage.

It was like crouching in a tomb. Ruthie had closed all the curtains. Either she wanted Harry all to herself or she didn't want anyone to know she was in his conveyance. Unfortunately, he knew the answer was the latter.

Harry took his time settling into his seat. He removed his hat, placing it next to him, spinning it around and around until it was in the exact middle of the cushion. Only then could Harry spread his knees comfortably and regard the nervous woman across from him. This Ruthie was almost the exact opposite of the one he'd met that awful night, although now she *was* dressed as a woman, which was a lovely change. Nevertheless, her body language was withdrawn and cagey, showcasing a shadow of the person who'd gone head to head with him at his club. Harry was afraid she would jump out of her skin at any moment. Her bonnet hid most of her face, and the few inches he could see were directed at her lap. She reminded him of one of those hermit crabs who had lost its shell, all anxious and bare, fragile as fine sea glass.

"Why are you here?" she asked finally. Her voice was hardly above a whisper. Irritation grew inside Harry, and he didn't know why, nor could he comprehend what to do with it.

"I told you." He reached inside his pocket for his ten-pound note. He held it out to Ruthie, but she merely stared at it as if he were offering her spoiled mutton. Harry tossed it in her lap, managing to keep his voice civil. "I lived through the night— thanks to you. You won the bet."

Ruthie's nimble fingers traced a line across the note. "I didn't care about the bet. I don't need this."

"That's not what you said that night."

Her gaze claimed his. Finally, those cornflower-blue eyes

came to life, and Harry inhaled long and deep. What was it about this rather ordinary girl that held him in such thrall? Harry could have anyone he wanted—and usually did—but this woman had him holding his breath. The carriage was stifling, the air was sticky with her condemnation, and Harry couldn't have wanted to be anywhere more. Just being near Ruthie made him feel safe, made him forget the whirling thoughts of dread.

"You're referring to my family's financial situation, I take it," she replied curtly.

"Naturally."

"That is none of your concern, since we are not at your club anymore, Mr. Holmes. I am glad to see you are healed and up and about, but you must understand the predicament you put me in by coming to my home—"

Harry opened his mouth, but Ruthie put up a hand to stop him. In her haste, two long tendrils of blonde hair fell over her right shoulder, taunting him.

Ruthie had no idea what those little pieces of hair were doing to him. Harry's fingers curled in his lap. The asymmetry was tortuous, and he couldn't do anything about it.

"And as for this nonsense about marriage, I... Well, I..." She blinked numerous times as she shook her head. The brim of her enormous bonnet made scratching noises against the upholstery, and Harry wondered if he would have to replace the fragile fabric after she left. He continued to stare at those wayward pieces of hair. "I don't think it's necessary," she went on. "You obviously have formed some idea in your head about needing to repay me for my services to you that night, but rest assured that I didn't do anything to warrant such a grand sacrifice. Your thanks is enough." She held up the ten-pound note. "And I'll take the money if it makes you feel better. A bet is a bet, after all."

Ruthie unleashed a ragged breath after her little speech, raising her chin toward him like she was slapping a period on the end of an overwrought sentence.

Harry scowled. Reading people came naturally to him, yet

this woman was…stubborn? Perverse? Insane? Or was it something worse than all those? Was Miss Ruthie an elitist?

Harry shifted in his seat. He snatched his top hat and placed it back on his lap, sliding his fingers over the sleek silk fabric, giving his fingers something to do.

"I'm sorry that I'm not Lord Dawkins. I thought you'd only be too happy to marry a man you wouldn't have to lean down to kiss."

Ruthie answered with a loud gasp. "What do you know about that?"

Harry couldn't drag his eyes from the hair, though he fought to follow the conversation. His fingers itched. His whole body itched. "Oh, I know enough. Everything, really. I make it my business to know, just as I made you my business." He crossed one leg over the other, setting his shoulders wide against the seat as the carriage bounced along. He cocked his head, studying Ruthie, loving the way she squirmed under his contemplation. "Miss Ruthie Waitrose," he began easily. "Twenty-two years old. Father is the late Lord Jeffrey Waitrose, Baron of Chiswick, and mother is Lady Celeste. You have an older brother named Mason who has grown an affinity for the card tables, though he's terrible at them, and a younger sister named Julia. Your father left you with nothing, and now your brother seems determined to leave you with even less." Harry's words came out hot, like he was firing bullets, but he had to give the girl credit. She didn't try to stop him, nor did she cower. If anything, Ruthie matched his gaze with equal intensity. "Your mother—who I hear is quite the beauty—is relying on you to make a good match to save not only the family's reputation but also the family house. Although, from what I hear, Berkshire can be nice this time of year—rather boring, but nice enough."

She sat up in her seat. "How did you—"

Harry dusted a fleck of dust off his knee. "I told you. I wanted to know everything. Now I want to know why you laugh at my proposal when my only competition is Lord *fucking* Dawkins."

He leaned closer. "Who, little birdies have informed me, has a hard if not impossible time keeping it up, if you understand my meaning."

"I most certainly do not!"

Harry's brow furrowed. "Oh. You've been spending so much time in gaming halls recently, I thought your education had expanded to bedtime activities."

The poor girl. There was no hint of freckles anymore. Her face had only one color—red. "I...I only played cards. I did not...talk to people of such things."

"Pity."

"I disagree, Mr. Holmes."

"Harry."

Ruthie found a smile, though it was more of a sneer. "I think, under the circumstances, Mr. Holmes is appropriate."

Harry grinned. "And I thought we knew each other better than to suffer through such formality. Though perhaps it's just *me* who knows *you*, which is why your prejudice is showing."

Ruthie laughed, causing Harry's stomach to flip. It was a deep laugh, full and throaty, a laugh without pretension. Harry had a thick desire to hear it again and again. He realized then and there that he would never grow tired of it.

Ruthie tapped her lap with the tips of her fingers. At first it alarmed Harry, though he could find no rhyme or reason in the act. Nothing like his tiresome routines. Ruthie tapped her fingers without even knowing it. How lucky. "You aren't the only one who did research," she said ominously. She let the words hang in the air, giving each one the proper time and space to hit him straight in the gut. "Your name is Henry Robin Holmes, and you were born in Ireland, though were settled in London quickly after."

A dismissive sound escaped Harry's mouth as he crossed his arms. "I told you as much."

"You did, indeed," Ruthie drawled. "But there's so much more to your story. Your mother raised you as a strict Catholic by herself, and you have no father to speak of. Your mother worked as a seamstress and never remarried. You left home around the age of ten, haunting the streets with fellow urchins, but your quick mind and unnatural grasp for numbers soon set you apart. After you opened the Lucky Fish, you became one of the richest men in England, though no one knows for sure how much money or land you actually have. Based on all the ancient tiaras and swords littering your room, I would assume you have matching castles for a few of them."

"More than a few," Harry replied. "And don't forget the vineyards. I have some of those, too. Good work, Miss Ruthie. Your cousin has kept you well informed, though you've told me nothing that I haven't heard before."

Ruthie rolled her eyes. "You have castles and vineyards and estates all over Europe—even America—but you don't use them. For a man with so much at his command, you ask very little. You never leave England—in fact, I have a sinking suspicion that you've never been on a train before. You live in a small room above your gaming hall filled with the loot you neither care about nor plan to use."

Ruthie's eyes swept over his body, and Harry had the odd notion that he was naked in front of her—and he didn't like it.

"Your clothes are impeccably made, but they are all the same—black. You dress as severely as one of your priests. You rarely touch alcohol, and never in your club. You eat the same bland food every day—chicken and root vegetables, porridge for breakfast. You curse like a sailor, live like a hermit, look like a monk, and never visit your mother, even though you bought her a home in Brixton."

Harry's hands clawed into his legs. "You were almost ten for ten. I did visit my mother—last month, before she died."

Ruthie's confidence faltered. "I'm sorry," she said, lowering her chin. "Losing a parent is never easy."

"You'd be surprised," Harry replied, stretching out the tension from his hands. He leaned forward again, attempting to regain his hold on the situation. Why had he allowed her to put him on the back foot? That was a stupid question. Harry hadn't let her do it; Ruthie had accomplished that all on her own.

Damn that gossipy cousin of hers. He must have been the person who'd showered her with all this information. None of the facts she tossed at him were that obscure; however, she'd used them to analyze him to a painful degree.

Ruthie squinted at him, biting her bottom lip as if unwilling to go on. "You have...*quirks*, though you try to hide them. You tap your fingers and...*touch* things...repeat your words."

Harry scoffed, but his voice was limp when he replied, "Everyone does."

"No." Ruthie shook her head. "Not like you. There's a method to it, a pattern. The number five. Like I said, you hide it well. I don't think I would have noticed if I hadn't spent the night with you."

Harry could feel something rise and bubble inside his chest. Hot and cold at the same time, he couldn't put a name to the sensation. So he ignored it. He ignored everything she'd just told him.

"Fine. Fine. Fine. Fine. Fine." Harry sucked in a breath, stifling a curse. *Get a hold of yourself, man! You're not a freak, so stop acting like one!* His smile was impossibly tight. "This is all well and good, but why don't we get back to the matter at hand? I take it your mother doesn't know that you slipped off to see me?"

"No," she said quietly. "I told her you that Reggie needed to speak with me and that I'd return quickly."

Harry whistled. "I doubt Ruth in the Bible would lie to her mother so convincingly. Perhaps she should have named you Eve."

"Eve didn't lie."

"But she didn't listen very well, either."

Ruthie pursed her lips. "You're right," she said. "I think it's time you take me home."

Harry chuckled. "But I don't have my answer yet."

"You can't possibly be serious about marrying me."

"By your own accounts, I seem like a most serious person."

"Yes...but..." Ruthie blinked wildly. Her wheat-colored lashes weren't long, but they were full, enticing in their own way. "I can't marry you. You have to know that. My mother...my mother would never consider it."

"Because of my poor upbringing?" Harry offered dryly. "I had no idea you peers were such snobs."

"You know very well they're snobs!"

It wasn't lost on Harry that she used "they're" instead of "we're," but he would ruminate on that for another time. He scratched his chin, hearing the telltale rasp. He already needed his second shave of the day. "I also know that peers' opinion of men changes depending on the amount of money in their pocket."

"You don't really believe that, do you? It doesn't matter how much money you make; they'll never accept you. They barely accept me."

"I don't give a fuck if they accept me," he replied, shocking himself with his harsh tone. "The majority of them are imbeciles, which is why I own most of their land. I don't care about them. I care about you—" Harry coughed. That was not what he'd planned to say at all.

Ruthie blanched at his choice of words. Harry hurried to finish. "I mean I only care about your opinion. Of me," he added. "Listen, please. I know this proposal is a bit of a shock. I know I'm not the man you ever thought you'd marry. I know I have"—he gritted his teeth—"quirks, as you say, but here I am anyway. Marriage was something I'd never really thought about until recently, but now that it's in my mind, I can't get rid of it. You say I can have anybody, but I don't want anybody. I want you. The kindness you gifted me that night showed me the kind of person you are, and that's the person I want as a partner. You are loyal and do what you say, forthright and relatively honest"—he smiled—"when you want to be. You aren't a silly girl with dreams of knights in your head. You're even-keeled and rational…levelheaded. Trustworthy."

Harry thought he was doing a fantastic job spoiling Ruthie with all these compliments; however, the more words that spilled from his mouth, the deeper she glowered.

"What's wrong?" he asked.

Ruthie sniffed. "It sounds like you want a dog—not a wife."

Harry sighed. "I want a companion, someone who will stay with me, someone who will be with me to the end."

"Again…that sounds like a dog." She scrunched her nose. "I hear dachshunds are quite nice."

"I don't want a bloody dog! I tried it once. It didn't work."

She cocked her head. "Why? Oh! Don't answer that. I don't care. And *I* don't want to marry a man who only wants me because he's afraid to die alone! You're just like my mother. You want Ruth from the Bible, someone who will devote her life to you, someone who will never leave you."

She whipped the wind right out of him. Ruthie continued to stare at him with that pitying expression.

"I'm not afraid to die," he retorted.

"Yes, you are," Ruthie replied gently. She reached across the carriage and laid her hand over his. He tensed at the action, grateful he was wearing his leather gloves. The warmth immediately soothed him, and Harry was instantly brought back to their night together. He wanted all his nights to be like that. He needed it. "A lot of people are scared," she continued.

"I'm not scared," Harry snapped. He sandwiched her hand with his other, loving the way they matched up so well. "I'm concerned, but it doesn't matter because I'm…handling it."

"How?"

"It doesn't matter," he said quickly. Harry slid back into his seat, letting her hand drop from his knee. "So that's it, then? Your answer is no?"

Ruthie's smile was awkward and wan. "I'm afraid so. We both know it's for the best, though I do appreciate the offer."

"I still owe you."

She searched for the ten-pound note and waved it with a flourish. "No, you don't. I've been properly paid."

Harry arched a brow. "That's nothing. How much did you say you needed to raise? Ten thousand…twenty thousand pounds? Have your cousin come to the club and I'll hand it over to him. There. Now you won't have to marry poor Lord Dawkins and spend the rest of your life minding his short, bald children."

Now it was Ruthie's turn to be lost for words. Her mouth dropped open like a trout's. "I couldn't… What do you… How could you…"

"What are you blathering on about?"

Ruthie scowled and tried again. "I can't take your money."

"Why?" he asked with a shrug. "If anyone offered me money, I would take it in a heartbeat."

"But you don't need it!"

"What the hell does that matter?"

Ruthie ignored his ridiculous question and peeked out the window. She played with her giant bonnet, fixing it straight even though it hadn't moved from its perfect position on her head. Harry would have known; he would have moved if it had. Her hair, on the other hand, was still driving him mad.

"So where does this leave us?" he said as the carriage slowed to a stop. "You have to let me give you something. I can't… I can't handle the lack of balance between us. You must allow me to make it right, make it even."

Ruthie reached for the door handle. Harry was almost certain she was going to jump out of the carriage like a thieving bandit, but she stopped to consider what he'd said.

"Is it true you made your fortune from gambling?"

"Not at all," he replied. "I started by stealing anything and everything."

Ruthie frowned. "I supposed I should be grateful that you're so honest."

"Only when it suits me."

"Yes, well…" She hesitated, her fingers dangling from the

silver knob. "You are also a skilled gambler? Is that a correct assumption?"

Harry nodded, growing uneasy.

"Then...then you could you help me...you know...gamble and win at your club?"

"No." The word came out like a cannon. Besides the fact that she was asking him to teach her how to beat his own establishment, Harry couldn't imagine spending more time with the lady while others were around. Alone he could suffer through his issues, but with her... Harry's concentration lagged and his quirks were more difficult to contain. She put his discipline to the ultimate test. Losing money was nothing. His bloody reputation was on the line. "No," he repeated, waiting for her fine wrist to bend and open the door where freedom awaited.

But that didn't come.

"You owe me," Ruthie reminded him. "You said yourself that we are out of balance. This is the only way you can make it right."

Harry threw up his hands. "Why can't I just give you the money?"

"Because I want to earn it. I want to do this for myself. I want to prove that I can just as easily make it as my brother can lose it."

"No one can do anything that easy," Harry muttered.

"Help me," she said.

"Not like that. Not like that. Not like—" Harry screwed his lips closed. "No."

Ruthie released a puff of sardonic laughter. "Fine, then," she said, swinging the door open. Late afternoon sun roared into the carriage like a lion, momentarily blinding him. Harry couldn't see Ruthie as she left him, couldn't hold on to an image to carry him home. Instead, he was left with her forbidding words. "You'll just have to live with the unbalance, then." She gave him a pointed look, then tapped her fingers against the door four times. Not five. *Four.* "I have a feeling it won't be easy."

Harry yanked the door shut and held the knob that was still

warm from her touch for as long as he could before performing his ritual. *Tap, tap, tap, tap, tap.*

He let out a sigh of disgust even as a faint smile made its way onto his face. *I have a feeling it won't be easy.*

"I'll be damned," Harry said to himself. "She really does know me."

Chapter Seven

RUTHIE ESCAPED BACK into her home, but that was as far as her energy could take her. She couldn't tackle the stairs, opting to lean against the door and close her eyes, waiting until her heart relaxed into a steady rhythm.

After a few minutes, she realized that was not going to happen—especially when her mother found her.

"Ruthie, darling!" Lady Celeste exclaimed, advancing toward her. "Where on earth have you been? I don't understand why Reginald has to take up so much of your time! Why doesn't he bother Mason? Or doesn't he have friends he can speak to without hounding you so much?"

Ruthie let out a desultory breath and raised a limp finger to tug at the bonnet ribbon fastened underneath her chin. Lady Celeste wasted no time taking it off her head and throwing it back to a maid to carry upstairs.

"I'm sorry, Mother," Ruthie replied wearily. "I was the only one he could speak to. We tried to make it quick."

Not quick enough.

Lady Celeste leveled her daughter with her unmistakable scrutiny. "At least you wore your hat," she said. With light pressure, Ruthie's mother tipped her face back and forth with her fingers. "I'll never understand these freckles," she mused. "They are as stubborn as you are. Sometimes I think I can barely see them, and then they're all I can see!"

"Sorry," Ruthie mumbled. Her head ached. All she wanted to do was flop down on her bed and sleep away this confounding day.

Lady Celeste dropped her hand. "What's wrong, darling? All of a sudden, you've turned quite green. Are you ill?"

Ruthie shook her head. "I don't think—"

"Because we can't have that. Not at all," Lady Celeste cut in, discreetly wiping her hands down the front of her skirts. "Not when Lord Dawkins is coming for dinner. Oh, don't give me that look. I thought it would be better than a walk in the park. More intimate."

"Mother, I don't think I can eat," Ruthie said truthfully. On a normal day it was difficult eating with the ancient lord whose fork tended to miss his mouth half the time. By the end of their meals, Lord Dawkins had more food on his face than Ruthie had in her stomach.

"Oh, you don't have to eat. Just sit there and smile. Ask him about himself," Lady Celeste replied blithely. "You know the lord prefers women with small appetites." Her face brightened. "Do you know what he told me today? He said that he admired your 'natural, delicate structure.' Isn't that marvelous?"

"Yes," Ruthie answered glumly. "Marvelous."

If only the good Lord knew he was being fooled. There was nothing *natural* about Ruthie's form. Only being allowed to eat the bare minimum for years would make anyone appear delicate and close to shattering. If her height and freckles would not bend to her mother's indomitable will, then her weight would.

Ruthie couldn't recall a time when she'd eaten more than a handful of food in one sitting. No…that wasn't true. Just recently, she'd gorged on deliciously sinful and mouth-watering goodies at the cricket clinic she'd hosted with Lady Anna. Anna's sister and aunts had baked an alarming amount of pastries and biscuits for the day, and Ruthie hadn't been able to stop herself from trying all of them. Actually, she hadn't tried to stop herself. The confections were there to be enjoyed, and Ruthie wanted them. It was that simple.

Lady Celeste didn't seem to notice the melancholic note in Ruthie's voice. Gently, she pulled her away from the door and nudged her toward the stairs. "I think a nap is in order," she advised. "And definitely splash some water on your face. We want you fresh and glowing with youth when the lord returns. Men like Lord Dawkins don't want young wives who look older than them. What would be the point of that?" She chuckled.

Ruthie held on to the banister for dear life. A sluggish pallor had enveloped her. She couldn't take one step knowing what it was all for—not when a bizarre man in a huge carriage had just offered her something so completely different. And she'd told him no. She'd laughed at him. In all honesty, she hadn't believed him. Because Harry Holmes didn't truly want *her*. He wanted the saintly version of her. He wanted the same Ruthie that her mother and Lord Dawkins wanted—the one that lived for everyone but herself.

"Ruthie! Be careful. What's the matter?" her mother exclaimed, rushing up the step. Her hands clamped around her daughter's arms just as Ruthie was beginning to sway.

The room was spinning, and, for once, her mother was keeping her on her feet instead of pulling her under. "I'm fine, I'm fine. I'm sorry, Mother. I didn't mean to alarm you," Ruthie said, taken aback by the fear in the older woman's face. Lady Celeste so rarely showed what was on her mind. This moment of panic gifted her a nurturing appeal, though it also made her look older...look her age. Ruthie's heart warmed, but it was a quick feeling, there and then gone, because it was a little slice of time she would never be able to share with her mother, since the woman would hate it for the same reasons that Ruthie cherished it.

Lady Celeste laid the back of her hand against Ruthie's forehead and each cheek, her countenance hardening. "No, no, no."

She shook her head as if she were having a fit. "This will not do. You can't see Lord Dawkins like this. A little red in the cheek is one thing—we could pass that off as a sweet blush—but this is too much. The man is horrified of death—"

Because he has one solid foot in the grave.

"—and he'll lose interest if he believes you are sickly."

Ruthie bubbled up with laughter. "I thought he appreciated my delicate form."

Lady Celeste raised an eyebrow. "A delicate form is one thing; a delicate constitution is quite another. He needs an heir, not another dead wife."

Ruthie winced. It wasn't like her mother to be so crude or frank; however, her plan had been foiled. Lady Celeste was a schemer, but she didn't do her best work under pressure. Ruthie almost felt sorry for her.

She wiggled out of her mother's grasp and, clutching the banister, attempted to trudge up the stairs once more. "I said I'm fine, Mother. I'm sure the lord won't mind me being slightly indisposed."

Hiding a smile, Ruthie glanced over her shoulder to find her mother staring up at her, aghast. "And this is the reason why you need me. You don't know men, Ruthie. You are far too young to understand how their minds work. They abhor sickness and cannot abide playing nursemaids. That is why women are the caretakers in the house."

Ruthie turned back to the stairs so her mother wouldn't see her frown. She didn't have one memory of her mother checking on her when she'd been sick as a child. It was always the nanny who administered the tonics and cold towels on her forehead.

"I'll reschedule right away," her mother stated. "I'll have him come by tomorrow. That will soften the blow. That's another thing men hate—waiting. Remember that."

"I will, Mother," Ruthie said as she continued to climb. Her legs were stronger now, the steps so much easier. It was remarkable how much more alive she felt knowing she wouldn't have to stare at Lord Dawkins's shiny head all night. "I will see you in the morning."

Lady Celeste had already moved on. She had almost made it to the drawing room—no doubt to pen her message to the lord—when a knock came at the door. She slapped her arms down at her sides. "Who could that be at this hour?"

Ruthie paused on the steps. Normally, visitors had nothing to do with her, but today had changed all that. In her newfound experience, anyone could be on the other side of that block of wood.

She calmed her nerves as the butler answered the caller, not giving any indication that this was anything more than a regular occurrence. He closed the door and walked up the stairs to Ruthie, offering her a crisp white envelope.

"For you, miss."

Lady Celeste's head peeked out from the drawing room. "Who is it from?"

There was no writing on the outside of the note. Ruthie's fingers trembled as she opened it. And as her eyes flew across the foolscap, she screwed her mouth shut because she knew if she answered her mother at that time her voice would have trembled as well.

"Ruthie?" the lady called again. "Are you going to tell me?"

Ruthie shook her head, hastily folding the letter back into a tiny square. "It's from…Mrs. Everett," she lied quickly. "Just news about the cricket club, that's all."

"Oh," her mother said, losing all interest.

With Lady Celeste out of sight, Ruthie pressed the letter to her chest and ran the entire way back to her room. She slammed the door shut behind her and jumped onto her bed, landing on her belly with a giggle. Opening the letter, she read it once more. And then two more times after that. Until the day she died, she would never forget the few short words imprinted in her mind.

Ruthie, I cannot live without balance. Meet me tonight. –H

enough to cut open skin. The only items out of place were the clothes on the bed that had obviously been stacked by Holly.

Holly went straight for them and shook them out with a flourish before holding them up to Ruthie's body. "They'll fit well enough," she declared appraisingly, tossing the navy-blue jacket back on the bed. "All right, then, it's time to make a man out of you."

Ruthie giggled as Holly set to work, untying and coaxing the clothes off her, incredibly adept and efficient at her job. This time it was Ruthie's turn to keep up the steady conversation. It felt too odd to have a woman she didn't know undress her in silence.

"Will you and...your man be joining us tonight?" she asked while Holly slid her petticoat down to the floor. Ruthie accepted her hand as she stepped out of the bell-shaped piece of clothing. "I mean Mr. Holmes and myself. I didn't mean to imply *us*. There is no *us*. Just Mr. Holmes and...well, me."

Holly's fingers stalled as they worked on the laces of the corset. Ruthie squeezed her eyes shut. *You sound like a besotted fool!*

Which she most definitely wasn't. She was merely interested in the man, that was all. He was interesting! Would a woman refuse a proposal if she was besotted?

Holly's fingers went to work again, and when she finished with the corset, she threw it in the corner along with the growing pile of clothes. Ruthie inflated her lungs, widening her torso to an exaggerated degree.

Holly came to her front, her hands on her hips. "No. I'm going to meet him at the pub. You *are* a tiny thing. I've never seen a woman your height have a waist so small. The corset didn't have to work too hard."

Ruthie coughed. The miserable corset had been working hard enough for her. "My mother says men prefer a small waist."

Holly snorted. "That hasn't been my experience," she replied. "Most men like to have a woman they can hold on to, if you understand my meaning."

Ruthie, in fact, did not understand her meaning, though she

nodded anyway so she didn't appear to be even more of a simpleton. And as she didn't wish to inquire as to what Holly did for Mr. Holmes and where she'd acquired all her experience, changing the subject seemed the safest route. "What pub will you be going to?"

"The Flying Batsman. Do you know it?"

Finally! Ruthie was on solid ground. "I know the place well. I'm good friends with Mr. and Mrs. Everett." She hesitated. "Well, maybe not *good* friends. Mr. Everett tends to yell at me a lot, and then Mrs. Everett—Myfi—yells at him for yelling at me, and then he yells at everyone on the team. It's really not as bad as it seems."

Holly cocked her head. "Are you one of Myfi's cricket club girls?"

Ruthie nodded enthusiastically.

"Well, then you know my man, all right. Benny Hardcastle."

"Benny's your man?" Ruthie squealed. Benny had worked as one of the team's assistant coaches last season. She understood that life had been rough for the retired cricketer who'd turned to drink after his career ended, but things were looking up for him now. Last winter he'd taken a position coaching for a men's county team, and now he had a lady on his arm. Once more, Ruthie had to marvel at how quickly change seemed to happen around her club.

Holly blushed prettily as she buttoned the clean linen shirt and helped Ruthie into her trousers. They were tighter than she would have liked. Clearly, these were clothes the old cricketer wore when he was a few stones lighter.

"No wonder Mr. Holmes has taken such a shine to you," Holly said absent-mindedly, focusing on getting Ruthie's blue necktie just right. "He and Mr. Everett are good friends. Business associates, even. He's donated plenty to help the club get off the ground."

"I know."

"I never knew why he donated quite so much," Holly said,

stepping back to admire her handiwork. She grinned. "But now it all makes sense."

"N-no, no, no," Ruthie stammered, holding out her hands. Holly easily evaded her. She snatched the jacket off the bed and swung it through Ruthie's flailing arms. "Mr. Holmes and I haven't known each other long—"

"Sometimes a minute is all it takes."

"We're barely even spoken to each other—"

"Sometimes that's best."

Ruthie sighed and stamped her foot in a most feminine way. "I saved his life! That's all this is."

Holly's mouth snapped shut. Ruthie composed herself, knowing that she'd *finally* got her point across.

But then something bizarre happened. Holly's eyes glassed over and her chin wobbled slightly. Her voice came out breathy and awed. "That is so romantic!" she said, clasping her hands together underneath her chin. "Falling in love with a man is like saving his life, isn't it? Are you a poet as well, miss? If not, you should write some of this down."

Ruthie's jacket-clad shoulders slumped in defeat. There was no getting through. Holly saw what she wanted to see. Perhaps she was so in love with Benny that she wanted everyone to share the bliss?

A fist pounded on the door—five times—causing Holly to jump out of her melodramatic stupor. "Holly?" came a deep voice from the corridor. A stark pause followed before the voice added with a cough, "Ruthie?"

"Damn," Holly muttered, hopping into action. "Just a few minutes," she called, hurrying to finish Ruthie's ensemble. She was like a whirling dervish completing the look. Ruthie was so dizzy that she could barely look at herself in the full-length mirror when Holly was done with her.

But it was worth the wait. Ruthie could hardly recognize herself—which she supposed was the point. Even with the tight fit, the jacket and trousers suited her much better than Anna's brother's castoffs. And the wig, thankfully, didn't itch. Made of human hair and not horsetail, it sat easily on her head, and didn't overheat her like the one Reggie had given her. The top hat was the cream on the cake, luxurious and stiff, and rested on top of her head snugly without feeling like it wanted to fall down to perch on her nose.

"I might have missed my calling," Holly mused, smiling at Ruthie's reflection. "Has anyone ever told you that you make a handsome man?"

"Surprisingly, no," Ruthie replied dryly. "Although my family tells me that I look exactly like my father."

"I'll bet he had all the girls running after him in his day," Holly said, slapping her on the shoulder.

Ruthie's laughter was halfhearted. "That's what they say."

With one last appraising look, Holly nodded and went to the door. She was just about to turn the knob when she twirled back to Ruthie. "I hope your family tells you that you're a pretty girl, too. Because you are." Holly brushed her hair out of her face, ducking her head. "I'm sorry. I shouldn't have said that. I didn't need to. You know how attractive you are." She flicked her chin to the door. "You've got men running after you too."

"I told you! It's not like that between us."

Five more knocks. "It's been more than a few minutes," Harry called out, his tone heavy with irritation. "A *few* generally means three or four. It's been more than three or four. Now, if you would have said *several* then I might have let this go. Time is up."

Holly raised her eyebrows and looked at Ruthie with a *told you so* smile. Ruthie ignored the teasing implication. "Have you ever noticed that Mr. Holmes…is not like other men? With the knocking and the counting—"

Five knocks pounded again.

They couldn't hold him off any longer. Holly finally lunged for the handle. "He's impatient to get what he wants," she said, opening the door. Harry Holmes loomed large and annoyed in the dimly lit corridor. "Seems like every man I've ever known."

Chapter Eight

HARRY BIT HIS cigar hard. "Are you even listening to me? I'm not granting you all this free knowledge for my health!"

Ruthie jumped next to him, and Harry darted at just the right second to stop her elbow from banging into his bad side. Crisis narrowly averted.

"I am. I am," she rushed out, running her fingers along her forehead. "It's just…"

Sweat.

Harry abhorred it on everyone. It quite literally turned his stomach, which was why he so rarely could be found on the main floor of the club in the final hours of the night. By that time, men were usually broken, and their sweat-soaked collars stunk worse than a packed ferry crossing a choppy channel during a storm.

Though as much as Harry couldn't abide the grease that leached out of men's pores, sweat was a practical ally. During his gambling days, it used to tell him so many things. Even if the men he'd played cards with did a halfway decent job of controlling the emotions on their faces, most couldn't curtail the nervous sweat that seeped through their jackets and clothes, crowding their upper lids and hairlines, mocking their austere acting. It made for easy pickings. Harry almost missed it. *Almost.*

But why was Ruthie sweating? And why wasn't he shuddering away from the sheen above her plump pink lip? It wasn't like the woman had anything to be nervous about. She was with him. No one would dare take advantage of her while she swanned in the sun of his company. All she had to do was keep her mouth shut and listen to his pearls of wisdom. Harry could never understand why people always had such a difficult time doing that.

"Do you need to get some air?" he asked.

She shook her head, her brow furrowing. "No. No, thank you. I don't mean to be ungrateful. I'm just nervous. You're giving me so much information. It's difficult to take in all at one time. I had no idea this game was so complicated."

Harry's expression must have been more incredulous than he'd thought, because Ruthie squirmed a step away from him. But it couldn't be helped. Vingt-en-un? Complicated? It being so *not complicated* was the reason why he'd chosen to start there in the first place. Vingt-en-un was a counting game, pure and simple. All one needed to do was concentrate.

"Let's go over it again," Harry said, secretly proud that he sounded so magnanimous. "You have to keep your eyes on the cards—all of them, not just the ones dealt to you. Only fools play that way."

"Yes, yes, I understand that," Ruthie said, her voice taking on an edge Harry didn't understand. Why was she irritated with him? Didn't she see how kind and patient he was being? "It's the counting that I can't grasp."

"Clearly," he said, lightening his tone at her glower. "It's simply a matter of probability of high and low cards. If more high and valuable cards are on the table, then it's more likely that low cards will be dealt soon, and vice versa. Now, remember, the dealer is only playing with one deck, and he won't reshuffle the entire deck after every game. So if you're counting the cards properly, accurately, you should have a greater chance of winning as the games go on. It's obvious."

When Ruthie's lips twisted, Harry almost admitted defeat.

Was she a bad student or was he a terrible teacher? Harry knew what his answer would be, but his answers so rarely coincided with other people's. "Here, look there," he ordered her. He grabbed Ruthie's upper arm and dragged her closer. Her citrusy perfume tickled his nostrils. Holly should have noticed the smell and wiped it clean. Gentlemen did not dab rosemary concoctions onto their necks. Still...the light smell didn't stop him from plastering her even more against his good side. On second thought, it wasn't that offensive, even when it mixed with her sweat. Actually, the marriage was quite...alluring.

"What am I looking at?" Ruthie whispered. Her words tickled his ear. So much tickling was happening! And for a man that hated to be touched by any and all, tickling was decidedly beyond the pale.

"Um..." Harry blinked past his cigar smoke. He twirled the cigar around in his mouth five times until his brain finally remembered its duty. His voice was oddly high-pitched when he continued. "Lord Harley." He cleared his throat. "Right in front of us. You can see his cards, yes?"

Ruthie nodded.

"He's holding a king and five, and he's asking for another card. He's asking for a blasted hit. The stupid man has even bet more money when he has no chance of winning."

"Don't you mean he has *little* chance of winning?"

Harry scowled. "I mean no such thing. He has no chance. He's going to get a ten, just watch."

Sure enough, the dealer dealt Lord Harley a card, and it was exactly as Harry said.

Ruthie gasped. Slowly, she tilted her head up to him. Her blue eyes reminded him of the little five-petaled flowers that grew outside his grandparents' cottage in Ireland. The memory was thin, and yet it stayed with him all these years later. He'd only visited the elderly couple once and been forced to wait outside while his mother pleaded with them for money. Luckily, he hadn't had to wait long. It had been raining. And cold. But the flowers had comforted him. He'd picked enough of them to make a necklace for her, but she'd brushed it from his hands the moment she emerged, tear-stained and despondent. Most of Harry's memories were shit.

"Are you...touched?" Ruthie asked, licking her bottom lip, making it wet and glossy. Christ, as if sweat wasn't enough, now Harry had to witness saliva? But, once more, he didn't shrink in disgust.

"Touched?" he repeated, staring at that ripe cherry of a lip, wondering what it would taste like if he nibbled on it.

"You know...by God."

"Oh, for fuck's sake!" Harry sneered, now having no problem jerking away from the silly woman. "Do you actually believe that rot?"

"Not usually," Ruthie said, frowning, doing her part to create even more room between them. "But how else do you explain it? That couldn't have been a lucky guess. How could you possibly know the ten of hearts was going to land in front of Lord Harley?"

Her expression was doing everything her sweat and her saliva couldn't. It was forcing him away. Because she was finally looking at him the way so many others did when he tried to explain the silly game. And the worst part was that he couldn't blame her. Harry had never met another person like himself. He'd met his fair share of lucky men and more than his fair share of crazy ones; however, Harry wasn't either of those things—despite what his mother and her church believed. It wasn't luck that had helped him win so easily all those years. It was something more. For better or worse, *Harry* was something more. And being himself was usually worse when it came to being with women or trusting friends—but never when it came to making money. When money was on the line, Harry was always grateful to be Harry.

"I didn't mean to make you upset," Ruthie said.

"Don't," Harry rasped when she tried to put her hand on his arm.

She yanked her arm back as if he were a cobra primed to strike. Harry rubbed a hand over his face. This was why he should have gone with his instinct and not invited her to the hall tonight. He simply couldn't control himself when she was around. He reverted to the child that couldn't help himself. The child that his mother couldn't understand and wouldn't love.

"Please don't be angry with me," Ruthie said. She was batting her lashes uncontrollably and looked on the verge of tears.

Christ, Harry, get control of the situation.

"You didn't upset me," he lied, softening his tone. He could feel half the eyes of the room on him. Everyone was always sneaking looks at him. He pulled the mask back over his face, exhibiting his customary bored, unbothered expression. "I just don't like to be touched." Was he apologizing? "And I was embarrassed."

Ruthie blanched. "Embarrassed? You have an incredible skill, the kind of skill that people would die to have. Why would you be embarrassed over it?"

"Not that," he replied gruffly. He tugged the handkerchief out of his jacket pocket and wiped his hands. He would have done it all night—wiping again and again—if he hadn't willed himself to shove it back in the pocket. "By the way you looked at me."

"How did I look at you?"

"Like I was an abomination from hell," he remarked flippantly.

"And I thought you said you knew me." Ruthie laughed. "Do you want to really know what I was thinking?"

Harry nodded. When her eyes sparkled like that, he was pretty sure he'd lost the capacity to speak.

She arched an eyebrow impishly. "I was thinking I've never been lucky in my life…until I met you."

TWO HOURS LATER, Harry was convinced of two important things: one, that Miss Ruthie Waitrose would never make a proper gambler, and two, that he was hopelessly in love with the woman. Fortunately, Harry was confident enough in his own abilities that he could change the first. Unfortunately, he was familiar enough with himself that he had no chance in hell to change the second. Once his mind latched on to something, it would take no less than ten Hercules to wrestle it from him.

But wasn't this a matter of the heart and not the mind? Surely that was a fickle, malleable beast, Harry thought as he sat next to Ruthie at the vingt-en-un table, watching as she asked for yet another hit that sent her over the eponymous number. This sudden, earth-shattering realization made him want to crawl under the table and hide. Only he wouldn't dare do that, because he might choose to peel off those ridiculously tight trousers she wore, and he had no bloody clue what he would do then— something not like himself, Harry was sure of that.

"Why do I keep losing?" Ruthie whined, tossing her cards down on the table. Harry hid a smile as a chorus of noncommittal grunts from the other players answered her. He continued to be amazed. How could they not know she was a woman? It was so strikingly obvious to him. The dullards weren't completely thick in the head; they'd picked up on her numerous tells, which was why they were beating her so soundly. Harry had tried to help her past them, but every time he'd pointed one out, it just made her angry. Then, as she attempted to bury one tell, another crept up to take its place. She went from bobbing her leg back and forth under the table to hiding her smile with her cards to licking her lips (Harry's personal favorite) to tugging on her right earlobe. The woman had absolutely no chance.

And neither did Harry.

Still, Ruthie wasn't completely hopeless. The girl merely lacked confidence. It was initially evident in her body language. She had a bizarre habit of shrinking when the attention was on her. Her shoulders would round forward; her neck would hang limp; her arms would draw close together, as if she were a note folding itself to be sent away. She made herself small, and it hurt Harry's heart to watch every time she did it. Nevertheless, that action didn't necessarily affect her card playing. Her indecisiveness did that in spades. Ruthie couldn't make a decision without immediately regretting it. Harry considered it his job to remember everything, and even he forgot how many times she'd told the dealer to hit her with a card before immediately apologizing and asking him not to.

What made the action more infuriating was that Harry knew she'd understood his little lesson. Before he'd allowed her to play with her own money, he'd tested her on his counting method, acting like a dog with a bone until her answers pleased him. Her mind wasn't the problem, and nor was her body.

Ruthie simply didn't have the audacity to believe in herself.

Harry hovered over her shoulder. "I think that should be all for the night," he said, sotto voce.

Ruthie eyed the coins left in her hands. She would come away with a few pounds, despite her limited gambling abilities. Leaving with more than one came with was always a decent night, in Harry's mind.

"Are you sure?" she drawled, raising her lovely brows in question. "It can't be *that* late."

The Lucky Fish lived in perpetual darkness. Heavy curtains covered all the windows and the lanterns on the wall were kept to a dim light, yet Harry sensed the sun ready to break over the city. His body could sense its rise. And the sweat permeating the room was starting to become unbearable. "You mean early," he said. "And yes, it is. You need to get home."

"Oh, let the lad play on," Jeremy Baker cried from across the table. By Harry's estimation, the moderately wealthy textile manufacturer was *not* having a decent night. He'd started with close to ten thousand and would probably only leave with a quarter of that—if he stopped now. And from the desperate look in Baker's eye, Harry was certain he wouldn't.

"Ya!" chimed in Simon Tolworthy, a prominent banker in the city with whom Harry was always glad he did not invest his money. "Let the boy play if he wants. Ah, excuse me, Mr. Waitrose. I meant no offense. I meant man, not boy."

"No offense taken," Ruthie replied easily.

"Waitrose?" Baker repeated, sliding his hand against his shiny chin. *Sweat.* Harry shuddered. *So much sweat.* Strike the previous guess. The man wasn't leaving with an *eighth* of his money. "Is that your cousin?" he asked, pointing over her shoulder.

Ruthie and Harry twirled around in their chairs at the same time, and he felt her entire being tighten in surprise.

"Uh, no," she replied stiffly, turning back to the group. "No, I've never met him before in my life. Must be a coincidence. Surely you're not related to all the Bakers in the kingdom?"

Fuck. Harry had allowed himself to get distracted. Usually, he knew every single person in his hall. How could he not have noticed that Ruthie's fucking degenerate brother had weaseled his way inside? Especially since said weasel was impossibly drunk and getting into a heated exchange with one of his insipid wastrel friends.

As customary, the louder their argument became, the quieter the room, so all could hear it better.

"I am not being ridiculous!" Lord Mason shouted with laughter. "Come now, Mike. We've bet on sillier things. Besides, you're the one who said it could be done. I'm just asking you to prove it!"

Mason's accomplice, Lord Michael, laughed awkwardly, squinting across the room.

"Anybody can knock the candle out of that sconce!" he replied. "I just don't want to take your money. I'm tired of taking it, friend. It's too bloody easy!"

Mason Waitrose's face went red, though he managed a guffaw to counter the sting. "You're just a coward, Mike. I may lose from time to time, but at least I'm a man who takes risks."

Out of the corner of his eye, Harry saw Ruthie's jaw harden

as she played with her coins on the table, picking them up and letting them trickle back down. She *tsked* loudly. "Ridiculous," she hissed a little too loudly, shaking her head. "Such a child."

Mason's glassy eyes fell on Ruthie's back. The room went silent, the air humid with expectation. "Excuse me, sir. Were you speaking of me?"

Harry's chair skidded sharply on the wood floor as he stood. "I'm surprised to see you here, Lord Mason. Last time I checked, you still held no membership here."

Mason hit Michael in the chest. "I came with Mike. I'm sure you know his father, the Earl of Waverly. Spector was at the door—he said it was all right."

Harry's eyes narrowed. His lips barely moved as he spoke. "It seems I will have to speak to Spector *and* Lord Michael."

"You do that, Holmes," Mason said, chuckling. "In the meantime, I would like to speak to that friend of yours, the one with the big mouth."

"I don't think that's a good idea—"

Ruthie swiftly came to her feet and went toward her brother. "Go ahead, sir. I am all ears."

Mason stumbled a step before catching himself. *Christ.* Harry eyed him closely. Did he recognize his sister? The disguise was decent enough, but surely a brother could see through it.

But Harry had misjudged Mason Waitrose. Or he'd misjudged how sotted the man was, because even though he blinked wildly, he showed no signs of recognizing Ruthie. His own bruised ego was the only thing he noticed.

"New to town, sir? I don't think that we've met, Mr....?" Mason sneered. He latched on to the top of the seat next to him, holding himself upright.

"Charles."

"Charles? Charles what?"

Ruthie hesitated, swallowing slowly. Harry hoped to God that no one else noticed the lack of Adam's apple in the act.

Her smile was withering. "You can just call me Charles."

Mason snorted. "Well, Charles with no last name from who knows where, I am not ridiculous. I am attempting to place a wager in a gambling hall. What could possibly be childish about that?"

"I meant no offense," Ruthie replied evenly, starting to sit back in her seat, but Mason's words stopped her.

"But you have," her brother cried dramatically. "You have offended me! So now you must right this wrong and be Mike's champion."

"His what?" Ruthie squawked, losing the gruffness in her voice. It didn't matter. The room was too fixated on Mason's drunken theatrics to care.

The man smiled, and Harry had to hold himself back from punching him in the face. The baron's son was quintessentially handsome, with his thick, light brown hair and arresting, soulful eyes. His body was broad and athletic, clearly from years in the saddle. Indulged and catered to, and ultimately lazy, Mason was everything Harry despised about the aristocracy. How could he and Ruthie have come from the same parents?

Mason pointed to the far wall. "Mike said that any man here could knock the candle from that sconce, and I said they are all much too tired, drunk, or dead. So"—he showed his teeth—"prove me wrong."

Ruthie shook her head. "I don't think I'm the man for you—"

Mason addressed the crowded room. "One hundred pounds on Mr.—uh—Charles missing. Who wants to take the bet?"

"One hundred pounds!" Ruthie gaped. "You don't have one hundred pounds!"

Mason rounded on her, his eyes like fire. "Of course I do!" he spat. "Who are you to tell me what I have and don't have? Are you one of the freaks at the circus, Charles? Can you see inside my pockets?"

The room erupted into laughter while Mason called out for someone to find him a ball. Harry flexed his hands into fists as Ruthie sank into herself. Her spine was like a tall building with floors falling into each other one by one. Furtively, he skimmed her elbow. "You don't have to do this," he whispered. "He won't even remember in the morning."

Ruthie refused to look at him. Her jaw was clenched in anger. "He doesn't have one hundred pounds," she spat. Harry watched a transformation take place. Gone was the scared little girl. Ruthie filled out her suit jacket, pulling her shoulders back and her chin up. "I'm tired of Mason always thinking he's right, always getting what he wants."

Harry tried to touch her elbow again—talk some sense into the woman—but she was already gone.

"Fine, Lord Mason," she announced, striding to her brother's side. "But I have to warn you. I'm a champion cricket player. You might want to think twice about betting against me."

Mason let out a loud laugh. "I try never to think twice about anything." A tall, red-faced man ran to Mason's side, handing him a shiny billiards ball. Mason tossed it in his hand before handing it over to Ruthie.

Harry tried to read her expression, wondering if she'd ever played billiards before. The balls were heavy. Would she even have the strength to get it across the room?

If Ruthie was nervous, she didn't let on. She lined up where Mason and Lord Michael insisted, a good ten feet from her target. The brass sconce was a decent size and to the right of the door leading out into the corridor. Everyone sitting at the tables in her path quickly moved, getting out of harm's way.

Ruthie scowled at the blatant cowardice. "Oh, ye of little faith," she said, rolling the ball around in her hand. Again and again, she massaged her palm with the ivory orb while she settled her aim on the sconce. Every conversation and breath felt suspended as the crowd waited for her move.

"Nervous?" Mason mocked her, standing at Ruthie's left side. Harry would have shoved the bastard out of the way, but she ignored his shameless interference.

"Not at all," she replied blithely. "Are you nervous that your pockets are light?"

Ruthie's eye came off the target and fixed on her brother. When he didn't respond to her jab, they stared at one another for a long few seconds. A sigh of impatience from an onlooker yanked her attention back to the sconce.

But something had changed. Harry was sure of it. Ruthie's demeanor was different; her focus had wavered, her anger abated. This time when she sized up the sconce, she didn't have murder and revenge in her eyes, only regret.

When she pulled her arm back and launched the ball forward, Harry didn't bother staring at the candle. He knew she missed the moment the ball left her hand.

Just as she'd planned to.

Chapter Nine

R UTHIE WISHED HE had let her walk alone. She preferred
Harry when he was odd and arrogant. Even his pretentious
lectures were better than the gallantry he was currently showing,
because not only was he accompanying her home, he was
tiptoeing around what had just happened in the Lucky Fish. The
man valued control, but even Ruthie knew that must have been
difficult for him.

For her, it was even more difficult. It wasn't like she didn't
want to speak about Mason; it was that she had no experience
doing so. Where her brother was concerned, there was no one to
confide in. She couldn't speak to *him*, since he was usually drunk,
almost drunk, or sleeping away his drunkenness. Lady Celeste
never wanted to hear anything negative about her darling boy,
and Ruthie hated causing her little sister stress in any way. The
girl still loved her older brother—believed he was the best of
men—and Ruthie wished for her to hold on to that innocence for
as long as she could.

Her cricket club friends were always helpful and supportive,
but other than Anna, Ruthie didn't know them intimately enough
to ask for advice regarding her disastrous sibling.

That left Harry. Who currently was walking down the footpath trying desperately not to touch anyone that passed by or step

on the cracks in the cobblestones. Ruthie didn't notice it at first, but once she saw it, she couldn't stop. Harry was usually so skillful at hiding his quirks, but around her, he struggled to keep up his smooth façade. Out of the corner of her eye, Ruthie studied him as he glued himself to the very edge of the street where the granite blocks were long and rectangular so that his feet could fit inside each one, never touching a crack or groove, leaving Ruthie to walk on the smaller cobblestones.

Was Harry Holmes *that* eccentric? All signs pointed to yes. How did no one else see it? How could she be the only one?

Regardless, it was quite evident that Harry had his own problems. He didn't need Ruthie to pile hers on—which reminded her...

"Did you ever find him?" she asked abruptly. Harry arched an eyebrow, and she added, "The man who shot you? Did you ever find out why?"

"Oh," he said, as if she'd asked him about the weather. He glanced down at his injured side and patted it gingerly. "Yes, I've got some leads. Haven't done anything about it yet, though. Been busy."

"I must confess, it's rather alarming that you're not more upset!"

He smirked. "Unfortunately, it's a hazard of the trade and something I've become quite used to."

"Being shot?"

Harry shrugged. "People wanting me dead. I've never actually been shot before. Stabbed a few times, yes. Beaten, definitely. But never shot. I suppose even murderers must change with the times."

Ruthie shocked herself by laughing. Harry turned to her and smiled. Again, she was reminded with how handsome he was...in that dark and forbidding way. Ruthie was accustomed to wanting. She was even more accustomed to not getting what she wanted. So she allowed this little flirtation on her end. What was the harm?

"How can you be so nonchalant about it?" Slowly she walked closer to him, testing her theory about cobblestones. If Harry didn't want his arm to touch hers, he would have to move and risk walking on the cracks. She'd changed back into her dress before they left the gaming hall, and her cloak was more voluminous than the jacket she'd worn. It skated against her forearm, creating a lovely rustling sound. Furtively, she waited. He balled his hands into fists, squeezing mightily, but didn't move. It seemed that touching her was the lesser of two evils. Or maybe he just wanted to touch her as much as she did.

Harry's voice was hard as he answered her, his words short and clipped. "I don't mean to be nonchalant, as you say. I don't particularly like being shot or stabbed or punched. But when you start from the bottom, you quickly learn that you have to be willing to do anything to climb up."

"And when you reach the top?"

His boyish grin made her skin hum. "You have to be willing to do anything to stay there."

Ruthie studied the cobblestone mosaic at her feet, the same one that the man next to her feared more than a bullet. "It sounds like a lonely existence."

"You sound like my mother."

"Your mother?"

Harry pressed his lips together as if he didn't want to release whatever was inside. Eventually, he went on. "She died—"

"I know. You told me, remember? I'm sorry—"

He shook his head. "Don't be. We weren't close. That's an understatement, really. She hated me. Anyway, for some absolutely absurd reason, she wrote to me a couple months ago, asking me to visit her one last time. I obliged because Ernest made me. He said I would always regret it if I didn't."

"He was right."

Harry snorted. "Nuns were taking care of her. It seemed that all the money I sent her over the years, she gave to the nearby convent. I almost walked out when I saw them, but they spotted me and ushered me in, thanking me for my overwhelming generosity." He rolled his eyes before sighing. "Anyway, I'd waited too long. She was nearly delirious in her bed. So, so small. It was odd because she always seemed so large to me when I was little, even when I outgrew her. But her anger... Well, that didn't shrink."

"Why was she angry with you?"

"Because I wasn't the son she wanted," Harry said—remarkably, without a hint of bitterness. He was matter-of-fact over his mother's lack of affection, as if he understood it better than she might have.

"Because you joined a gang?" Ruthie asked.

"Fuck no," Harry replied. "Because I was different. An odd boy that everyone laughed at, a boy who shuddered away from her hugs and never cared when she began to withhold them. She said I never could give her what she needed, could never be the son she wanted. I tried, my God, I tried, but I just...couldn't."

The words shook Ruthie to her core. If she could understand anything, she could understand disappointing a parent. "Did she say anything to you when you visited?"

Finally, Harry lost his ambivalence. "Of course she did. She must have been reserving her strength for it. She grasped my hand even though I... Well"—he glanced down at his gloved hand apologetically—"even though I don't appreciate that, and yanked me down to the bed. I remember staring at her teeth—she'd lost so many. The ones that remained were so yellow they were almost green. She told me she'd had a vision from God and that I was going to hell if I didn't repent. She'd seen me there. I was going to die, alone and helpless, unless I found favor in the Lord. Bloody rot."

Ruthie was too stunned to speak. She had her issues with her mother, but she couldn't imagine Lady Celeste speaking to her so vindictively. Ruthie continued to watch Harry as he stepped on his stones, his gait confident and unwavering. For a moment, she allowed herself to look beyond the gray hairs and stubbled cheek, beyond the haughty, handsome façade, and find the little boy who must have been terrified of his overzealous mother. So terrified that he'd abandoned her to make a life in the cold alleyways of London. So terrified that he grew into a man who considered murder attempts to be a "hazard of the trade."

Ruthie trembled and hugged her cloak tighter. "So that's your hurry to be married—your fear of death. You laugh and call it rot, but deep down you believe your mother's right." She paused, feeling undeniably hurt. "That…that is why you asked me to marry you."

Harry stopped walking. He turned to Ruthie, meeting her squarely. She tried to hide her disappointment, tried to put on a brave face as well as he did, but she knew she failed. "It wasn't the only reason," he said.

He stood there for a long moment, watching his sweet words sink into her. Ruthie attempted to keep them at bay; she reminded herself that this man was only trying to soften the blow, and yet…and yet those words found their way to her heart, easily and surely. Giddy and nervous, Ruthie broke the silence and began to walk once more. "You were so brave to leave when you were so young," she said, clumsily changing the subject.

Harry blanched, squinting at her ruefully. "How bizarre that you consider leaving home to become a thief as brave. Most would think otherwise."

"Well, I don't," Ruthie replied, lifting her chin.

"I didn't feel very brave at the time," he continued. "Really, it was a matter of necessity. I'd overheard her discussing exorcisms with a priest from our church." Harry scratched his chin. "I didn't think it would be wise to stay and be a part of one of those. I had a feeling that it might not end well for me."

"I should think not." Ruthie laughed. "But you shouldn't be modest. I don't think I would ever have that much courage."

"You would."

Ruthie pictured her mother lavishing all her attention and grace on Lord Dawkins while gesturing with wild eyes for her daughter to do the same. "No," she said glumly. "I couldn't. Can I tell you a secret?"

"I'd be most disappointed if you didn't."

Ruthie gnawed at her bottom lip. A minute ago, she'd told herself not to burden the man, and now she was confiding in him. Did she have any control of herself in his company? But Ruthie's heart was heavy; her soul felt even worse. She needed to talk to someone, and Harry Holmes was the only person who didn't mind listening. He might be a different, eccentric sort of man, but that counted for something, didn't it?

"I missed on purpose tonight," she said, watching closely for his startled reaction. When nothing happened, she went on, "My throw. I missed the sconce on purpose. I could have hit the candle off. Easily. But I decided not to at the last second."

"I know."

"You know?"

Ruthie stumbled over her feet. Usually, it was difficult for others to keep up with her pace; however, this night she was finding it a trial to stick with Harry's gait and conversation.

"Of course I know. I saw your mind change right before you threw the ball. Why?"

She angled her head. "Did you really believe I could hit the candle?"

Harry's expression turned guilty. "Well…not at first, but then it hit me."

"What?"

His smile was self-satisfied, as if he'd solved an ancient riddle. "You were always vaguely familiar to me. I swore I knew you from somewhere, but I couldn't place you. It was driving me quite insane, actually. I *hate* not knowing things."

"And?" Ruthie prodded, hiding a smile.

"Oh, yes. Then you mentioned cricket tonight. You're one of Samuel's darling cricket girls, aren't you? I must have seen you play last year. And I figured you had to be good if Samuel could stomach you. He's quite the snob about cricket."

"Yes, he is. But…" Ruthie bobbed her shoulders. "I'm not one of the better players, although I wouldn't say I was bad."

Harry cast her an appraising look. "Truly inspiring words."

"I'm sorry! But you can't expect me to… I mean, it's not right to speak about oneself in such a way…to be an egotist."

"Why?" Harry asked, truly baffled. "I do it, and it works just fine for me."

"Yes, but you're you and I'm me. We're very different people."

"Thank you for clarifying that," Harry returned dryly. "And you're right. I would have never let my arse of a brother win. Why did you?"

There it was. The question Ruthie had been avoiding, the one she didn't want to answer out loud. Because it would make her even more ashamed of herself than she already was.

"You wouldn't understand."

"I could try."

She turned to him. "Could you? There seem to be a great many things that you don't like to do, but your body compels you to do them anyway. How much control do you have over yourself?"

Harry had kept walking. When he noticed Ruthie was behind him, he looked down at the stones and changed course. He stopped right in front of her, the tips of his boots narrowly missing her own. "It's not as easy for me as it is for other people. It's not as simple as just *wanting* something."

"Wanting something isn't easy. Some of us try not to want with everything in our bodies, but still can't help it."

"And what do you want, Ruthie?"

What did *she* want? In her entire life, had anyone ever asked Ruthie that question? If so, had she ever dared to give her answer out loud? Could she do it now?

"I…I don't know," she stammered. Oh, but she did. She wanted the kind of life that other girls took for granted. It wasn't a grand life full of wild adventures on the Continent or schoolgirl fantasies involving pirate ships and turquoise waters. She wanted love. Pure and simple. Ruthie wanted a husband who adored her. A man who was excited to ask her about her day, who valued her opinion and wanted to build a life with her. She wanted a companion who knew how to make her laugh, a confidant who knew when to let her cry. A person to snuggle into when she was cold and a shoulder to rest her head on when she was tired. A lover to share her nights, to covet her days.

Ruthie wanted a man who asked her what she wanted. And she wanted the strength to accept him.

Harry's eyes darted over her, reading her. She felt herself turn warm; it was a slow, steady burn growing in the deep reaches of her belly. His voice was gentle, as soft as the pillow she laid her head on alone each night. "What do you want, Ruthie?"

You.

The word was at the tip of her tongue. How Ruthie yearned for this man to sweep her in his arms and kiss it free. Open her to a new world of freedom and enlightenment.

Harry cocked his head, waiting, ever patient—interested. Could anybody truly understand what a gift that was? To have someone desire to hear her answer rather than just branding her with theirs?

He leaned down to her. Ruthie opened her mouth to speak, only the words wouldn't come. Harry's smile was kind, so kind it hurt. And for a moment, she actually believed that if she told him she wanted him to kiss her, he would do it. That he would *want* to do it, too. He wouldn't grimace as his arms folded around her, and he wouldn't flinch as his boot straddled a crack in the stone, and he wouldn't falter as his lips fell to hers. And he wouldn't be disgusted as she devoured him with her aching, overwhelming *want*.

The picture Ruthie painted was nice. More than nice. Decadent. Sinful. No, not sinful. Beautiful.

And so very, very terrifying.

Harry's eyes fell to her lips, and fear rushed in, dashing all her hopes to the side. Ruthie stepped away, remembering that she was not a courageous woman. She was Ruthie. The loving daughter. The good friend. The sympathetic sister. The rock that willful people broke themselves against.

Harry stretched his arm, making to grab her elbow and bring her back inside the bubble of their moment, but it stalled halfway. His expression changed, almost like he were a man waking up from a long, unlikely dream.

So Ruthie answered him the way she was supposed to, the way she'd been told to her entire life, the only way she knew how. "I lost so my brother could win," she said, walking once more. "It's his destiny."

Chapter Ten

THE HAIR ON the back of Ruthie's neck had been at full attention all evening. She couldn't put her finger on it, but the mood was curious, and not a little bit terrifying.

Lord Dawkins was hardly a loquacious fellow—it was one of the traits that Ruthie appreciated most about him—however, tonight, as he sat across from her at the Waitrose family table, he was positively chatty.

And Lady Celeste was loving every second of it. Clad in a simple gold gown that served to make her dark hair gleam even more than usual, Ruthie's mother was practically glowing over the lord's constant stream of conversation. She didn't seem to notice, or mind, that Lord Dawkins never made a point to ask others their opinions; her smile was as unbreakable as British steel.

And that was the real reason keeping Ruthie on edge. No one found the Corn Laws that exciting—especially after forty-five minutes.

Sitting at Lord Dawkins's right, Ruthie's little sister, Julia, made the most of her time being ignored and stretched her tongue out long in an attempt to touch the tip of her nose. Ruthie snorted into her water, splashing some into her face. She had to give the little devil credit—she almost made it.

Lord Dawkins flinched in his seat, startled by Ruthie's unladylike performance.

Quickly, she used her napkin to wipe the water off her cheeks. "Excuse me," she muttered, feeling the hot poker of her mother's gaze stab her right in the chest. "I am just so in awe of your knowledge on the subject, my lord. You are such a…" Ruthie wished someone could come behind and squeeze the words out of her body. "You are a worldly man. So much more than me."

Lord Dawkins returned a patronizing smile, his beady eyes never traveling higher than her clavicle. Not for the first time, Ruthie wondered if there was something the man didn't like about her face. Too many freckles? Too long and masculine? Her chest couldn't be that inspiring, could it? She'd certainly never thought so, had always assumed it was just like every other woman's.

"Sometimes I forget how young you are, Miss Ruthie," he said, casting Lady Celeste an approving, knowing look.

"It feels like she only just left the nursery," Lady Celeste replied with a sanguine smile. "But you know how we mothers are. It's so hard to let go of our babies."

Luckily, Ruthie wasn't holding her glass, because she was certain she would have snorted again.

"I understand completely," Lord Dawkins said. His head was shiny and slick with the kind of greasy sweat that would have made Harry Holmes tremble. *Ha!* Ruthie smiled at the memory. Harry's aversion was evident to anyone paying attention—and Ruthie was. Whenever anyone had the ill grace to mop the sweat from their brow or temples, Harry's upper lip would curl back in utter disgust. The movement was small, infinitesimal—and Harry would most likely deny ever doing it—but Ruthie was becoming a quick study of the gaming hall owner. And what she learned continued to surprise and delight her.

Unlike her current dining companion, whose pale face grew ruddier with each passing minute. The room was pleasant enough, not too warm or cold. Was all the talking tiring the lord out? If so, he wasn't ready to give up yet. "Young people need an education," he went on, puffing out his paltry chest. "Someone to take them in hand and show them the ways of the world. Someone they can trust."

Julia perked up. "Mother, Mason mentioned that he was going to take a trip to the Continent next year. Do you think we can go with him? He could show me the ways of the world!" She clasped her hands together and pressed them to her heart. "I cannot wait to see Paris. I hear it's the most beautiful city in Europe!"

"How could it be?" Lord Dawkins scoffed. "It's full of Frenchmen, and stinks even worse!"

He broke into peals of belly laughs that ended in him coughing uncontrollably into his plate of half-eaten sole and peas. Earlier, he'd apologized to Lady Celeste for his lack of appetite, but his gout was flaring terribly.

Lady Celeste tittered jovially. Paris had been her favorite city. One of Ruthie's most beloved memories was her parents, in one of their détentes, telling their brood stories of their adventures in France while sharing secret, scandalous looks with one another. Julia was much too young to have the same memory, though Ruthie had done her best to recount the stories as best she could over the years.

At the rebuke, the girl sat slumped in her seat, crestfallen and disillusioned while shoving her own peas around her plate with her fork.

"You're too young to go to Paris," Lady Celeste answered, lowering her voice to soften the sting. "Your brother is a young man and not an appropriate chaperone. I could hardly expect him to look after you."

"Especially when he can barely look after himself," Ruthie muttered, shocking her mother so much the woman dropped her fork.

The room lapsed into a bewildered silence. Instead of frightening her, the sharp emptiness emboldened Ruthie to go a step further. "Where is our dear brother, by the way? I find it hard to believe he's not hungry. He couldn't possibly be thirsty with all his late night carousing—"

"That's enough!" Lady Celeste barked. Swiftly, she turned to Lord Dawkins, breaking the awkward moment with a startling laugh. "Those two," she said in a long drawl. "They are the best of friends, always teasing one another. And where do you think a lady should travel, my lord, for her spiritual and social education?"

It wasn't a perfect segue by any means; however, the lord was only too glad to pivot away from the family squabble. "Ah…yes, let me think. You know, I've been to so many places, it's so hard to say. My friends always tell me that I'm one of the best-traveled people they've ever met."

This time it was Julia's turn to snort in her water when Ruthie rolled her eyes so hard her head almost toppled to the table.

"I'm sure we would agree with them," Lady Celeste replied, throwing a scowl at her insubordinate daughters. Still lost on the Continent with his adoring friends, Lord Dawkins didn't notice the furtive exchange. "Travel gives a person an unmistakable substance," she continued. "Everyone should make it a priority. It is a fault of character if they do not."

"I didn't know you valued it so much, Mother," Ruthie remarked, exaggeratedly biting the fish off her fork.

Lady Celeste shook her head at Lord Dawkins playfully. "You know very well that I do. Don't be absurd, Ruthie. I cannot wait for you to see the world. You'll be better for it."

It was so difficult not to be charmed by her mother. The lady was simply too beguiling, too lovely. Her handsomeness provided the perfect mask for her subterfuge. Like a moth to a flame, Ruthie couldn't help but fall for her light and found herself believing her mother…or wanting to.

"Do you really mean it?"

"Of course! You know I only want the best for you—for all

my children." Once more, Lady Celeste's laughter was nervous and for Lord Dawkins's benefit. "How can you ask me that?"

Ruthie stared at her food uncertainly, maintaining even breathing. If ever there was a time, it was now. "Then I have something I'd like to discuss with you," she began evenly, trying to mask the hope in her voice. "I've been approached with a chance to travel—it's not to Paris or Rome, but it's still very exciting."

Lady Celeste's smile didn't budge. It was as if Ruthie had morphed into Medusa and her serpentine words had turned her mother to stone. "Now isn't the time, my dear. Let's speak on this later."

But later would never come, Ruthie was certain. Pressing her mother now in front of their guest was her only chance. "Oh, but you don't mind, do you, Lord Dawkins?"

The odious man opened his mouth, but Ruthie beat him to it, unwilling to let him speak and ruin her moment. Who knew when he would stop? "I wouldn't have to go far or be away that long—three weeks, maybe four," she said. "The cricket club has been invited to play exhibition matches in a few cities around the country. It's an honor that they want us to come. You know how much the club means to me, Mother."

Lady Celeste's smile fell. "My dear—"

Ruthie cut her off, leaning over the table. "All the travel expenses have been paid for by a benefactor, and we would be staying with good families—good *ton*," she added, though she had no idea if that last part was true. It *probably* was. "Mrs. Everett and Lady Bramble will act as chaperones. And it isn't for a few more weeks, so I won't be missing many social events, since the Season is almost over, and you always say it's important for me to meet new people, and this would be a great opportunity to do that— and did I say we wouldn't be going far? Only to Exeter and Bath and maybe Ipswich and Manchester."

She sucked in a breath. If she didn't, she was afraid she might pass out. But she'd had to get it all out before her mother could reply. She had to lay everything on the table so Lady Celeste could hear all the facts and give a fair and rational answer. Ruthie had to make her mother see not only how important this was to her, but also how beneficial.

The silence was no longer encouraging. The longer Lady Celeste stayed quiet, the more Ruthie wanted to bang her head on the table. Julia's eyes had doubled in size during Ruthie's never-ending speech, while Lord Dawkins scratched at a food stain he'd found on his jacket.

Ruthie shrank under her mother's scrutiny. Lady Celeste filled the eerie silence by lifting her wine glass and taking a long sip. She licked her bottom lip and regained her smile. But it was thin and mirthless.

"Meet new people?" she repeated curiously, lifting her eyebrows. "In *Manchester*?" Lord Dawkins chuckled, but Lady Celeste didn't shift her focus from her wayward daughter. "I'm afraid it's out of the question." She returned her wine glass to the table; the dull thud gave her words extra finality.

"But how? Why?" Ruthie asked. "You don't need me here."

"That's correct. *I* don't." Her mother cocked her head, sharing a knowing grin with Lord Dawkins, whose face flared as red as a beet.

Ruthie's stomach dropped. *No. No. No. No.*

This cannot be happening. Not now.

Her next words felt like they were covered in broken glass and were cutting her throat as they left her mouth. "I…I don't understand."

But Ruthie did. All too well. She just didn't want to. Because she knew once her mother explained the truth of that smile then it would all be too real. And Ruthie couldn't handle that. Not now. Not when she'd been working so hard on a plan to rid herself of this man and the unfathomable future as his wife.

Nevertheless, Lady Celeste would not spare her. "I wanted to wait to tell you after dinner," she said, mercifully relenting on her smile. "I assumed that Lord Dawkins would want to do the honors, but he thought it best that I told you the happy news."

"What happy news?" Julia asked.

Lady Celeste didn't take her eyes off Ruthie. It was as if she were willing her oldest daughter to be overjoyed, begging her not to embarrass the family by being anything other than grateful. By sticking with the plan. By having purpose. "Your sister is going to be married."

Julia frowned. "To whom?"

"To Lord Dawkins, of course."

"Lord Dawkins?" Julia exclaimed, scrunching her face up in confusion. "But he's so ol—"

"He's so perfect for her!" Mother interrupted. "Yes, I know. That's why this is such wonderful news."

Sweat.

Lady Celeste's temples were sweating. Ruthie lost herself in a tiny bead as it trailed down the side of her mother's face, fading away under the crevice of her sharp jaw. Even Harry Holmes would have a difficult time finding Lady Celeste's sweat unappealing. The woman had once had the very best of London eating out of her palm. Men had come from miles away just to witness her awe-inspiring beauty. She'd had adoration; she'd had excitement; she'd had true love.

And now she was selling her daughter off to the highest bidder—to the only bidder. Did it upset her to know her daughter would have none of those things? Even under her delighted façade, Lady Celeste had to be aware that Lord Dawkins was incapable of loving anyone but himself, and his years of excitement were decades behind him. And as for adoration… Did Lady Celeste now contend that it was a childish emotion best left to young men and over-stimulated spinsters who read too many novels?

Ruthie's marriage would be a quiet one. Respectable. One-note and reserved. And she must be grateful. Always grateful.

And never satisfied.

Never. Satisfied.

Never happy.

Never…wanted.

But that wasn't what Ruthie wanted. Ruthie wanted more.

"This is terrifying," she said softly.

"I'm sorry, dearest. What did you say? You have to speak up," Lady Celeste said.

Ruthie lifted her head. "I said I'm terrified."

Agitated, her mother shook her head apologetically at the lord. "Every girl is nervous to leave her home and be married. It's completely normal to be a little scared of the exciting future ahead, but don't worry. You will be a wonderful wife and mother."

"I'm not nervous, Mother. I'm terrified—" Ruthie's words broke off as she held back a sob. She would not cry in front of Julia. She wanted her sister to remember this moment and be proud of her one day.

More importantly, Ruthie wanted her sister to know what courage looked like.

She placed her napkin on the table and stood up from her seat. "But I don't want to be terrified anymore," she said, proud that her voice was so even. "And I don't want to be a part of your plan. For *once* in my life, I want to be brave."

Lady Celeste pursed her lips, her calm façade vanishing. "What are you talking about? Sit down!"

Ruthie ignored the order. "Lord Dawkins, thank you for your proposal, but I cannot marry you."

The man answered with a blustery, disbelieving chuckle. "Whyever not? You have to be aware that I'm the only one who wants you."

"No," Ruthie replied, astonished that his words didn't hurt her. She was wearing a shield, and they merely bounced off. "You don't want me. You *need* me."

"What the devil does that mean?"

Ruthie smiled. Unlike her mother's, there was no chill to it, no mask. It was a true smile born of true happiness. Because

Ruthie had no idea how she would feel in the morning. She didn't know what the future had in store. She only knew that at this moment—this one small moment—she felt alive and happy, and she valued herself and her decision.

She was betting on herself.

RUTHIE DIDN'T LOOK over her shoulder as she walked down the street. No one was following her anyway. Her mother had been too stunned; Lord Dawkins had been too stumped. No one had tried to stop her when she fled the dining room. Most likely, Lady Celeste was too busy placating the lord over her daughter's bewildering and rude behavior. A gentleman's ego was a fragile thing; it would have to be massaged.

Ruthie hadn't exited the house right away. She'd made one stop to her room to pen a quick letter to her sister, explaining where she was going and how Julia could contact her if needed. In the end, it wasn't necessary, as her sister's light footsteps could be heard outside Ruthie's bedroom just as Ruthie was signing her name to the note.

In her haste, she hadn't shut the door, and Julia paused through the small opening staring at her older sister with a mix of awe and alarm.

Ruthie had dropped her pen on her desk. "I'm sorry you had to see that."

"I'm not," Julia replied, taking tentative steps into the space. "It was like being on the stage during a play."

Ruthie laughed. "But it wasn't a play," she said, trying not to relive everything she'd just done. If she did, she might regret it and run back downstairs to apologize. "It was very real, and I'm not sure what the repercussions will be."

Julia shrugged. "Mother will be furious. But she'll forgive you. She has to."

Sweet young girl. "No, she doesn't."

Julia played with the ends of her braid. "Perhaps you should keep to your room for a few days. Stay out of her sight until she cools down and realizes that what you did was for the best. She couldn't possibly expect you to marry that old man. He's...*old.*"

Ruthie laughed despite herself. She walked over to her sister and enveloped her in a bone-crushing hug. "Thank you for understanding."

Julia's words were muffled against Ruthie's chest. "You've never done anything like that before. It's like you're a different person."

"I *feel* different," Ruthie said, resting her chin on Julia's head. Too bad she didn't know if that was a good or bad thing.

"What were you writing?"

"A letter. To you."

"To me?" Julia pulled away. "Why?"

Ruthie's body tingled. So many emotions were running through her veins, threatening to overwhelm her fledgling calm. Her sister's innocent question was almost too much. Tears pooled along Ruthie's lids. "I can't stay here. I'm leaving. Tonight."

"But where will you go?"

"I have a plan," Ruthie said, avoiding the question. "You don't need to worry."

"Will you come back?"

"Of course!" Ruthie had lied to Julia before, but they'd always been small and inconsequential. They were falsehoods for her own good. This one was different. This lie was for Ruthie's peace of mind, because she couldn't leave the only home she'd ever known believing she would be allowed back. "I need to do this," she said, pulling her sister in for one more hug. "I'll always regret it if I don't."

Julia murmured against her heart, "And you promise that you will be fine?"

Tears had finally slid down Ruthie's face. "I do," she'd lied again. "Better than fine."

Now, with the moon overhead, Ruthie lengthened her stride as if the memory was nipping at her heels. More tears threatened to come, so she dashed her sister from her mind. She couldn't look back. Forward was all she had now. She'd made sure of that. Her old life was gone. She'd burned it to the ground. Ruthie hadn't the heart to tell her sister that their mother would never forgive her for this. Lord Dawkins had been the family's lifeline. Lady Celeste had been counting on the lord's money and protection.

But Ruthie could fix that. She had an idea—all she needed to do was convince her mother to trust her. Easier said than done.

Ruthie turned on St. James Place. The area hummed with people enjoying themselves, carriages picking up and dropping off revelers as the night commenced. The closer she came to the Lucky Fish, the closer doubt came to tripping her up. What if Harry said no? What if he'd changed his mind?

That was another thing Ruthie refused to contemplate. She steeled her body and her mind as she sidestepped a group of disheveled, clearly inebriated men engaged in an argument. She was about to tackle the club's stairs when a voice called to her.

"Miss Ruthie?" Ernest emerged from the middle of the heated group of men. "One moment, gentlemen," he said to them, quickly walking toward her. "I won't let them inside until they go home and change," he explained, nodding to the group. "The Lucky Fish has standards, after all, and their combined smell is offending all of them."

She nervously reached out to grab the butler's hands. "I need to speak to Mr. Holmes. Is he here? What am I saying—of course he's here."

Ernest spoke in a low voice. "Is everything all right, Miss Ruthie? You look...*unsettled.*"

Ruthie tried to smile but could see it did little to quell his worry. She took a deep breath. "I'm fine, truly—I just need to speak to Mr. Holmes. It's of the utmost importance."

Why wasn't he running inside to do her bidding? Why did he continue to regard her as if had just escaped the asylum? Ruthie patted the hair off her face. Her hair had come undone during her walk. She must appear crazed and disheveled.

"Did you walk here, Miss Ruthie? It isn't safe. Let me call a carriage for you so you can go home."

Ruthie squeezed the butler's hands so tightly she heard a knuckle pop. "Listen to me, Ernest. I am not going home. I am never going home again. Now, if you don't take me to Mr. Holmes this minute—"

"What the hell are you doing here?"

Ruthie turned to the doorway where Harry stood, arms crossed, the pale light of the hall silhouetting his intimidating figure. He swiftly descended the steps, his annoyed features becoming more apparent the closer he came. "You can't show up announced. It isn't safe."

"That's what I just told her!" Ernest cried.

Harry flicked his head, and the butler immediately left, returning to the group of men who still hadn't stopped their squabbling. He loomed over her, and the exquisite relief Ruthie felt was palpable. His nearness served as a balm for her worries. His concern—masked in irritation—almost sent her to her knees.

But Ruthie couldn't fall yet. She pulled at her reserves, knowing that this was it. This moment would alter her future. She would see it through with clear eyes and heart. She hadn't planned it, but she'd jumped at it nevertheless.

"Well?" Harry asked. "Do you have anything to say for yourself?"

Ruthie's lips trembled. Anxiety was a cold, cold thing. "I...I lied...when I told you what I wanted."

Harry didn't speak. As always, his expression was blank, but she knew him better now. The way his eyes darted back and forth between hers, the way his tendon jumped in his neck, the way he pretended not to swallow—he wanted her there. He wanted to hear what she had to say.

"Will you let me play cricket?"

He replied instantly, "Yes."

"Will you let me see the world? Will you let me live the life I want to live? Will you let me be who I want to be?"

Ruthie didn't know where these questions were coming from. She hadn't meant to ask them, but once they came out of her mouth, she recognized how important they were. As did Harry. It was a small change, but his face softened, and an understanding floated between them like a gentle breeze.

The last question proved to be the hardest to get out. "Do you still want me?" Ruthie asked.

"Yes."

"Good."

Ruthie closed her eyes. And then she moved.

She closed in on Harry, wrapping her hand around his neck, pulling him toward her. Ruthie's lips landed on his with single-minded determination. She pressed into Harry with a lifetime of yearning and something, tasting the bitterness of his cigar, the sugary sweetness of wine. His mouth was warm and inviting, the lips lush and pillowy against hers. Ruthie had never kissed a man before; she'd assumed Harry would be all prickly skin and rough angles, but as he breathed against her, he succumbed to her desire, canting his head to hers, taking all the uncertainty and emotion inside her and guarding it with his strength.

He opened his mouth, catching her gasp as he swept his tongue inside, swallowing her surprise and coaxing a response. Harry's neck trembled under her palm; his stomach tensed and flexed as she placed her other hand on him, fighting an urge to search for the skin she'd once sewn back together.

The night disappeared around them. Ruthie had lost all sense of time. She could have kissed this man forever if the world let her. She was so lost in the kiss, she only slightly noticed that Harry's arms didn't circle her as she would have wanted, nor the fact that he'd positioned himself in between cracks in the pavers beneath them. Those little things didn't matter. The passion was undeniable. The thrust of his tongue, the growl in the back of his throat, told Ruthie the one thing she needed to know.

A whistle dragged her back to her senses. Harry's lips paused on top of hers. He sighed and slowly retreated, his disappointment obvious. He made to kiss her again, and Ruthie closed her eyes in giddy anticipation, but then he spoke.

Her letdown was quelled by the kindness in his voice. "How does it feel to finally be brave?" he asked.

Ruthie's laughter was dismal. "Absolutely terrifying."

Harry chuckled. "Yes, that sounds about right."

Chapter Eleven

ALTHOUGH HARRY HAD no taste for religion, this situation was precisely why he allowed a select number of clergymen to enter the hallowed halls of his club. You never knew when you would need a priest—even if it was a drunk one.

Ernest was at their heels as Harry towed a flushed Ruthie inside the club. "Who's here?" he called over his shoulder, dragging his fiancée toward the stairs.

"Father Brian, Father Samuelson, and several others, I think. I'll find out," Ernest said, earning his substantial salary. Even though Harry's thinking could run a bit wayward at times, Ernest never had a difficult time reading it. He knew exactly what his employer was planning.

Harry stopped halfway up the stairs, cushioning Ruthie while she bumped into him. He gave his butler a pointed look. "Find one quick," he said, before adding, "Preferably one that can still stand and doesn't reek of perfume."

"Certainly, sir." Ernest nodded and hurried down the staircase. Harry appreciated the man's speed. It matched his own. There was no time to waste. He finally had Ruthie in his home; he aimed to keep her there.

When he got to his room, Harry finally released her hand. Going straight to his bureau, he opened the side door, brought out a small black case, and carried it to his desk, using both hands so as not to upset its contents. He could feel Ruthie's eyes on him as he took out a small set of keys from his breast pocket and located the one he needed.

The case opened with a thrilling click. Harry appreciated jewelry even less than he appreciated clergyman, though he admitted that it, too, had its uses every once in a while. Glorious and resplendent rings of every color and size glittered up at him.

He turned to face Ruthie. Hands clasped in front of her, she appeared lost and a little frightened standing alone in the middle of the space. He couldn't believe she was still here. She'd chosen him. Harry had a feeling he'd been the lesser of two evils, but he wouldn't complain, and nor would he look this gift horse in the mouth. Most of the people he came into contact with thought he housed a little bit of evil—what did it matter if his wife did as well?

"Come," he said gruffly, moving out of the way, giving her a full view of the rings. "Pick anyone you want...or all of them." Harry rubbed the back of his neck, an odd feeling of inadequacy coming over him. "I suppose they're all yours now anyway."

Ruthie's steps were short and tentative as she did as he ordered, though when she made it to the table, her fingers remained strangled together in front of her, almost as if she were afraid of the precious metals. She leaned over the desk. Her eyes widened, but they still weren't as round as some of the stones in the case.

"How did you... I couldn't possibly..." Her breath was hushed and fast. "They're too grand. How do you have these?"

Harry frowned. Did she not like them? Did she not want them? Suddenly, it occurred to him that he desperately wanted to put a smile on her face. Not doing so seemed like the ultimate failure. "You know how I have them."

Ruthie shook her head, and more hair broke loose from her bun. Harry closed his eyes, refusing to let the asymmetry ruin the moment. When he opened them again, he watched Ruthie run her fingertips over a tiny stone the size of a red-berry mistletoe. "How could people just give these away?" she murmured.

Harry shrugged, confused by her sobriety. The last thing he wanted was for her to feel sorry for reckless fools. He needed her to feel lucky that all of his was now hers. But he hadn't counted that Ruthie would mind if everything he owned came from the misfortune of others.

He stood next to her and picked up the ruby ring, holding it up between them. In his fingers, it seemed such a dainty thing, not worth the tremendous debt it had been used to clear. But just as beauty was in the eye of the beholder, so was a thing's worth. What was priceless to one person was trash to another. To a man who grew up on the streets, Harry understood more than most that value was given and not born.

He took Ruthie's hand and placed the ring at the tip of her finger. Her nails were shiny and clean, her fingers long and elegantly tapered. He remembered how well they'd fit together that first night they shared, how scared she'd been of him, how much he asked of her, how much he continued to ask.

And she'd still come to him.

"People give me their most precious items because they have to make a choice," he said, staring down at the ring, trying to find the courage to inch it further on her finger. To find its home. "They find themselves at a wall. They can either turn back and face the consequences or find their courage and climb it."

Her hand began to tremble. "It doesn't seem like that hard of a decision."

"Every choice is difficult," Harry growled. "Every choice is the ending of one life and the beginning of another. Each day is filled with these tiny deaths and births, these new versions of the person you choose to be. I suppose right now I'm asking you to be the person who would spend the rest of your life with a person like me. And that won't be easy. But if you bet on me, right here and now, I promise that you will never lose. Not once."

Ruthie's smile was winsome, gentle. And because Harry

lacked the courage to do it, she was the one who slid the ring down her finger.

The sparkle in her eyes rivaled the ancient stone. "As I said, it isn't a hard decision."

HARRY COULD FEEL his butler panting down his neck like an asthmatic dragon, but he kept his eyes on the bustling room. "Yes, Ernest?"

"It's just…" The butler fidgeted, his breathing growing heavier, causing Harry to wince. "Don't you have someplace you should be?"

Harry glanced at his pocket watch and sighed. He didn't know why he even looked at it. He knew the time perfectly well. He could have told Ernest what it was down to the second. One thirty-two in the morning. On his wedding night.

Harry lifted his chin, avoiding his butler's all-knowing eye. "I'll be up shortly."

"That's what you said an hour ago," Ernest pointed out. "And the hour before that."

"I'm busy," Harry snapped. "Being married doesn't change that."

"I understand well enough, sir. I do," Ernest returned in not nearly enough of a placating manner. The word "but" hung in the air. Harry didn't have to wait long for it. "But," Ernest continued, "your new bride might not appreciate that fact. She might be lonely up there. She might want some company from her husband. Poor thing has had a bit of a day, if you don't mind my saying."

Harry did mind. Of course he minded! No one's butler should speak to him in that impertinent manner. But Ernest wasn't an ordinary butler and Harry was no ordinary master. Besides, the incorrigible servant was right. Ruthie had had "a bit of a day."

And Harry was, no doubt, only making it more trying.

The wedding certainly hadn't helped. If Ruthie had come to Harry hoping for romance and chivalry, he'd failed her. Giving her the ring had been damn near perfect. Unfortunately, every moment after had left much to be desired.

Harry hung his head at the memory. *Father Brian. Fuck.* Why had it been Father Brian, of all people?

"The ceremony wasn't all that bad," Ernest said in a nails-on-a-chalkboard conciliatory tone. "I'm sure Miss Ruthie didn't mind."

Was his butler a mind reader now? How could he know that the ceremony was running on a loop in Harry's head? Oh, right. Because it had been a fucking disaster. A calamity of errors of epic proportions.

Ernest's words continued to scald the back of Harry's neck. "On his best days, Father Brian has issues with his memory. The man is seventy-five, after all."

Harry's fists tightened at his sides. "He couldn't remember one name?" he spat. "One fucking name—the bride's! He called her everything under the sun except her own."

"He called her Ruby once... That was rather close."

"And he swayed like a goddamned tree in a storm!"

"It was barely noticeable."

Quick as lightning, Harry spun on his butler, his heart nearly beating out of his chest. "Do you think she noticed when he got sick all over the floor in front of her?" he shouted. He was causing a scene. He could sense eyes veering toward him, but the visions of his tragic wedding ceremony blocked everything neatly away. All Harry could see was Ruthie's dainty silver slippers. He'd fixed on them as she'd jumped out of harm's way, lifting her skirts from the mess when the priest heaved all over himself. They'd seemed so delicate and innocent...so deserving of something better than a sick priest and hasty, clandestine nuptials.

Harry's shoulders fell. He closed his eyes, running a hand though his hair. If he could have torn out every inch from his scalp, he would have. That pain was nothing compared to what was going on in the hells of his conscious.

His words came out in a rasp. Pitiful. "She deserved better."

"Yes," Ernest agreed. "And she also deserves a husband on her wedding night. Is that why you're not going to her? You're embarrassed?"

Harry huffed. *Yes.* "Embarrassed? Hardly."

"Then why are you still down here? Vine can handle it. I'll let you know if we need you, although you know we won't."

Harry lifted his head to the stairs. All he had to do was take them. Just a few little steps and he'd be exactly where he wanted to be. With Ruthie. But his feet were soldered to the floor.

When his master didn't speak, Ernest took it as a sign to continue pleading his case. "Miss Ruthie will forgive you. She laughed when you threw the priest out of the room."

"What else was she going to do?"

Ernest seemed to consider it. "She could have screamed. She could have cried. I understand that women can fall into hysterics."

"Not Ruthie."

"No, not Miss Ruthie. Or should I say, not your wife. Not Mrs. Holmes."

Harry's spine clicked straight. He liked the sound of that, *Mrs. Holmes*, More than he cared to admit. It felt incredibly right coming out of his butler's mouth. Everyone in the entire world should say it with equal reverence—from the pope to the queen.

Harry looked back at the stairs. "You'll tell me if anything happens down here?"

Ernest would never roll his eyes at his master in public, but Harry could tell he wanted to. "You know I will."

Harry stared at him for a few long seconds before finally nodding. "Good." He turned toward the staircase, taking a deep inhale.

He heard Ernest chuckle behind him. "Most brides and grooms are nervous on their wedding night. It's natural, sir."

But Harry couldn't laugh. He couldn't find anything funny about this situation. Ernest had no idea what he was talking about.

Nothing was ever natural for Harry Holmes. And, unfortunately, his bride was about to find that out.

Chapter Twelve

HARRY KNOCKED ON his bedroom door. It seemed the right thing to do. Decorum was called for. After the evening Ruthie had had, politeness was needed.

He waited until a little voice invited him in, and even then, he took it slow. The room was cast in shadows, with only one thin candle lit on the table near the bed. The atmosphere was similar to the carriage ride they'd shared on the day he first asked Ruthie to marry him. Harry's footsteps felt aggressively loud as he walked across the room. His bride was in his bed—her bed now. Her hands were folded primly in front of her as she leaned against the headboard.

Had she been waiting for him?

Of course she has, you fool.

Harry would have to thank Holly in the morning. She'd been busy. Before scurrying away after the ceremony, Harry had ordered her to see to everything Ruthie would need that night to be comfortable. He wasn't sure where Holly had come up with it, but Ruthie was wearing a modest white nightgown that fastened under her neck with capped sleeves that gave Harry a bountiful display of long porcelain arms. He itched to move closer, yearned to see if freckles dappled those charming arms as much as her face.

Ruthie's hair was plaited in a long braid that ran down her right side, sloping over the small mound of her breasts. The asymmetry failed to nag at him. The picture was too beautiful. In the scant light, the coil appeared as silver as moonshine, and, again, Harry desired to be next to her, to cradle that rope of hair in his hand and see if it felt as smooth as it looked.

Ruthie's soft words interrupted Harry from his romantic musings. "I wondered if you would come."

Harry's guilt tugged at him. That was one thing a bride should never wonder on her wedding night. Thoughts, apologies…*condolences*…swarmed through his head, all fighting to be blurted out first. He shifted his stance, feeling like a lonely actor on stage about to give his triumphant soliloquy.

Eloquence, tact, was needed.

"It…ah…it smells better in here."

Harry slapped a hand over his face. Eloquence and tact were not to be had.

From outside the cavern of his palm, he heard a bubble of nervous laughter. "Yes," Ruthie returned lightly. "Holly saw to it. She wouldn't let me back inside until it was cleaned properly. I hope Father Brian is feeling better."

"Father Brian's lucky he can still walk."

Ruthie's forehead crinkled. "Is he that bad off?"

Harry waved a hand in the air. "Oh, he's fine. I just meant that he's lucky I didn't break his legs into a thousand pieces."

Ruthie's expression froze, almost as if she didn't know if she should believe him. *She should.*

She fiddled with the edge of the bedsheet, and Harry noticed her ring. His heart jumped in his chest. "One can't help being sick," she said. "It wasn't his fault."

Laughter choked out from Harry's throat. "Yes, but one *can* help drinking a bottle of gin before midnight."

"Oh."

"Yes, oh."

The laughter died quickly on his lips. A small fire whimpered halfheartedly from the hearth, though sweat broke out along Harry's temples.

Ugh, *sweat*.

He wiped his forehead with a handkerchief and then neatly folded it and placed it back in his jacket pocket. "The heat is oppressive, don't you think?" he muttered.

Ruthie bolstered herself higher on the bed. "Not particularly."

Harry reached for his handkerchief again. Christ, he was sweating like a maniac. Surely Ruthie wouldn't want him to touch her now.

Touch her.

Fuck. How the hell was he going to tell her?

It didn't help that his little bride looked so sweet and beguiling in his monstrous bed, like a cherubic lamb waiting patiently to be slaughtered.

Ruthie's eyes were round and wide as she waited for him to do something—anything. She barely even blinked. The only things that continued to move were her fingers, and their fiddling betrayed her nervousness. Nervousness that Harry's bumbling behavior was certainly not helping.

Best to just get on with it, then.

Harry swallowed the lump in his throat. "I…ah…I'm sorry it took me so long…tonight—"

"It's fine."

"I'm very busy—"

"It's fine."

"I can't trust people to take care of the den for me—"

"It's fine."

"And I wanted to wish you goodnight because I won't be joining you tonight—"

"It's f—" Ruthie's word stalled on her lips.

Harry stifled a curse. He was hoping her amenable behavior would continue until he escaped out of the room. His entire body tensed as he waited for her to finish her sentence.

"What do you mean?" Ruthie asked slowly, a distinct edge in

her tone. "Why?"

Harry locked his hands behind his back, taking a few steps closer to the bed. Five small steps. It was a bad decision. At this new angle, he realized his bride's nightgown wasn't as modest as he'd thought. The fabric was thin and flimsy, providing him with an advantageous view of the plummy flesh that lay beneath. His body had reacted to her the moment he'd entered the space; now, he was positively throbbing with expectation.

His voice came out high. Weak. "I thought you might prefer it."

Ruthie cocked her head, her expression curious. "You thought that I would prefer to sleep away from my husband on my wedding night?"

Did she have to say it like that? So…damning? He was being considerate, for fuck's sake.

"I thought after the day you've had…"

Ruthie didn't miss a beat. "That I might need the comfort of my husband?"

Harry's wide shoulders slumped on an exhale.

"I thought that men usually wanted"—Ruthie waved her hands around the bed—"this."

"They do."

She frowned. "My mother—"

"What about your mother?"

Ruthie's face pinched. "If we don't"—again with the hand waving—"do this, then she might try to have the wedding annulled. I don't want to risk it."

"We can just tell her we did." Harry regretted the words the second they came out of his mouth.

"Is it me?" Ruthie asked, the hurt in her voice making Harry feel lower than he'd ever felt. And then he saw it. He watched her close in on herself, becoming so small on the bed he thought he could lose her.

Harry was an ass. He was worse than an ass. He was a coward. "Christ, Ruthie. How can you think that? Of course it's not you. It's me. It's always fucking me."

She coughed out a laugh. "Sure," she whispered.

She wasn't going to make this easy for him. Again, Harry searched for eloquence and tact. He searched for a way to salvage this piss-poor night. He searched for a way to make her believe him when he said he wanted her more than he wanted anything, but he was too fucking defective to treat her properly.

Harry latched on to his wife's dejected face as he searched for the perfect, compelling explanation. Nothing came to him.

"I don't fuck like other men."

Again, eloquence and tact were not to be had this night.

Ruthie regarded him warily. Her fingers were no longer playing with the bedsheet. Her knuckles were white as she clutched the fabric for her dear life.

Harry's jaw clenched under her abject scrutiny. *Well…she asked.*

His bride blinked. And then blinked again, slower this time, as if she were also trying—and failing—to find the perfect words. Harry certainly hoped she had an easier time of it than he had.

She licked her lips. "Ah…sorry…just how different?"

Harry groaned. With both hands he rubbed vigorously at his face, disturbed by how wet his hands had become. *Still fucking sweating.*

"This is not what I'd hoped to talk about tonight."

"You brought it up," Ruthie pointed out.

"Yes, but…" Instantly, Harry surmised that hell must be dealing with awkward situations over and over again for all eternity. "I only tell you so we're on the same page. It's for your own good. You don't have to spend your night worrying—or any night after. I won't… I won't subject you to it."

"Again," Ruthie began, "how different? And why *exactly* wouldn't I want to be subjected to it?"

It was true that Harry didn't have experience dealing with highborn virgins, but he couldn't be the only person of his ilk who assumed an explanation wouldn't be necessary. Most would have just taken what he'd said and offered a thank you. Not his young bride. No, Ruthie Waitrose wasn't terrified or grateful. She was curious and—by the set of her pointy jaw—interested.

Which only made Harry's lower half burn even more.

With a ragged sigh, he threw himself down on the couch against the wall—his legs were shaky all of a sudden. Not to mention it was much easier to hide a cockstand that way.

"I didn't think you'd need all the details," he answered, feigning a bored, put-upon voice.

"You've intrigued me."

"That was the opposite of what I intended to do."

"You failed."

He had. Harry felt that tug again, that pull toward anguish and despair over how the night had gone. He'd married the girl—got what she'd wanted. But all he'd done since he put that blasted ring on her finger was disappoint her.

"What's wrong?" Ruthie asked.

"Nothing."

"Tell me."

"The wedding. I swear to you, darling, for the rest of your life I'll give you anything you want just to make up for that fiasco—"

She flopped her hands against the bed. "I don't care about the blasted wedding, Harry. I care about why my own husband won't sleep with me!"

Startled, Harry laughed. It wasn't funny. None of this was. "I already told you—"

"Yes, I heard you the first time. You don't fuck like other men—" Ruthie slapped a hand over her mouth, though she was anything but disturbed over repeating the filthy word. Even from the couch, Harry could see her blue eyes twinkling mischievously.

Some men in his acquaintance didn't approve of women using such profanities. They considered it uncouth, a definite turnoff. Not Harry. He realized that he fucking loved it. But, then again, he found that there was very little he didn't love about his new wife.

He leaned back against the cushions, rubbing his sweaty palms against the tops of his legs. "What do you want me to say, Ruthie?" he asked tiredly.

If she saw a defeated man, it didn't sway her. "The truth. Tell me—" She bit her lower lip, and Harry wondered if she was going to use that word again. "Tell me what you mean. I won't let you leave until you tell me."

She was leaning over her lap now. The bedsheet was low and wrinkled along her hips. The swell of her breasts outlined the linen of her nightgown, and Harry's mouth watered at the forbidden fruit that he'd already sworn he wouldn't touch. As enticing as she was, Ruthie was equally frightening. And he believed her. If he left without telling her, she'd surely follow him—modesty be damned.

Harry started slowly, picking his words carefully. "You've mentioned my foibles before. You called them quirks." He waited until she nodded. "Well, there are many of them, more than you can ever imagine. I deal with them all day long, and it's always been my mission to keep them from others to the best of my ability. Men in my line of work don't succeed when others think they're"—Harry pursed his lips—"freaks."

"You're not a—"

Harry lifted his hand, cutting her off. "For some reason, it's harder for me to control them around you. Or maybe you're more observant than others. There's the tapping, the counting, the not stepping on cracks or lines...the need for order and symmetry."

"Many people need that."

"Not like me. And that's only the start. There's the issue with touching. I can handle it with gloves and clothes, but skin-on-skin contact makes me...uncomfortable."

"How uncomfortable?"

"Very."

Ruthie frowned, fixing her attention on the ceiling. "But you touch me," she said quietly.

"Yes."

She met his gaze. "You kissed me."

"Yes."

"Did you...did you..." She ducked her head. "Did you not like it?"

"It was the single most beautiful moment of my life." The words whipped out of him like a fierce wind. So startling. So true.

Ruthie's cheeks turned pink. "If that's the case, then why can't we..." She waved her hand between them.

How did one tell an innocent that there was a difference between theory and practice when it came to sex? Ruthie was proving her mettle by hanging in this difficult conversation, but Harry hadn't the slightest idea how she would take hearing him explain to her that he got off on watching. It was only after encouraging and coaxing a woman to touch herself and reach her own fulfillment that he would come inside her, losing himself for that one brief moment in a luscious body—all while remaining perfectly clothed. His always-running mind never allowed him anything more. The connection was always brief, perfunctory. Harry was a slave to his foibles and, over the years, this was the only method he'd used in the bedroom. It worked, and he'd never had cause for concern or a need to fix it.

Deep down, he was scared that he wouldn't ever be able to. And even more petrified to have to, one day, tell her that.

So, instead, Harry replied pathetically, "It's complicated."

"I see."

He shook his head. "You don't."

"You're right. I don't. But I want to. I *want* to."

Ruthie slipped out of the bed. Her nightgown covered her from head to toe, though Harry would be damned before he found anything else as revealing. He never believed he'd be so enamored by toes. Little white toes peeked out from underneath the flimsy material as her never-ending legs brought her to stand in front of him. And her arms—dear Lord, her arms were indeed covered in pale freckles, the kind that charted a course directly to his heart.

Harry sucked in a breath as she towered above him, all words lost and forgotten in the deep recesses of his dark soul. He didn't deserve this woman. He knew that as faithfully as he knew the sun would rise tomorrow. But he'd taken her. Ruthie Waitrose was his. Why couldn't she be happy with just that? Just his name.

Ruthie had risked everything tonight. She'd taken a chance on him. Now, gambling was in her blood. Harry had lived among gamblers the majority of his miserable life, and he knew one thing to be certain—one win was never enough. They always craved more.

And Ruthie craved him. He could still feel the want in her kiss from earlier. He could see the ember of desire flickering in the blue flame of her eyes. The air sparked and nipped at their skin from the electricity flowing between them.

"You don't know what you're asking."

Ruthie's lips curved. "You told me that you would do anything for me. I'm calling in your marker. I want this. I want you."

Harry's willpower was on a thin leash. He couldn't figure it out: was his new wife desperate, or was she a seductress?

Ruthie pulled her nightgown up and over her body, tossing it to the floor, and Harry decided the answer didn't matter. His wife was naked in front of him. Tall and statuesque, rosy and tight, she wasn't so much thin as lithe. There was a strength that belied her small bones, an athleticism that suggested stamina and speed. Characteristics Harry valued—in life and in the bedroom.

Ruthie began to whistle. Her patience had effectively ended.

As had Harry's well-meaning resolve.

To his mind, he only had two choices. He could order her to get back into bed or he could ask her to lie down on it. The chasm of difference was known only to him. And, as usual, the devil on his shoulder won out.

Harry's lips were impossibly dry. What he said next was barely audible. But Ruthie clearly heard him, because she broke into a self-satisfied smile and turned toward the bed. Her luscious behind cried out to him for the shortest of moments before she turned back and sat on the edge of the mattress. Very briefly, she hesitated. Harry recognized the trepidation on her face—here one heartbeat, gone the next—as she gingerly reclined, lying on the bed.

He watched her chest pump up and down for a few breaths as she waited for his next order. He struggled to contain himself. *Go slowly.* But the anticipation was too great. The picture in front of him was too tantalizing. Ruthie was pure sex.

And not a good listener.

"I told you to hang your legs off the bed," Harry said, harder than he'd expected. Well, that couldn't be helped. Everything about Harry was harder than expected at the moment.

"Oh." Ruthie wiggled down until her knees bent along the edge. Harry's bed was higher than most, but the tips of her adorable toes still skirted the hardwood floor. "Like this?" Her voice was breathless. Nervous. Again, theory and application were two very different things.

"Now, open your legs," Harry said, ignoring her question.

Her breath came faster now. Another pause. Harry was just about to repeat his order when Ruthie's knees began to tremble. Then, inch by blessed inch, she widened her thighs, granting him a view he would forever be grateful for.

"Like this?" she asked.

But Harry couldn't answer her. His voice—his mind—was momentarily lost. He could only stare into the heat of her. The deep pink folds of her body that were made to welcome him, to hug him in their vicious clasp.

His response fell out of a thin exhale. "Yes…g-good," he stammered. Harry's skin felt too tight. The *world* felt too tight for the emotions banging inside of him. "Now, I'm going to tell you something, and I'm only going to say it once," he started. "I'm going to ask you to do things. Things to yourself. And I want you to do them. They'll only give you pleasure; I promise you. I don't want you to think. Just do."

Ruthie came up to her elbows to level him with a dark look. The tips of her breasts hung deliciously toward him. Harry had never put one in his mouth before—had never wanted to until now. What would Ruthie's breasts taste like? His mouth watered at the exotic possibilities.

"Will it give *you* pleasure?" she asked.

"You have no idea."

"You're right," Ruthie said, reclining once more. She studied the ceiling. "So, give me an idea."

Harry leaned forward in his seat. He rested his elbows on his knees as he took in this feast. He didn't have to tell Ruthie to do anything. He was already knocking on the door of his limit. He would spend the moment she whimpered, but that would be selfish. This night wasn't about him anyway. It was for his bride. And he wouldn't stop until she was as limp and satisfied as he was.

"I want you to touch yourself."

Ruthie giggled. "I am touching myself."

"No, not on your stomach." Harry gritted his teeth around his next words. "Touch yourself…between your legs."

Ever the good student, Ruthie acted right away. Harry watched as she caressed herself down the lines of her hips to her thighs. Time seemed to stop as her hand paused at that swath of land, as if she were deciding whether to move forward.

"Keep going," Harry urged.

He could hear her swallow. Eventually, she grabbed hold of her courage and sent her fingers further along the inside of her thighs. She played with the skin there for a few tantalizing seconds and then meandered to her center, sliding her fingertips through her curly patch of blonde hair. Her movements were smooth and focused as she dipped one tip along the seam of her body, caressing the sweet line with cautious care.

It was a small gesture, so tiny one could almost miss it, but Harry heard the uptick in her breathing, the hitched catch of her voice that escaped out of the back of her throat. True surprise. Flawless excitement.

Harry clutched his forearms while he continued to take in the erotic scene. Ruthie fumbled at first, yet that somehow was equally enticing. Because this wasn't an exhibition. She wasn't on display to him. With the bite of her lower lip, the frown upsetting her brow, the woman was exploring herself. For herself *and* him.

In all his forty-two years, it was the most courageous thing Harry had ever seen.

"Good girl," he purred, perched on the edge of his seat. "Use two fingers. Pet yourself. That's it. Doesn't that feel fucking good?"

Ruthie's voice shook along with her legs. "I…I-I don't know."

"Yes, you do," Harry said, almost feeling the wet friction of her caresses. His stomach clenched. His balls were impossibly tight inside his trousers. "Let yourself enjoy it. Have you found the spot yet?"

"Wh-what spot?"

"That means no." He chuckled lazily. "You'll know when you do. It's toward the top, hidden away along with all of life's pleasures. It is the cliff, both daunting and alluring. Frightening and persuading. Once you climb to the edge, you're powerless to stop. You simply have to jump. Nothing matters except the little death."

Ruthie's breathing quickened. "You're speaking in riddles," she rasped.

"I only speak the truth," Harry said. "You'll know soon enough."

It didn't take long, and Ruthie didn't have to tell Harry once she found it. Her toes curled along the wood as she unleashed a harsh mewl.

Harry's grin reached to each ear. "That's it," he said. "Press there, just a little. Then more. Rub yourself until you burst apart."

Just as Harry was. It was almost too much, watching Ruthie

work herself. Her skin was heated and burnished against the hearth's light. For once, Harry concluded that sweat had a time and a place after all. His wife's limbs were slick and shiny as her hips bucked against the mattress, her fingers pumping faster and faster. Her back arched, sending her breasts bouncing toward the ceiling, her nipples taut and pointed.

Peaches flashed in his head. Yes, Ruthie's breasts would taste like peaches, all tart and ripe, swollen with nectar.

Her sounds were louder now, more aggressive and disjointed. "I can't," she sobbed, squeezing her thighs against her hand. "I don't know…"

"Don't stop," Harry ordered her, his tone urgent and hard. "You're almost there." Over his trousers, he cupped his shaft in his hand, squeezing, not allowing himself to tip over the precipice. *You can do it. Keep going, darling.*

Ruthie had lost control. Her entire body was moving restlessly on the bed. Her neck was arched, her eyes squeezed shut as she continued to reach. Harry could hear her slickness, hear the slide of her fingers.

And then she screamed.

Harry leapt out of his seat. With a couple of flicks, his trousers were unbuttoned and pushed down, releasing his engorged cock. He had to blink a few times to make sure he wasn't truly dreaming. The sight underneath him was too good to be true. Ruthie's arm finally lagged as little, tiny vibrations erupted inside her body. Her lips were plump and red, her mouth open in awe and astonishment.

But the time for admiration had passed. Harry shifted in between Ruthie's legs. He dug his hands into her thighs, grabbing and pulling her until her pelvis was flush with his. He reached for his shaft, placing the tip at the center of her opening. One thrust was all it took.

He slammed forward, sheathing himself in her impossibly wet and tight opening, all breath leaving his body for one cataclysmic second.

Ruthie screamed out again, this time in pain, and later, Harry would thank the heavens for that sound because it brought him back to some semblance of reality. Hidden in her depths, Harry stared down at his wife, waiting, waiting for...he didn't know what.

As her body clenched around his shaft, he searched her for disdain, repugnance, anything that would force him to stop. Force him to heed the angel on his shoulder, the small semblance of control.

But there was none of that. Ruthie showed no signs of distress or distaste, only a small wince of discomfort and the awkward moment of what to do with her hands. She moved to place them on his shoulders but stopped herself in midair.

"Hold your breasts," Harry grunted.

Instantly, Ruthie did as he said, a secret smile forming on her lips. And just seeing that, along with the nipple peeking out from between her fingers, was enough for Harry to fall into oblivion. He pulled out slowly and arched back inside, once more, losing his rhythm from the heady act. Finesse was forgotten. Skill and sophistication were thrown to the wayside as he pounded against her, taking, slaking his need.

Ruthie held him with her hips, guided his thrusts with her inner thighs until it was Harry's turn to scream.

It came hard and fast, guttural, pulled from his body like a stunned confession. He spilled himself inside her, almost pitching forward onto her chest in the effort. At the last second, he caught himself, punching his palms into the mattress on either side of Ruthie's body.

Their chests heaving, they could only stare at one another, each in wonder and astonishment over what had just happened. Harry would never be able to put words to it. Housed somewhere between this world and the next, it was both primal and ethereal, of the body and the spirit. Animal and God.

Animal and God.

Animal.

Ruthie noted his tension. Her eyes narrowed as he studied the connection of their bodies, the smudge of blood on the inside of her thigh, the growing red welts of skin where he'd held her. Ruthie raised her hand again. It was pure instinct. Harry jerked angrily as she tried to run her fingers along his forehead. His shaft fell out of her, and he stumbled away, dropping her legs so they flopped back to the side of the bed. He caught her grimace, the confusion on her face.

He recognized the disappointment. "I'm sorry," he said, quickly stuffing himself back in his trousers. He tucked his shirt in and buttoned everything to controlled perfection. Shame built up inside of him. Shame for who he was. Shame for who he could never be. Shame for what he could never give her.

Ruthie reached for him again, but he swiftly evaded her. "Don't leave," she said.

"I'm sorry. I'm sorry," Harry repeated, head down. He clamped his mouth shut, stopping more of that nonsense.

He couldn't look at her, couldn't bear another one of those looks. So he did what he should have done the moment she'd taken off her nightgown.

Harry turned on his heel and left.

It was rude. It was blunt. It was unspeakably cold.

But it was the only thing he could do. Speaking wasn't an option. Chances were that if he opened his mouth in front of Ruthie, he would say something he didn't mean. Or worse, say something he did. And then keep on saying it until he forced himself to stop.

Gambling was for fools.

Chapter Thirteen

RUTHIE WOKE THE next morning feeling intolerably sore, and it had nothing to do with her body. As the sun streamed in through the window, she grabbed her pillow and shoved it over her face. She couldn't face it. Her heart hurt too much, and it was only exacerbated by the profoundly lovely feeling her body continued to enjoy. Every tiny movement elicited a flood of memories that made her stomach flutter and her fingertips curl into the cool sheets. Even the innocent touch of those silky sheets awakened something deep inside of her. Two days ago, that harmless occurrence would have been disregarded; now, it was like a siren's cry of possibility and change.

But that wasn't the only reason Ruthie lolled in bed. There was also the little problem that she had not the slightest idea what to do with herself. Despite leaving her home in spectacular fashion the day before, she couldn't call Harry's famous den of iniquity her home either—especially since he'd left her and hadn't come back.

Was someone supposed to wake her? Even though Holly had been more than helpful last night, Ruthie didn't believe that she was her permanent maid. One would have to be found. Had Harry thought of that? Probably not. A bachelor for so long, he most likely wouldn't have a clue as to the needs of a wife—

especially in the limited timeline that Ruthie had given him.

Ruthie *hmphed* and squirmed onto her belly, burying her face into the sheets. There were many things that Harry would have to learn, she thought dismally. Like how to treat a wife after lovemaking. Would he always turn tail and flee like that? Was it her fault?

Ruthie hadn't meant to reach for him. She'd lost her head, so overcome by what she'd experienced—by what they'd shared—that she merely wanted to touch him, to let him know what she was feeling.

But he hadn't wanted that. Harry hadn't physically pushed her away, but by the expression on his face, he might as well have. Ruthie understood that she'd stepped too far. There was an invisible line, and she'd crossed it. Now she had to decide if toeing the line was worth it, or if she would demand her new husband draw a new one. Worse, she didn't even know if he could.

Luckily, a knock on the door saved her from delving deeper into her mysterious husband.

Tucking the covers under her chin, Ruthie was relieved to find Ernest on the other side, along with a young, pretty maid she remembered from the night Harry had been shot. The girl bobbed with a tray in her hand and placed it next to the bed. Ruthie didn't think she'd ever been so excited to see toast, butter, and a pot of tea in her life.

Ernest's smile was brighter than the sun as he waited for the maid to finish. "And how you are this lovely morning, miss? I mean"—his eyes twinkled as he coughed into his fist—"Mrs. Holmes."

Ruthie couldn't contain her blush. "F-fine, thank you, Ernest," she replied, mustering all the decorum her mother had drilled into her. She smiled at the maid. "Thank you…"

"Jessica," Ernest answered for the maid, who bobbed again and swiftly exited the room. "She won't be your full-time maid, but I will hire one today as soon as possible. You, of course, will get the final decision."

The butler's generosity struck Ruthie. She'd never been given the final say on any of her mother's servants. "I'm sure whoever you choose will be fine," she replied.

Ernest nodded. He glanced at the door before turning back to her. "Well, then, if there's anything else…"

"Where's my husband?" Ruthie asked. She fixed her gaze on the light blue teapot as embarrassment blazed across her cheeks.

"He left early this morning, ma'am. He likes to do that. Start the day with the sun." He flicked his head to the window. "He should be back this afternoon. I'll let him know you were asking for him."

Ruthie's hands flew out in front of her, nearly upsetting the tray. "No! Please, don't do that. I…I mean… I hate to bother him."

"I'm sure it's no bother at all."

"I just mean…" Ruthie searched her mind to salvage this dismal conversation. Suddenly she felt young and immature, incredibly naïve, and was certain that Ernest knew it. "I don't want Mr. Holmes to think I'm following him. I just… I'm not sure what my duties are, is all. We, ah, didn't have time to discuss it."

"Duties, ma'am?"

"In the house."

Ernest frowned. "This isn't much of a house, ma'am. It's a gambling hall. Mr. Holmes and the rest of us just happen to live here. It was my understanding, or at least my opinion, that you would live in the Belgravia townhouse."

"Belgravia?"

"Yes, ma'am," Ernest replied. "I doubt Mr. Holmes would want you to stay here."

Ruthie's chest tightened. "Oh, he wouldn't, would he?"

Either Ernest missed the anger in her voice or he dutifully ignored it. "It would hardly be proper, ma'am, for a woman such as yourself. A baron's daughter."

"My husband could have mentioned that pertinent fact to

me," Ruthie muttered.

Ernest hesitated, tapping his teeth together. "Last night was rather...abrupt. We were all taken a little off guard by the pleasant circumstance." His ebullient smile came back. "No matter now, though. We'll have everything worked out as quickly as possible. You'll feel at home in no time. Just let us take care of the details for you. You won't have to do a thing."

ERNEST COULDN'T HAVE known it, but doing nothing was one of the things Ruthie had hated most about her old home. Lady Celeste ruled the household—as was her right—but she also ruled her daughter's life, down to the amount of food she ate each meal. Ruthie was tired of doing nothing, tired of allowing others to make decisions for her. She'd thought marrying Harry and taking her future into her own hands would solve that problem, but that giant leap was only the beginning. She hadn't considered that every day after she would need to find the confidence to make her own decisions. But it was like Harry told her: *each day is filled with these tiny deaths and births, these new versions of the person you choose to be.*

Ruthie had chosen this new life, and she would have to continue to choose it. And her first choice was to not allow her husband to dump her in Belgravia—not unless he came with her. She had wanted freedom, but that didn't mean she wanted to be alone.

With that decided, Ruthie's spirits immediately lifted, as if a load had been released from her shoulders. Suddenly, getting out of the bed didn't seem so difficult anymore. In fact, nothing seemed difficult.

With Jessica's help, she got ready for her day. She washed and dressed in what she'd worn the day before and set off for a walk. Her body was restless, anxious, but in a good way. Energy coursed through her. She needed to think, and moving was the best thing for that.

Nevertheless, it only took one foot out the door for Ruthie to realize something was wrong. The impression wouldn't go away; it was heavy and cumbersome, which didn't make sense, since Ruthie felt impossible light. The morning was chilly without a cloak, but the sun was bright and toasty—

Sunny. That was it.

Her bonnet. Or her lack of bonnet.

As Ruthie made her way into St. James Park, it finally came to her. For the first time in *forever*, she was out of the house without one of her mother's gigantic bonnets wrapped around her head to ward off the sun and prevent more freckles. Such a silly little thing, but it seemed monumentally liberating. And Ruthie could *see*! She didn't have to tilt her head at odd angles to make out what was happening at her sides. The park was grand and delightful, already filled with riders and walkers catching the unlimited potential of morning.

Ruthie had always considered the night to be her favorite part of the day. That was the time when she believed anything was possible. Now, as she skipped off the well-worn path and her slippers grew damp with the morning dew, she realized she might have been wrong. And that wasn't a bad thing. Because experience taught her that. And she was now a woman with experience.

A married woman.

A woman who'd...*made love* to her husband (she still wasn't sure if she could use that foul word again).

A woman who was now on the receiving end of many odd stares.

Chuckling to herself, Ruthie returned to the dirt path and attempted to appear somewhat presentable. Experienced women didn't have to be eccentric, although it gave her an inner thrill that she could be if she wanted.

Maybe some other time. She was busy. Logistics had to be considered. For instance, her clothing. She didn't have much, but she should write a letter to her mother, asking her to send along her things—minus the bonnets. Would her Lady Celeste acquiesce, or would she ignore it? On second thought, maybe Ruthie didn't need her old clothes. Nothing was stopping her from asking Harry to purchase her a new wardrobe.

Although…that didn't sound very brave. She would have to face her mother sooner or later—especially if she wanted to see Julia.

But did that day have to be today?

Ruthie shook her head, enjoying the unencumbered sensation. *No*. It could be tomorrow. Or even the day after that. She was sure she'd be feeling much braver by then.

"Miss? Miss? Would you mind?"

Ruthie turned to see she wasn't alone on the path. Two little girls were following close behind, each with a palm outstretched. Their faces were clean, and their hair was pulled back into dark black plaits down their backs, but their dresses had seen better days. Threadbare and thin, they offered very little in the form of comfort, and even less warmth.

Arresting Ruthie's attention, the taller of the two came forward, thrusting her little hand in Ruthie's chest. "We're hungry, miss. Please, have mercy."

Her accent was unmistakably Irish. It wasn't a foreign sound to Ruthie. So many Irish were moving to England, especially since the famine had decimated the small country's potato crops. Ruthie winced. She hadn't only forgotten her bonnet. She also forgot her reticule. "I'm sorry," she said lamely. "I wish I could help you, but I have nothing."

The older girl eyed Ruthie's clothing warily. As modest as it was, her dress clearly showed her status.

"Orla! Maeve!" Dust kicked up behind the girls as a woman with matching raven-colored hair came running down the path. She grabbed their arms and yanked them away from Ruthie, swatting the fronts of their dresses as if to rid it of dirt and sin. She looked up at Ruthie with guilty desperation. "I apologize, miss. They got away from me. I'm sorry if they bothered you."

"Not at all," Ruthie said, recognizing the concave cheeks and frank hunger the mother wore as easily as her daughters. "I'm just sorry that I cannot help."

The woman nodded absent-mindedly, towing her daughters away. "We don't need charity, miss. The girls know that. We're not beggars."

"I know you're not," Ruthie said, scurrying after them. "They were just hungry."

"Please don't be telling anyone about this, miss," the woman pleaded, grimacing when she noticed Ruthie following her. "They won't be bothering you again."

"They weren't a bother," Ruthie said. "If you'd only stop, maybe I can help you. I live close by. If you come with me, I can get the children something to eat."

"No thank you—good day, miss."

"But Mam!" the older daughter whined, tugging her arm out of her mother's clutches. "We're so hungry."

"Be quiet," the mother snapped.

"Ruthie? Ruthie, what's going on?"

Ruthie spun around to see Harry watching a few feet behind them, watching the entire scene with a confused scowl. Dressed in an overcoat and top hat, he was decidedly better outfitted for the day than she. And exceedingly handsome.

She twirled a few loose ends of hair around her fingers, wishing for the safety of a bonnet, before throwing up her hands. "I'm just trying to offer them something to eat. They won't listen to me. They're hungry, Harry."

Her husband's steps were measured as he came up to the group. He reached into his pocket and revealed a handful of coins.

The mother instantly backed away. "We don't want any problems, sir. We weren't following your woman."

"I know that," he said gently. "Where are you from?"

"London," she replied quickly, focus bouncing between Harry and his money.

He smiled softly. "Where are you really from?"

The youngest girl gasped at his pronounced accent and wiggled her mother's hand. "He's from home!" she whispered.

"No, lass," Harry replied wistfully, "I haven't been there for a long, long time."

"We left a month ago," the woman said, her sadness tangible. Her face was impossibly tired and had more wrinkles than anyone her age deserved. "We came from Wexford. Thought we'd have more of a chance here."

"Ah," Harry said, rubbing his smooth chin. "I'm a Kilkenny man, myself, but I won't be holding that against ya."

The mother laughed, and it was a brittle sound, as if it hadn't been done in many days, and for one brief moment, Ruthie saw the years of toil and stress leap off her narrow shoulders.

Harry nudged the coins into her hand. "Get the girls something to eat. And find a safe place to stay tonight."

The money seemed to frighten the woman. "I can't take it, sir. It's too much."

"Take it," Harry said once more. "I know how hard it is here. You'll need it to get started."

The girls didn't need to be told twice. They jiggled their mother's arm until she accepted every coin from Harry and then began to drag her down the path in case she changed her mind.

Ruthie watched them go, not taking her eyes off the family until they were out of sight around the bend of the trees.

"Thank you," she said, turning to Harry. "They needed that."

He shook his head, still looking off toward the bend. "It won't be enough." He reached into his pocket and brought out a small ledger and pencil. He swiped through a few pages and made a small mark before returning it to his pocket.

"What was that?"

"Nothing." Harry began to walk toward the park's exit. "What's different about you today?" he asked, squinting at the top of her head. "You look…incomplete, for some reason."

Ruthie's hand whipped to the top of her head, and she felt

herself blushing. "I'm not wearing a bonnet," she replied. "Now, don't change the subject. What was that? What did you write down?"

"It's nothing."

"Harry!"

Her husband groaned and dropped his head playfully. "I keep a ledger."

"I can see that. Of what?"

Harry stared ahead, his easy gait becoming stilted. "Of my good deeds."

"Your what?"

His expression was like thunder. "You heard me. I like lists, and I thought keeping one of my good deeds would be beneficial."

"For whom?" Ruthie had to hold back her laughter. Something told her that this wasn't a laughing matter to her husband.

"For me, obviously," Harry snapped. "If or when I find myself before my creator, I thought it would be helpful to have a list I could give him...so I could plead my case...show him that I wasn't completely useless."

"Plead your case?"

"Please stop repeating everything I say as if I'm crazy. I'm not crazy. I'm resourceful. And"—he lifted his chin—"I've been attempting to spend more of my money more charitably these last few months, and I don't want to forget anything."

"Yes, I remember that now."

"How did you know?"

"Myfanwy mentioned it while we were visiting Lady Anna a few months ago." Ruthie scrunched her nose. "She isn't convinced it will work."

Harry scoffed. "That woman is never going to stop hating me no matter what I do."

Ruthie cocked her head. "Can you blame her?"

A year ago, Harry had been the reason Myfanwy showed up late for the cricket club's match against the matrons. He had placed a bet on the matrons, and he'd hoped that by locking Myfanwy in her house, the matrons would pull off the win. Unfortunately, Myfanwy had escaped, helped her club beat the married women, and had, as yet, refused to forgive him.

Harry squirmed under Ruthie's scrutiny. "I was going to let her out eventually."

Ruthie couldn't believe she was laughing. "I don't see how the person in front of me could do something that diabolical."

Harry flashed a devilish smile. "You don't know the half of it, my dear. But that reminds me. Now that I have you here, I have something to tell you."

"I have something to tell you too," Ruthie said, remembering her decision from the morning.

"I need you to spend my money."

"I'm sorry?"

Harry's footsteps stalled, his expression slightly bashful. "Well, not all of it. But I really don't have time, and you women are supposed to know all about these types of charities and things. I don't care who you give it to, just let me know and I'll handle it. I trust you."

Ruthie blanched. "I'm glad you trust me, Harry, but I don't know that much about charities. My mother wasn't much for giving."

Harry dashed a hand in the air. She zeroed in on his gloves. The gloves he needed to touch her. Suddenly their night came pouring back to her, the way he made her feel when he was with her—and, unfortunately, the way he made her feel when he left.

Harry was too lost in his grand idea to notice the change in her demeanor. The words spilled out of his mouth. "You don't have to know anything about charities. Start your own. I don't care. Hire anyone you need to help you."

"But shouldn't it be a personal endeavor? I don't see how I could become involved in something that I didn't feel passionate about or have a genuine interest in."

Harry grimaced as if she'd just told him he'd have to hug

every person in his club that night. "Personal? Charity isn't personal, and nor would I want it to be. Just come up with an idea and be sure to tell me everything you spend. I'll want to write it down."

Ruthie was becoming more and more flustered. How could he make charity seem like such a remote venture? In her experience, it had been the exact opposite. The time that she'd given to Anna's cricket clinics had been immensely rewarding, not only because she had enjoyed helping but because she'd believed in the end result. Introducing little girls to cricket and showing the value it could bring to their lives was a noble and important goal. How could he expect her to put that energy and drive into something any less substantial to her? The philanthropy would suffer. "I've never started a charity before. Who would even listen to anything I had to say? You just saw me. I tried to give those little girls food, and they practically ran away from screaming."

"You're being dramatic."

"I'm not!" Ruthie cried. "I'm not a natural leader. People don't like to listen to me. You're not even listening to me right now!"

Harry jerked straight, his mouth shutting into a grim line. With a frown, he regarded her closely, almost like her mother used to when she'd count her freckles after Ruthie came inside from a walk.

Only, his attention never made her want to cower in shame. It made her feel seen...in a good way. Now was her moment.

"I'm sorry that I tried to touch you last night," she said.

Harry ducked his head. "Don't apologize."

"I forgot. It won't... Last night won't happen again. You tried to tell me, and I didn't listen."

"It won't?" he asked softly, almost sadly.

"No."

Harry released a torrent of a breath, as if he'd been just as insecure over what happened as Ruthie. "Yes. Fine. Good."

They stood there for a few seconds, unsure of how to act, how to move forward. Harry took off his top hat and rolled it around in his hands, tapping its brim five times before placing it back on his head. He was nervous, Ruthie concluded. She was beginning to understand that the tapping was a sure sign of that.

He glanced at the exit. "Should we go home now?"

Ruthie didn't budge. She wasn't done yet. "Home?" she asked slyly. "Or Belgravia?"

Harry jerked. "Belgravia isn't my fucking home."

"But is it mine?"

He sighed and dug his hands into his pockets. Ruthie didn't know where all this strength was coming from. She'd never had the courage to stand up to her mother; how could she do it so easily with Harry Holmes?

Because I'm not afraid of him.

He continued to contemplate her before grabbing her hand with his glove. "Your home is with me."

He held her the entire way to the club. To their home.

Chapter Fourteen

"WILL YOU STOP flitting around here, fussing?" Harry hissed as Ernest refilled his wine later that evening. "We know how to eat. You don't have to wait on us!"

"Oh, I don't mind," the butler said eagerly, rushing over to Ruthie's side of the table, adding a splash of wine to her glass even though she'd barely touched it. "I just want to make sure the lady has everything she needs."

"That's what I'm for," Harry seethed, slicing his beef with his knife. He stabbed a piece with his fork and chewed it harshly, imagining it was his butler's neck. "If the lady needs anything, I will get it for her."

"Truly, Ernest, you've done enough. I don't think I can eat another bite anyway," Ruthie said, dotting at her lips with her napkin. "It was delicious."

The butler reminded Harry of a puppy being scratched by its owner—all he was missing was a wagging tail. "Really? Did you really think so?" Ernest asked, arching a brow at Harry's plate. "It wasn't too bland? He doesn't like any seasoning or sauces. Meat and vegetables are all he ever eats. Are you sure you don't want dessert? Mrs. Fox makes a wonderful pudding. He won't have any. He says it's an issue of texture, but just tell him to look away while you're eating."

LOVE SPORT

Harry slammed down his fork. "Will you get the hell out of here? I'm having dinner with my wife. *My wife.* Not my wife and my butler."

Ruthie giggled, hiding her smile in her napkin. Harry noticed that she'd made that delightful noise for most of the dinner. It could have been the wine that Ernest kept topping up, or she could just be happy. As he'd planned. And all he'd had to do was mention eating dinner together in his room. It was that simple.

"No dessert for me, thank you," Ruthie replied. "Perhaps tomorrow."

Ernest shuffled away from the table. "Oh…" He looked at Harry. "Will this be happening again tomorrow?"

Ruthie glanced back and forth between the two men. "Is dinner not a usual occurrence?"

Ernest scoffed, answering before Harry had a chance to open his mouth. "Hardly. This one eats standing up."

Ruthie's expression faltered, her lashes flickering wildly. "I'm sorry. If you're busy with the club, you don't have to sit here entertaining me. I'm sure I would be fine by myself."

"I want to be here," Harry said instantly, hoping for the smile to return to her lips. "And we can eat together from now on." He glared at Ernest. "I never made a habit of it before because I never had anyone suitable to eat with."

"Quite right. Quite right," Ernest agreed, ignoring the fact that Harry was obviously putting him down. "Well, this is quite exciting, then. You're like a real gentleman now, sir, enjoying the fruits of your labor. Good for you!"

Harry dropped his head into his hand. He really needed to get another butler, one that showed more respect for his employer. "Just take these plates and get out of here."

"Right away, sir," Ernest said, lunging for the china. "And I'll bring up some dessert as well…just in case."

Ruthie laughed that time, and Harry decided it was almost worth being annoyed by Ernest just to see her so relaxed in his company. After last night…he didn't think that would happen.

151

However, that was all behind them now. As she'd informed him in the park, there would be no more nights together. He'd tried and he'd failed. Harry was just thankful that Ruthie still wanted to spend time with him. That had been the entire point of this marriage, hadn't it? Companionship. The end of being alone. Love and sex had no place in their world. They were too out of Harry's control.

Case in point was his ravenous body that refused to listen to reason.

Harry changed positions in his seat for the umpteenth time as Ruthie shyly wiped her mouth once more with the tips of her fingers. How could something so innocent whip his body into such a frenzy? Especially when it had to do with the mouth, something Harry made a point of never staring at. All that saliva…chomping…food stuck in teeth. But with Ruthie… With Ruthie, none of that seemed to matter. The gentle slope of her mouth kept him transfixed. The faint wine stain on the bottom of her lip made him want to lick it clean.

"Do you really think he's going to bring up more food?" she asked, thankfully having no idea of his erotic thoughts.

"I have no doubt," Harry replied stiffly. "The man can't stand not knowing what we're talking about."

Ruthie nodded. "He's a good friend."

"He's my butler!"

She gave him the kind of look one would give a child. "He's also your friend."

Harry didn't agree, but now wasn't the time to begin an argument. "You know—"

The door banged open, cutting Harry off. Vine entered in two determined strides before halting like he'd hit a brick wall. "What the hell?" he asked, staring at Ruthie as if she had two heads. "Ernest said you were having dinner?"

"And?" Harry asked.

Vine blinked. "I didn't know what that meant."

"It meant I was having dinner."

Now Vine looked at Harry as if *he* had two heads. "But you should be at the club."

"Not tonight."

"But you're always at the club."

"And tonight, I'm not."

Harry scowled at his second-in-command, waiting for realization to filter across his ugly mug. Only it didn't come.

"What should I tell the others?" Vine finally asked.

"Perhaps you can tell them that he's having dinner?" Ruthie added helpfully, only it was obvious that Vine didn't find the suggestion helpful at all. His wandering eye slanted to Ruthie in a way that Harry didn't appreciate.

"I'm not going down tonight. You can handle it," Harry barked. "Now leave us."

"Have you forgotten that someone's trying to kill you?" With a sly glance at Ruthie, Vine opened his coat to show Harry the pistol he carried in his pocket. "How can I keep an eye on you if I don't know where you are?"

"Christ, man, you couldn't keep both eyes on me if you tried. Now, you know where I am, so let me eat with my wife in peace!"

Vine's cheeks ballooned like he were a squirrel filled with nuts. His complexion blazed to a shocking red. Harry muttered a curse. He shouldn't have mentioned the eye. Of all the things, why had he mentioned that lazy fucking eye?

Cracking his knuckles, Vine charged out the door, slamming it behind him. Harry sighed. He didn't look forward to dealing with that mess tomorrow. However, he could understand Vine's irritation. Like Harry, he was used to a certain way of doing business, and change never came easy.

Still, if Vine didn't like it, he could fuck off like all the others. Harry would miss him, but insubordination would not be tolerated—even from an old friend.

Harry chuckled and jabbed his thumb at the door. "Believe it or not, *he's* my friend. Are you *sure* you don't want to pack up for

Belgravia? Think of the quiet—think of the proper servants. I have other places, you know. All over. I hear they're quite nice."

Ruthie's blue eyes fixed on him. "You *hear*? Haven't you seen them?"

"I don't need to see them. I have papers that tell me what they're worth."

Ruthie placed her napkin on the table and leaned back in her seat. "Do you ever want to visit them? Get away? Do you ever get tired of doing the same things every day, seeing the same people, eating the same food?"

Well, that was quick. Harry's pessimistic side had guessed that it would take a few days for Ruthie to realize that she'd made a mistake. He tapped his fingers on the tabletop, waiting until the disappointment mellowed enough for him to speak. "My life isn't as boring as all that," he retorted, angry at how petulant he sounded. "You're not a prisoner here."

"No! That's not what I meant," Ruthie exclaimed. She wore the same yellow dress she had on yesterday. She reminded him of a sunflower, so tall and buttery, always so quick to make someone smile. "I'm not bored. How could I be? I've only been here a day. I was just asking. I'm trying to understand how your mind works."

Harry scoffed. *Good luck with that. He* still didn't understand it. He thought to laugh it off, make a joke of his little idiosyncrasies, but found that he craved honesty instead.

"It's tiring," he began, surprising himself by how tired he sounded. "I'm always exhausted. Sometimes it feels that everything is hitting me at once. Everything is always so noisy. So I learned long ago that simple is better. I keep my life small. I keep order. I keep control. It...helps."

"Like your walk this morning in the park? Does that also help?"

"Walk?" Harry frowned. "Oh, no I wasn't walking. I mean, yes, I was walking, but...I like to start my day sitting. I prefer to go outside where it's quiet, since this damn place never is, and I close my eyes. I try to keep my mind still and underworked. Does that make sense?"

"I think so," she replied slowly. "Yes, it does. And it really helps you? Closing your eyes? It's the best thing that helps you block out the noise in your head?"

"Other than sex, yes."

Ruthie blanched. She cast her eyes down at the table. "Oh, yes," she said nervously.

Shit. Harry had been doing so well. Now last night was back to the forefront. He should have quit while he was ahead.

He stood. "I should be going. Thank you for dinner. I've never eaten dinner with my wife before. I...I rather enjoyed it."

Two spots of pink dotted her cheeks. "Thank you. I did as well. But you told Vine you weren't going down to the club tonight."

"I'm not. I figured I might as well get some sleep." He shrugged. "Maybe read a little."

"But I don't understand. This is your bedroom."

Harry stared at Ruthie, searching for guile. Was she trying to make a fool out of him? Did she want him to spell it out? "You already told me that we wouldn't be sleeping together anymore. So I just assumed that I would take another room."

"I never said that."

"You did."

"I did no such thing."

Harry planted his hands on his hips. "I remember perfectly well. At the park. You said specifically that last night wouldn't happen again."

Awareness dawned on Ruthie, and she let out a patronizing chuckle. "I meant that I wouldn't try to touch you anymore, but I still want to be with you. Honestly, Harry, we're not back to that, are we?" She got up from the table and mirrored his stance with her hands on her hips. "I want a real marriage, Harry Holmes. I won't take anything less."

He still didn't understand what she was saying. But he doubted she did either. "But l-last night…" he stammered. "Last night…last night…last night—" *Fuck, the repeating!* Harry bit his lips together.

Ruthie's irritation dropped. "It's fine. Last night was wonderful, and I would have told you that if you hadn't left me like you did."

"I didn't know what to say. I thought you were upset—"

"I *was* upset," she said. "I was upset that I didn't listen to you. You told me not to touch you, and I did."

"I hurt you."

"Not much. Just at the end. The beginning was…enlightening."

"I was only involved in the end."

"That's not true. Harry? That's not true."

He looked up to find her staring at him, her eyes so gentle and captivating, filled with such concern and understanding, it nearly broke him. Very few people had ever understood him; very few cared to try.

"I pushed you too far last night. I should have given you time, but that was my mistake—"

"You didn't make a fucking mistake—"

"Shh, please," Ruthie said. She reached out to hold him, but stopped herself and hung her arms at her sides, shaking them as if to rid herself of the temptation. "Let me get this out. I should have been gentler with you. Slower. But you've given me an idea, and I'd like to work on it. If you…" She glanced down shyly. "If you want to try again, we can continue to do it your way, or…we could try something different.

Want to? *Fuck.* That was *all* he wanted to do. But Harry curbed his excitement. "I don't want to disappoint you again."

Ruthie released a deep, throaty laugh. "Harry Holmes, you could never disappoint me. I chose you, remember? Now take off your necktie. I think I've come up with a better use for it."

〉〉〉〈〈〈

RUTHIE TIED THE knot at the back of her husband's head. "That's not too tight, is it? I don't want to hurt you."

"No, no, it's fine," he answered tentatively. "It's incredibly odd, but not uncomfortable."

"Good." Ruthie retreated from the bed and stood in front of Harry to admire her handiwork. She'd wrapped the necktie around his eyes to block his vision and had him seated on the edge of the bed. Other than his jacket, he still wore all his clothes, along with his trusty black gloves.

"Now what?" he asked, expectation high and apparent in his tone.

That was a good question. Ruthie wasn't exactly sure. She hadn't got that far in her theory. It had only come to her when Harry mentioned that he liked sitting alone in the park. The man seemed sensitive—more sensitive than others—when it came to outside stimuli, and it affected him in a most discombobulating way. If Ruthie could quiet his mind when he was alone with her, help him feel safe, then maybe their lovemaking wouldn't be such a source of stress. Maybe he could learn to enjoy the entire act instead of just the end. And maybe, just maybe, one day he would allow her to touch him the way that he'd taught Ruthie to touch herself.

She crossed her arms. "Do you trust me?"

There was no hesitation. "Yes."

His easy response gave her confidence to go on. "Good." She knelt in front of him and held her hand out just inches from his chest. "I'm going to touch your chest, Harry. That's it. I'm not going to do anything more. I won't unbutton your clothes or go any further. I'm going to put my hand right over your heart. Can I do that?"

She watched his throat bob as he licked his lips. "Yes. You can touch me. Now?"

"Now."

Gently, with great care, Ruthie rested her hand on his heart, marveling at the way she could feel its strong, insistent beat through his linen shirt and waistcoat. "Is that all right?" she asked.

"Yes," Harry replied. "Yes, this is fine. It's good."

"You're trembling."

He shook his head. "Not in a bad way. I...I'm getting used to it. I'm...I'm..."

"Maybe this is enough for today." Ruthie moved to stand, but Harry caught her hand and pushed it back to his chest, holding it there against his thundering heart. She smiled to herself and spread out her fingers, capturing more of him, taking all that he was willing to give. Her hand looked so small on his chest, and yet she felt immeasurably strong, strong enough to keep a man like Harry safe.

Locked in this embrace, Ruthie could feel her breath pumping faster, the communion of this moment affecting her in ways she didn't expect. She studied Harry as he pulled her closer, her torso as close to his as possible without touching. It was a lovely thing to stare at someone without their knowing, to appreciate the beautiful uniqueness of the other without embarrassment getting in the way. How Ruthie wanted to run her fingers along the gray shards of hair that weaved through his temples; how she wished to kiss the deep lines that fanned out from his eyes. She wanted to rub her hands over the chin stubble that forced him to shave more than once a day and caress the lips that had made her entire body tingle with one taste.

Harry's lips fell apart the tiniest bit, and Ruthie could see the tips of his white teeth. She leaned in, moving her face toward his, always mindful of his margins. "Is this too close?" she whispered in his ear.

Harry shook his head slowly. She took her hand from his and ran it up his chest. When she found his skin at the base of his neck, he shuddered.

"Do you remember what you told me when we first met?"

Ruthie asked, sliding the tips of her fingers along his throat, riding its wave while he swallowed. "You said that I make you feel safe. Do you feel safe now?"

"Yes." His voice was shallow and reedy, but Ruthie felt the huskiness all the way down to her toes.

Ruthie's fingers made it to his chin. She grazed them against the line of his jaw, loving the grating effect of his whiskers on her sensitive pads. "Is this too much? Do you want me to stop?"

Once more he shook his head. "Keep going."

Ruthie allowed herself to be brave. She traveled up his cheeks, lightly skimming the bridge of his straight nose and sharp cheekbones. His skin was soft, supple, youthful. A map that had so much more life in it. Ruthie was sure that if she asked Harry what kind of book he was, he would tell her a tragedy, but she only saw a blank page waiting for their happy ending. Waiting for her to bring some romance into his pragmatic life.

She made her way down to his lips, hesitating briefly before tenderly caressing them. She was transfixed and attentive, mesmerized by their wide, lovely bow shape. Such shocking, filthy words had come from these lips, but they'd only ever made her feel lightheaded and cherished. They'd only ever made her feel wanted.

His mouth twitched against her, fluttering against her palm.

"Can I kiss you, Harry?" Ruthie asked. Her voice was just above a whisper, as if she were casting a wish upon a star, floating a prayer into heaven.

"Christ, you better soon. I don't know how much more of this I can take."

Ruthie flinched away. "Is it bad?"

He yanked her back to his face. "It's too fucking good," he said before capturing her lips.

This kiss was so very different than the one they'd shared on the street. That one was desperate and carnal, filled with open-ended questions and hasty panic. Maybe it was the way Ruthie had been touching him, but when Harry opened to her now it was exquisitely soft, undeniably sure and tranquil. With a gentle surge, he swept his tongue around her mouth in a luscious massage that touched Ruthie's heart.

It was a sweet kiss. A kiss of dreams. A kiss of sweetness and sincerity. A kiss of intention.

Ruthie continued to skim the side of Harry's face with her fingertips, and somewhere in the back of her mind she knew his hands stayed at his sides. Even then, even lost in their kiss, he wouldn't allow himself to touch her. But she cast that thought from her mind for another day. They had time. There was no rush.

In this room, surrounded by other people's wealth and misfortune, Ruthie felt like the luckiest girl in the world. Because even though she could taste the need on her husband's tongue, she could also taste the want. Harry Holmes *wanted* her.

And that wanting surged. Soon the kiss became deeper. Their teeth clashed together as a primal, naked yearning took the reins. Harry groaned as he pressed against her, capturing and containing her desire, guiding their kisses with less restraint, less reverence. Ruthie could feel the heat building in him, feel the control slipping.

She told herself to pull away, but she wouldn't heed her own warning. There was something so beguiling about finding herself on this edge of danger. Not knowing was like a kind of drug.

And she only wanted more. Her fingers shook as they worked on the buttons of his waistcoat. There were five of them. Had he done that on purpose?

Harry wasn't stopping her. Was it Ruthie's imagination, or was he even backing away to give her more room to work? She was almost there. Just one more and then his shirt would be the only thing between her and his chest. Suddenly, she wanted nothing more in life but to place her hand on his heart again, only this time skin to skin.

The fifth button came undone in her hands.

"Harry!" A frantic pounding came from the door. "Harry, get

out here! You have a problem that needs attention. Now!"

Vine.

Damn.

Harry's head jerked away, but Ruthie hadn't released his waistcoat. He yanked the necktie off his head and looked down. His eyes widened as if he were startled by what was happening. Slowly, Ruthie dropped her hands, and he instantly replaced her, doing the buttons back up.

"You should go," she said, coming to her feet.

"Yes," he said.

She wandered back over to the table, where Ernest never had left her the dessert. She wondered if it was too late to ask him for a taste of that pudding.

By the time she looked back at Harry, he was back in working order with his jacket on and his expression blank, as if the past few minutes had never happened. But they had. Ruthie could still feel them in her bruised lips, in the shakiness of her knees.

Harry walked to the door but stopped to face her as he reached for the handle. He cocked his head, a crooked smile on his face. "You said that people never listen to you?"

Ruthie's heart pounded against her chest.

"It's all I want to do." He hauled open the door. "Tomorrow, then? Same time? Same place?"

Chapter Fifteen

"HOLY FUCK, WHAT is he doing back here?" Harry yelled, landing on the ground floor of the club. He fixed his glare on Vine, who turned away, obviously not wanting to face his employer's furious question.

Mason Waitrose was back again. Three sheets to the wind again. And creating yet another disturbance in the Lucky Fish.

"Where is he?" the sotted fool called out, stumbling in the center of the main room with his hands outstretched. A group of friends—all equally sotted—surrounded him, including Lord William, who laughed and urged on the antics. They were making quite a show for Harry's customers, and he didn't appreciate that at all. If people were ogling Mason, then they weren't losing their money to him. "I want to speak to him now," the man screamed. "Get him out here so he can face me like a man!"

"He's upstairs with your sister," came a voice from one of the tables. "But I wouldn't worry. They're just talking!"

Laughter ricocheted between the tables. "Sure," another man teased from his seat. "Just talking. They've been talking *all night long!*"

Mason's face flamed so red it was purple. He slammed his fist down on the roulette table, bouncing the little white ball from its wheel. "Don't you dare talk about my sister," he said, tripping into Lord Michael's arms. His friend hoisted him back and made a show of dusting off the back of his jacket. "My sister is a chaste, good girl—"

"Sure she is."

"Not anymore."

The teasing only egged him on. Mason's tirade was stronger than his sense of self-preservation. "My sister is a saint. My sister has been corrupted by the devil!"

"My wife is upstairs sleeping, and you are being very rude," Harry said, stepping into the center of the floor. He didn't raise his voice. He didn't need to. The club always stopped for him. "It's time for you to leave."

He locked his hands behind his back in a casual fashion belying the raging violence that threatened to lash out from his body. How dare this bastard come to his club and call him out—and worse, embarrass his own sister!

Looking into Mason's face, there was a moment—one sliver of a moment—where Harry thought he saw something…grief, anguish, regret…but it died swiftly when Mason opened his mouth again.

"I'm not leaving without her," he said as nobly as a man could with a crooked necktie and sweaty hair matted to his brow. He lifted his chin to the crowd and pointed a finger at Harry. It was bare. No signet ring. No doubt that was Mason's possession upstairs in Harry's bedroom. "This man takes our money. He takes our possessions. And now he thinks he can take our sisters? He is not one of us. You know this. And he never will be."

"Ah, sit down, Mason. Have another drink!" a voice called out.

"I will not!" he replied, jerking Lord Michael's hands from his shoulders.

Harry's glare was as icy as his veins. "I don't take your money or your possessions. You lose them. I accept them. And as for your sister—"

Mason tripped forward. "Don't you dare mention my sister. You aren't fit to say her name."

"Maybe so," Harry replied. "But she is my wife now, and you will respect her decision. *Her* decision. Her decision." He clapped his mouth closed. Fuck this bastard for making him repeat himself.

No one seemed to notice. All eyes were still on Mason, everyone waiting for Harry to beat him to a bloody pulp. He wanted to. He wanted nothing more. But then he would have to touch Mason, and, more importantly, he'd have to explain to his wife why he'd maimed her brother. Harry was new to marriage, but even he knew that that wasn't a proper *second day of marriage* topic.

Mason shook his head, crossing his arms like a surly child. "I'm not going until I see her. I'm not going until she tells me with her own lips. It is my duty as the man of my family to take care of her."

Harry laughed then, a great, booming laugh that cut through all the tittering in the room. "And what a great job you've been doing. You're a wastrel, and a poor one at that. How do you think you've been helping your family by throwing all their money away? You don't understand the meaning of duty."

His last sentence was low and menacing, but the entire room guffawed mercilessly. Mason's eyes darted nervously over all the peers, people he considered his equals, people who were supposed to laugh behind his back and never to his face. Rules were being broken. Unwritten ones that had been followed by their fathers and grandfathers.

"At least I have a title," he retorted, jutting out his chest. "I have a name. I'm not just another Irish brat off the boat with no food and no father."

It was like a glass had been broken, so quickly did the levity drop. Breaths were held. Every eye was fixed squarely on Harry. His fingers tapped against his trousers. They wouldn't stop. He couldn't make them. This was why he preferred to watch from the shadows. So much easier to hide things.

Suddenly, the exhaustion that was always nipping at his heels caught up with him, and Harry's legs almost went out from under him. Catching himself in time, he found one of his men. "Deal with him, Spector," he said.

"No!" a voice screamed.

Harry turned to the staircase. There, Ruthie stood, clutching the banister as if her life depended on it, as if her body were as drained as his, or maybe it was her spirit. She must have followed him down soon after he left their room.

Ruthie's face was pale and haunted as she closed her hand over her mouth, staring at her brother with an equal mixture of disbelief and pity.

Mason was the opposite. He broke out in a sloppy grin, lifting his arms once more. "Ruthie. There you are! Let's go now. Mother is worried. You've been very naughty."

"Mother?" Ruthie rasped from behind her palm. Harry couldn't watch this any longer. He went to his wife and tried to usher her up the stairs, but she refused to move. Her eyes remained glued on her brother. "Did Mother send you here?"

Mason shrugged. "What does it matter? I'm here. Now let's go. Don't make me wait. You're embarrassing yourself, my dear."

Ruthie blanched, then let out a mirthless laugh. "No, Mason. It's the other way around. It always is. Go home."

Harry's heart thumped. Had he actually been worried that she would leave with the bastard? *No.* It was still nice to hear it, though.

Mason bumbled toward the staircase. "Can't you see? Darling, I'm here to save you from this blackguard. Now, let's go. I'm not leaving without you."

"You're going to have to," Ruthie returned easily. "I'm married. I know you've heard. You've generously shouted it to everyone who would listen tonight."

Harry flicked his head to Spector, who took Mason in hand, dragging him to the exit. "Don't worry, boss," Spector said eagerly. "I'll make sure no one finds the body!"

"Good," Harry replied reflexively.

"No!" Ruthie said, slamming her palm on the banister. "You're not going to kill him."

Fuck. "Right. Try not to kill him, Spector."

Harry reached inside his jacket pocket, but his wife's words stopped him. "Don't you dare write that down in your ledger! *Not* killing my brother does not go on your list."

Slowly, Harry dropped his hand back to his side as he watched Spector wrangle Mason out of the club. The man was stronger than he looked, and withstood Spector's pushing for a few seconds.

Ruthie's soft voice cut through the tussle. "Have you no shame, brother?"

Mason sobered instantly. Then he chuckled, though it was halfhearted and limp. "Shame, you say?" he replied as Spector grabbed the back of his neck. "Shame is my destiny, sister. And now it's yours as well."

⟫⟫⟪⟪

THE FOLLOWING MORNING, Ruthie hurried out of bed as the sun was rising. She tiptoed around the room, dressing herself even though she needn't have bothered. There was no one to disturb. After the night's upheaval from her brother, she'd gone back to her room and cried herself to sleep. Harry had slept elsewhere.

Later, Ruthie resolved to ask him about it. It was a bad routine they were getting into. She looked forward to the morning when she could wake to her husband's warm body. She didn't have to touch it; she had a notion that staring at it would be enough. But today...today she had more pressing matters.

As determined as Ruthie was, her feet still dragged as she made the short journey. Her anxiety was enough to kill the chill in the air, but not her trepidation. She'd never knocked on her

166

own door before. At this hour, her mother would be waking from her drug-induced sleep, clamoring for her tea. Ruthie needed to face Lady Celeste while she still had puffy skin and sleep in her eye. It was when her mother was most vulnerable.

Her knock was light, but the butler answered it at once, unable to hide his displeasure at Ruthie's appearance. She attempted to walk past him, but he closed the door just enough that she couldn't squeeze through.

"I would like to see my mother," she announced.

The butler nodded. "Lady Celeste has been waiting for you. I will get her. She asked that you wait here."

Ruthie waited on the doorstep. The wind picked up, slashing at her arms, and she couldn't contain the shivers while she listened for footsteps. When her mother finally came to the door, she was already dressed in a crimson day robe, her hair fashioned in a handsome, plain bun at the base of her head. Her skin was as luminous as ever, although more tired looking than usual.

She clutched the frame of the door, as if ready to slam it at a moment's notice. "Why are you here?"

Ruthie's nerve faded quickly. "I…I…" she stammered.

Lady Celeste's brow arched more with every bumbled word.

Ruthie inhaled through her nose. "I came to speak to Mason. To see if he is all right."

"Your brother is fine. He is sleeping," her mother replied tersely.

"I'm sure you heard about last night."

Ruthie could see her mother's tongue root around inside her mouth as she mulled over her words. "I've heard a great many things these last few days. As well as having to deal with a few *unwanted* visitors."

Ruthie returned a questioning frown.

"Oh, didn't your husband tell you? He paid me a visit yesterday," Lady Celeste announced the same way one might announce a cockroach. "He told me all about your nuptials, how he would look after you…something to that effect. He tried to be charming. He failed."

"That was good of him," Ruthie said meekly, feeling so intolerably sorry for her husband having to deal with her mother. Why hadn't he told her?

"He came like a beggar, which, now that I know where he's from, shouldn't surprise me." Lady Celeste laughed. "He asked for your clothes, your personal items. I told him you didn't have personal items. You wore clothes that *I* gave you. They're mine. Or now they're Julia's. I'm sure she will put them to better use. Find a man whom I can acknowledge in public."

"Oh," Ruthie said. "Yes, I see." She couldn't think of anything else to say. In her mind, she always had these long, drawn-out battles with her mother, but now that the chance presented itself, she'd come up with nothing. Because it didn't really matter what she said. Her mother's opinion would always be the only one of import.

Ruthie craned her neck to peek over her mother's shoulder, but Lady Celeste closed the door even more. "Is Julia awake?" Ruthie asked. "Can I see her before I go? She never wrote back to my letter."

"And she won't," her mother replied with harsh finality. "Honestly, Ruthie, what did you expect would happen? That we would all just rejoice in your hasty, poor decision? You married beneath your class. Your actions have threatened to ruin us. And you thought you would come here, and we would forget all that. You are not the prodigal son, and I am much too busy picking up the pieces that you so casually broke. I'm trying to save us so your sister can have an honest, good life."

Tears clouded Ruthie's eyes. "I want to help! Let me help you now. Harry is a generous man. I know he will come to your aid if I ask!"

Lady Celeste curled her lip in a sneer. "He didn't tell you that either, did he? Yes, well, I know more than most that men have their secrets. He already asked me to take money. Commanded me, more like it. And I refused."

Ruthie's stomach dropped. "You refused?"

"Naturally!" her mother scoffed. "I could never take that man's money. He's so…"

"What, Mother? What exactly is he?"

"He's different—that's it. I don't care how much money he has. The man is *different*."

Ruthie wasn't surprised that her mother had noticed. She was a keen watcher of people. She'd probably spotted all of Harry's quirks in minutes and judged him even quicker. "Just because he does…odd things from time to time, that doesn't make him different. He tries so hard not to show anyone. The repeating, the tapping, the aversion to touching people… It's not such a curiosity. They're just little quirks. It's who he is."

"No touching?" The lines around Lady Celeste's lips wrinkled. "Are you saying he doesn't touch you?

"No, that's not what I said."

"What kind of man doesn't want to touch his wife?" Her eyes narrowed. "*Oh.*"

"What do you mean, 'oh'? He does things in his own—"

Her mother reached for her. "What things? Depraved things? What is he making you do in that wretched house?"

Ruthie wriggled her arm free. "He's not depraved. I'm trying to tell you that he's a good man. Just different."

Lady Celeste shook her head. "He's a freak. I knew it. He is not good enough for you. We are better."

"Are we?" Ruthie asked, her anger growing. "Because you've had men in your life, Mother—your husband and now your son—let you down, *continually* let you down. And finally, there is one that tries to help—*wants* to help—and you deem him unworthy? What an odd view to have."

Lady Celeste straightened her shoulders. "Yes, well, it is the only view I have."

Ruthie snorted. "Then I suppose I should be grateful that I'm on the outside looking in now." Her head dropped. "Goodbye, Mother. Please tell Julia I came to see her. Tell her…tell her I love her and that I tried."

Without waiting for a response, she trudged down the door-steps, eager for the door to slam and the conversation to be over. When it didn't come, she looked over her shoulder. Lady Celeste remained at the threshold, watching her daughter with an expression that Ruthie couldn't read. It looked too much like regret.

"Everything I did, I did for you. You know that, don't you?" she asked. "I only wanted the best for you."

Ruthie turned to face her. "I believe that you believe that."

Lady Celeste stepped out onto the porch, letting the door close behind her. She wrapped her shawl tight around her frame. "I married for love, and it made my life unbearable. I never wanted that for you. I wanted you to have a comfortable life, one where you didn't have to worry about bills and creditors." Her face tightened. "Or whom your husband was spending his nights with. I wanted you to be free from all that."

Ruthie climbed a step. She only needed one to be on the same level as her mother. But even then, she felt incredibly large, and so much stronger than the petite woman who now trembled from an inconsequential bluster of wind. Ruthie didn't shiver. Not anymore.

Her legs were too long, her posture wasn't perfect, her hands were big and mannish, but she could withstand *so much*. She could take her mother's constant judgments, her father's constant failings, her brother's frailty, and still remain standing.

Because she was bigger than other girls. Because she was taller. Because she was stronger.

Stronger than she'd ever believed.

"I *am* free from all that," Ruthie explained. "You're just angry because I didn't do it on your terms. And I can't change that now. And I can't make you forgive me or let me help you."

Lady Celeste rolled her eyes, returning to the door. "You think you're free? You are far from it."

Ruthie told herself to let her go, but she couldn't help calling out, "I didn't marry for love."

Lady Celeste spun around and eyed her daughter, then she snorted. "Oh, you poor, silly girl. Of course you did. And trust me, that odd man of yours will make you regret it."

Chapter Sixteen

"I CAN'T BELIEVE you didn't beat the brother senseless," Samuel Everett remarked wistfully, never taking his eyes off the pitch. "No doubt in your colorful career you've *retired* men for slighter offenses."

Harry reacted with an infinitesimal nod. That was a polite way of putting it, which was odd, since Samuel Everett was rarely polite. He was also rarely seen much these days, as he was expecting his first child with his wife, Myfanwy. And when he wasn't attempting to keep her safe in their home, he was at the London Ladies Cricket Club screaming at his players.

Standing next to him on the boundary while Samuel hollered at the poor girls was as close to having a heart-to-heart conversation with a friend as Harry could get. They hadn't always been on friendly terms—there was that prickly situation between Harry and Myfanwy—but the men had grown closer over the past year as they became business partners and Harry had become a greater benefactor to the club.

Harry would never tell Samuel this—and Samuel wouldn't care to hear it—but he valued their time together, even when Samuel barely acknowledged him. Harry needed this sense of balance in his life, especially since Samuel Everett never gambled and remained as far away from London's underbelly as he could get. Harry found the man unusual, exasperating, and refreshing, their talks even more so.

"I wanted to smash my skull into his sweaty face," Harry admitted. "But I didn't think my wife would appreciate it."

"That's rather magnanimous for a man who was at death's door a couple weeks ago. As to that, did you ever find out who done it? Who wanted to take a bite out of you this time? Bennie told me it was one of Dugan's men, but I thought you'd worked everything out with them."

"So had I, but I didn't come to talk about that," Harry said. He didn't tell Samuel that he'd actually held a meeting with Dugan that morning at the man's favored pub down by the docks. Over a drink, Dugan swore that he hadn't been behind the shooting, nor had he heard who was. A large son of a bitch, Seamus Dugan had hair the color of a carrot and hands like potatoes, thick and knobby. He was young and impetuous, quickly making a name for himself in the underworld—but he wasn't a liar. Harry believed that the dangerous man would sooner slice a throat than utter a falsehood when his character was in question.

So Harry had done all he could do. He'd taken Dugan at his word, finished his drink, and shoved off, no closer to knowing who'd spilled his blood than he had the day before. Vine must have got bad information. It happened. Or someone was trying to frame Dugan. That happened just as often. Regardless, Harry didn't feel like dumping all this on Samuel's door. Not when he had more important things to talk about—like money.

"Holly told me that orders keep pouring in for the miracle muscle-relaxing tincture. She's finding it difficult to keep up with demand. I told her to hire more workers. She wants to expand as well, has some ideas about other tonics that the girls at the club use, for their hair and other things. What do you think?"

"Fine, fine, that's fine. Whatever you decide is best," Samuel replied absent-mindedly before taking four angry steps forward. "No! Two hands! Two hands, Maggie! Christ, you can barely catch the ball with two hands. What makes you think you should do it with one? Think!" He backed up again, in line with Harry. "Sorry about that. Now what were you saying?"

Harry regarded his friend, shaking his head. "Do you care about anything other than cricket?"

Samuel snorted. "Obviously. She's over there on the sidelines glaring at me because I won't let her play. You understand; you've got a wife now. How the hell did that happen, by the way?"

At the mention of Ruthie, Harry searched for her among the players. It didn't take long. He found her by herself, far out in the field, fielding. Her hands were clasped in front of her, as if she were praying no one would hit the ball in her direction.

"What do you mean, *how*?" Harry said. "I asked. Eventually, she said yes."

"Ha!" Samuel snorted again. "I doubt it was that easy. Miss Ruthie doesn't seem like your type."

"It's Mrs. Holmes now. And what exactly is my type?"

Samuel squinted against the sun, holding his hand up above his eyes. "I don't know. Someone...worldlier."

"Worldlier? Like a whore?"

Samuel finally turned to him. "No! That's not what I mean. I just...thought you'd want someone more talkative, less afraid of her own shadow. And yes, maybe a whore."

"Ruthie's not afraid of her shadow. She can be quiet, but she's not a wallflower by any means."

Samuel gave him a dubious look. "The woman never speaks in front of me. She's terrified of me."

"Because you're a terrifying fucking person!"

Samuel chuckled. "That's rich coming from you. I've seen one look from you make a man piss his pants."

Harry crossed his arms. "Well, my wife is stronger than you think. And I think you've spent too much time around Myfanwy, who throws out her opinion whether anyone wants it or not."

Samuel nodded, focus back on the field. Harry rolled his eyes as he watched the besotted man's expression soften. "My wife is an assertive woman, that is true. And I wouldn't have her any other way."

"Neither would I have my wife any other way."

"Well, that's lovely to hear," Samual replied. "I'm so glad everything is working out for you. Truly, I am. I just love it when one of my players finds her knight in shining armor and throws her life into chaos right before a new season."

Harry tensed at the blatant condescension, especially as Samuel crept closer.

"But your wife—*my player*—has dropped two catches today and was dismissed three times without scoring any runs. Ruthie isn't my best player, but she tries. She tries so damn hard, and that means everything to me. A person can't ask for more. So you can understand why I'm confused that she'd played so poorly when I know she's a hell of a lot better than that." His voice sharpened. "If you do anything to ruin her game—*upset her*—I will stomp your fucking teeth in. Do you hear me?"

Harry nodded.

Samuel grinned. He slapped Harry on the back and charged onto the field. "I'm glad we understand one another. Congratulations again!"

"I DIDN'T KNOW that you were coming," Ruthie said, falling into step with her husband as she left the field. She waved goodbye to Anna one last time as Anna's husband helped her into their carriage.

"I thought I would surprise you," Harry said. "Was it a good surprise?"

"Of course," Ruthie replied. "I just... I didn't play well today. Samuel was upset."

"Samuel's always upset," he remarked dryly.

"He's always so patient with me. I just don't want to let him down."

"You won't. You just need to show more confidence. Look like you're ready for the ball. Like you *want* the ball."

"But I don't want it!" Ruthie cried, wringing her hands. "Every time the ball comes near me, I panic. I'm afraid I'll make a mistake and let down the team."

"That's horseshit," he replied. "You need to want the ball. You need to believe that you're the best person who can make the play. You need to imagine yourself hitting the game-winning runs. And then it will happen, trust me."

"I don't think I could even imagine that," Ruthie joked.

He nudged her with his elbow. "And I bet you never could have imagined being married to me, either. And look at you now. Confidence, darling. All it takes is confidence."

Harry let his advice sink in, and they walked side by side for another few seconds, each lost in their own thoughts. He felt oddly content, but then again, he always enjoyed walking on grass. No cracks to be found.

When it became apparent that Ruthie wasn't going to divulge anymore, he broke the silence. "Was there something on your mind today? Something that made it difficult to concentrate on the field?" He hesitated, annoyed that Samuel's comment had got to him. "Something that I did?"

Ruthie's brow pinched as she stared at her. "No. Why would you think that?"

He shrugged.

She sighed. "If you must know, I spoke to my mother today."

"Ah."

"Indeed," she replied. "And she never disappoints."

"At what?"

"At being herself."

Harry locked his hands behind his back. The urge to tap was growing. "I could sense that about her when we met. I went by the house. I didn't tell you. I wanted to...but it didn't go as pleasantly as I would have liked."

Ruthie laughed darkly. "Yes, she told me. You shouldn't have gone. I could have saved you from being treated that way."

"Oh, I'm used to being treated that way. Your mother just had the nerve to do it to my face."

"Yes, the woman has confidence," Ruthie muttered. "She's never lacked for that. I suppose it's because she's so beautiful, used to everyone jumping to do her bidding."

"She's an attractive woman, but beautiful? I don't think so."

"Harry," Ruthie drawled. "You don't have to pretend to make me feel better. Everyone with eyes can see how lovely she is. Do you know that Eugene Delacroix asked to paint her once? My grandfather wouldn't let her because the artist insisted she be nude!"

"Huh." Harry chuckled, rubbing his jaw. "I think your mother might be lying to you. Now that I've seen her up close, she bears a startling resemblance to *Liberty* in his masterpiece."

"Oh stop!" She laughed, slapping his arm playfully. "Oh, I'm sorry. I didn't—"

"Quite all right," Harry said. He reached for her hand and placed it on his arm like they were any other couple enjoying a walk together. Who knew? Maybe they could be. As long as he wore his gloves.

"Why did you go to her?" he continued. "What did you need? I hope you're not worried about your clothing. I've already told Ernest to go shopping for you today. He was beyond excited."

Ruthie's smile was purely for his benefit. "Nothing. I mean, I asked about my clothes and things, but that wasn't really why I went there." She flicked something from her eye. "I went there to help, or to at least offer help, and she turned me away. She told me that she didn't want anything from me—us. She said I'd ruined everything, ruined the family in Society."

Harry took out his handkerchief and handed it to her. After wiping her tears, Ruthie gave it back to him, and he took it at once. Without hesitating, he put it back in his pocket, not even shuddering while he did it. He would have smiled if he wasn't sure she would have taken it the wrong way.

"You didn't ruin a damn thing. Do you think anyone will have the balls to slight my wife? Your place is safe, believe me. You might not be drinking tea with the queen anytime soon, but I'm sure I can work on that if it's what you want."

That got a truer smile out of her. "I don't need to take tea with the queen."

"Who, then? The prime minister? The archbishop?"

"No, thank you."

"Just as well. The man's breath is terrible."

"How do you know that?"

"How do you think? He loves the roulette table. Can't get enough of it."

"Oh," Ruthie said quietly.

Harry was getting desperate. He hated seeing her so down and plaintive. He wanted to order his wife to make a list of all her problems so he could go about fixing them in an organized manner.

Her fingers curled into his arm. "Why is it," she started slowly, "the people that need the most help never accept it?"

"Pride, I suppose," he answered. "Also, charity is a tricky thing. Most people want to feel like they've worked for what they have, that they've truly earned it."

"I never thought it would be this difficult."

"People are difficult."

"You're not."

Harry shot her an incredulous look. "I am the *most* difficult."

Ruthie shook her head. "Not to me. To me you've been nothing short of perfect."

"I doubt that."

"Well, maybe not perfect. But"—she blushed, glancing at his necktie—"you're trying. And that's more than a lot of people do."

Squinting, Harry leaned away, appraising his wife dramatically. "Look at you, Ruthie Holmes. You sound positively worldly."

She slapped him on the arm once more, wearing a shy smile. "Why are you so surprised? I *am* worldly," she announced. "Very worldly."

And Harry, who once considered change to be the root of all evil, was trying.

He wondered what Samuel would have to say about that.

Chapter Seventeen

"**G**ET THE FUCK out of here, Ernest. I swear to you, I will toss you out in the streets if you're in this room for a minute longer."

Plain as day, Harry could see the debate going on in his butler's head. Ernest's eyes narrowed in contemplation while Harry glared at him. There he stood in the doorway with two plates of dessert in his hand—both ostensibly for Ruthie, since he knew that Harry wouldn't touch the gelatinous goop.

Harry needed this man out of his room for the rest of the night. He only wanted his wife's attentions.

He was in the mood to try a little bit more.

Ernest made the wrong decision. He hurried into the room, arranging the sickly-sweet plates in front of Ruthie as his employer leapt from the table. Harry's arm snaked out, but only caught air as the butler careened out of his grasp and fled to the door, closing it safely behind him.

Growling, Harry slammed back into his seat, nearly upsetting it. He tore out his ledger from his pocket and opened it to a fresh page.

"Where was the good deed in that?" Ruthie asked between fresh bouts of laughter.

Harry scribbled away. "I didn't kill him. That's important. I wanted to. I could have. I didn't." He closed the ledger with a flourish and shoved it back in his pocket. "The Lord will appreciate that one, I'm sure of it. Now then…"

Ruthie's blue eyes bored into him. Expectantly. She cocked her head. "Now then."

Harry's hands went to his necktie. He held her gaze as he worked slowly, untying the thin piece of fabric. He slid it off his neck and tossed it on the table. "I remember saying something about same place, same time?"

Ruthie's chest rose on a breath. "I remember that as well."

Harry stood from the table. He walked to his wife's side and offered a hand. She stared at his glove for a heavy second before accepting it and allowing him to lift her to her feet. She was wearing one of the new dresses that Ernest had bought for her that afternoon. Made of midnight-blue satin, it served to accentuate the color of her eyes, make them more seductive, more forbidding.

Not for the first time, Harry admired her height, the way she could look at him squarely. Taunt him. Confront him. Challenge him. In all the best ways.

"I take it you didn't mind our little lesson last night?" she asked. Not forgetting the necktie, she glided to the bed, towing Harry faithfully behind.

"You know as much," he replied.

She turned around wearing a devilish smile and nudged him lightly until he was seated on the mattress as he had been the night before. Ruthie wasted no time winding the cloth around his eyes and fastening it securely.

Once more housed in darkness, Harry found his awareness tingled and acclimated to the new sensations. Everything became so finely tuned. The earthy notes of Ruthie's perfume tickled his nostrils; the feel of her body vibrated in the air surrounding him. Her very being covered him like a blanket, and she hadn't even reached for him yet. And it didn't frighten him. At first, he thought the blindfold would make him claustrophobic, but it did the opposite. It freed both his mind and body. It allowed him to focus on one thing at a time—on the way his wife made him feel, one touch at a time.

"Are you ready?" Ruthie asked. She was close. So very close. He could smell the tart apple on her breath, the cherries hidden in her wine. Now, he wanted to taste them.

Harry nodded and could sense her smile, sense her confidence growing. "Just tell me what to do," he said, amused at the wobble in his voice. "I'll listen to you."

"I know," Ruthie replied. "I know. I know."

He frowned, wondering if she'd been hit with the same affliction as him—the damned repeating. However, there was no annoyance in her tone. If anything, she seemed content to repeat the words as if they were a spell she was weaving over him.

Ruthie gave him no warning this time. She placed her hand over his chest, and Harry hauled in a giant breath. In the past when people put their hands on him it always felt like an enormous weight, a shackle that he couldn't wait to break out of. Not with Ruthie. She felt like liquid, like a cool spring he swam in, refreshing and awakening. Like he was a new man, a real man living more than a half-life.

"Harry?" she asked as her fingers ran up his throat, taking the same road they had as before. It was easier this time. No longer surprised, Harry could enjoy the way she played with him, harvest the glorious sensations she evoked.

"Keep going," he said. "Don't stop."

He heard the laughter in her voice. "We forgot to lock the door."

"The next person who barges in gets stabbed," he remarked wryly.

"I thought you didn't approve of stabbing. Too…intimate?" She caressed his mouth, coaxing the next words from him.

"There's a time and a place."

Harry licked his lips, catching a patch of her skin. He tasted her briny flesh, the unmistakable flavor of blood rushing to the surface, heightened anticipation. And he wanted more. He was thirsty, so very thirsty, and wanted to taste everything that was her, everything that would tell him who and what she was.

"Take off your dress."

Ruthie's fingers stalled. She shifted away from him, taking her warmth, but Harry wouldn't be deterred.

"Do it."

Her giggle was nervous, but Harry heard the rustle of clothing, the sound of clasps being unlatched. "I thought you were supposed to be listening to me," she said.

"I *am* listening to you," Harry replied, hearing silk flutter along the hardwood. "I'm listening to everything you're doing."

Her movements stopped. She was waiting for him to tell her what to do. Harry wouldn't take that away from her. He could only hope that she wanted the same thing that he did.

"What do you want, Ruthie?"

A memory came to Harry, of his asking her that question before. She'd been so taken aback by it, so seduced by it.

"I want to kiss you again."

"Then what the hell is stopping you?"

Ruthie sat down on the bed. Harry canted his head to her as she leaned into him. Her soft, supple breasts grazed his chest as she placed her lips on his, opening them softly. But Harry wasn't in the mood for soft. Nor did he have the patience for gentle. His blood was high. His need was too great. He plundered her mouth hard, filling her with his tongue, sipping on her passion.

Harry continued to clench his hands at his sides as their kiss turned fierce and primitive. He couldn't get enough of her. Again and again, he stormed inside her, mingling his tongue with hers, sampling the flavors of her fervor.

He wanted to lose himself in her, to plant his shaft so deep inside her that he couldn't know where he started and she began. His chest began to tremble and his heart pumped wildly as they exchanged breaths. His cock strained against his trousers, screaming to put an end to the torment.

But this wasn't torment, Harry realized. Kissing this lovely woman, feeling her nipples skim across his chest, wasn't a means to an end.

It was just the beginning. And Harry wanted more.

Tearing his mouth off Ruthie's, he caught his breath at the base of her neck. "Give me your breasts," he rasped. "Let me taste them."

Ruthie arched away. He was completely alone as she made up her mind. In those few seconds, Harry felt undeniable grief, lost and untethered. Because he finally had what he desired, and it had slipped from his fingers.

But then she moved. Ruthie shuffled on the bed, going to her knees. And then he felt her once more. The tight bud of her nipple grazed his mouth, and Harry reacted at once. He opened wide to take her. He had never tasted a woman's breast before, and the feeling was both novel and a revelation. Never had he encountered something so soft and succulent, enticing and delicate. He licked her skin, circling the sweet nipple with his tongue before biting down until he heard her gasp. Ruthie's hands circled the base of his neck, pulling him closer, all while Harry stroked her sensitive mounds, sucking against the weighty flesh, appreciating the idea of peaches and cream for the first time. She bucked against him, growing more and more restless.

And, again, Harry was having his fill, but he was not satisfied. He wanted to experience more.

Ruthie gasped as they tumbled back to the bed. With his gloved hands he dragged her body to the edge, situating himself in between her legs. She rocked her pelvis against his cock, her inner thighs squeezing him closer. Ruthie leaned up, reaching for the buttons of his trousers, but he nudged her hands away.

Her breathing slowed. He could hear the question on her lips as he backed away and knelt in front of her. Ruthie's knees knocked together, and Harry had to coax them apart, kissing the knobby ridges. "Open for me," he said, sliding the tip of his finger down her long calf. "Let me kiss you more."

Ruthie made indecipherable noises in the back of her throat—but none of them were *no*. Slowly, her legs separated, and Harry took his time, savoring the rich, salty aroma of her body. There was no thinking. He licked her seam, delicately opening it just as he had her legs. She convulsed at the invasion while arching for more. Ruthie opened to his mouth. He was the alchemist, transforming her body into liquid gold.

Ruthie's fingers found his head. They wound into his hair, pulling, anchoring her to this mortal plane. And Harry feasted on her. He licked and teased all the hidden places that he'd watched her touch days before. He would never give up that vision, but this feeling, this act, was remarkable in itself, binding them together in ways Harry couldn't have imagined.

Ruthie's motions became more erratic. She thrust her pelvis against his mouth, and Harry listened. He fluttered over her sex with his tongue; he massaged her while she screamed with abandon, pressing her knees to his ears, pumping her fulfillment through the pores of her skin. And still Harry kissed her. Because he wanted to taste the difference between the edge and the fall. He wanted to know everything about this woman—his woman. He wanted nothing to stand between them in this moment.

And when he spilled in his pants like an overexcited lad, Harry could only laugh at himself. He was too content and proud to do otherwise.

Finally, he pulled the necktie from his head. Ruthie lay back on the bed, her eyes shuttered, her lips curved in a sweet smile. Harry took his time arranging her on the bed, tucking her under his covers. Her breathing was regaining its normal rhythm, but she wasn't asleep. Her body was languid and heavy, sated and at peace, and as Harry stretched out next to her for the first time—close but not exactly touching—he allowed his body to do the same.

As he stared at the ceiling, a rush of sensations slammed into him. They came on him fast, unbidden and unrelenting. Harry grabbed at his heart, thinking it would pound out of his chest.

The anxiety was crippling.

Until Ruthie moved. Her arm grazed his, a wisp of a touch. And Harry was rewarded with the only feeling that mattered.

He wasn't alone.

Chapter Eighteen

"I DON'T UNDERSTAND what we're looking for," Maggie grumbled, twirling her parasol in her hand. "We've walked this path a thousand times already. My feet hurt."

Ruthie scowled at her teammate as they ambled along the path in St. James Park. "Earlier at practice you told me you have nothing to do!"

"That didn't mean I wanted to spend it traipsing around the park like some debutante searching for a husband." Maggie's eyes narrowed dangerously. "We're not doing that, are we? You haven't turned into one of those newly married women who only want to help their single friends find husbands now, have you?" She started to backtrack, her fear vivid under her plain bonnet. "I'm aware I don't know you very well, Ruthie, but I thought you were better than that!"

"Oh, calm yourself!" Ruthie chided. She spun in a circle once more to spy anyone coming down the path. "I'm the last person who'd foist marriage on anyone."

Maggie chuckled bitterly. "And why is that? Is it not every-thing you dreamed it would be? I'm sorry to say, but you wouldn't be the first woman who realized that pertinent information a little too late."

"No, not all." Ruthie could feel her cheeks warming under

her very small and very unassuming bonnet. "It has been most...enlightening."

It had been a week since Ruthie woke up next to Harry in their bedroom. And each night after had been just as...*enlightening* as the last. They still hadn't made love again, nor was Harry ready to take off his gloves yet, but the intrepid man was trying. And Ruthie couldn't ask for more than that. It was only a matter of time before he let her touch him. Maybe even a matter of time before he told her that he loved her.

Because Ruthie was surely falling in love with him. And the more she spent time at the club getting to know her husband, the more she became aware of that fact. She barely even noticed his quirks anymore, although she could always tell when he was irritated with them and the lengths to which he went to keep others from recognizing them. There were two Harry Holmeses—the one he showed to the world and the one that he saved for her...and Ernest.

The one that frightened other people, and the one that frightened himself.

Ruthie couldn't help but wonder if that was the reason he was always so exhausted by the end of the night. Hiding your nature day in and day out seemed a Sisyphean task, resulting in a crazed, paranoid mind.

At first, she had balked at being her husband's lodestone. She'd hated the idea of his only wanting her as a means of solace and protection. But something had changed in their nights together. Harry still took from her, but not without giving so much more. In the end, Ruthie had to ask herself if that would be enough. If he never grew to have romantic feelings for her—the kind she'd dreamed about as a young girl—could she be satisfied? Her answer scared her. Because she felt close—so close. And the closer they became, the more she wanted.

Perhaps she was just like her brother and father—bad at gambling. From her time at the Lucky Fish, she'd learned that a good gambler knew when to stop pushing. He knew when enough was enough. He knew when to walk away from the table.

And although Ruthie felt stronger than she ever had in her life, she didn't know if she would ever be able to do that. And that unfortunate realization reminded her of her mother's words during their last conversation, and the underlying pain that was still so very evident whenever she mentioned Ruthie's father.

"Enlightening," Maggie grumbled. "I don't think I like the sound of that."

"Is there anything that interests you about marriage?"

"I'm not *against* marriage," Maggie protested. "I'm sure it would be fine to find a nice man who loves me for who I am, like my father loves my mother."

Ruthie regarded her new friend. With her rich chestnut hair and sleepy doe eyes, she warranted many second looks by men of the *ton*. What could be the problem?

"Just fine?"

Maggie shook her head in irritation. "The men in our group don't like me. They never have. They call me a tomboy and say I prefer mud to dresses just because *one* time when I was seven, I accepted a dare from Lord Michael that I could ride a pig better than he could ride a horse. I could! And they've never let me forget it."

"Lord Michael?" Ruthie asked. "The Earl of Waverly's heir?"

Maggie rolled her eyes. "Of course you know him. Everyone knows Lord Michael."

"He's very popular in the set, isn't he?" Ruthie said. All the girls knew or wanted to know Lord Michael. "And he's good friends with my brother."

"Oh, so your brother's a pompous ass too?"

Ruthie scrunched her nose. "I'm afraid so."

"Ah, well, that's all right," Maggie said, strolling a few determined steps ahead. "It is too nice of a day to think about pompous asses. Now why don't you tell me who we're looking for so I can actually be of some assistance?"

Ruthie scanned the park. She'd come back every day since

she'd encountered the little girls and their mother and only seen them one other time at a distance. By the time she'd made it to their end of the grass, they'd vanished. "I'm just hoping I run into some people again," she said. "I wish to speak to them."

"Then why don't you write them a letter like a normal person? Oh!" Maggie covered her mouth with her hand. "I'm sorry. Did someone cut you in public over your marriage? Is that why you can't write to them? Well, don't worry about me or the other girls in the club. We're made of sterner stuff than that. In fact, when I told my mother I was spending time with you today, she was intolerably excited. She said that father owed your husband too much money for us to be uppity. She can be such a cow, but I love her to death."

Ruthie laughed despite the rambling, off-putting speech. "Thank you so much," she replied dryly. "And no, no one cut me—except my mother, I suppose. No, I'm here because—there!"

Her arm shot out as two little girls with dark braids came into her line of sight. They were wearing the same thin dresses as before and didn't appear to have put on one ounce of fat. If anything, they looked smaller. Ruthie tore off down the path with Maggie close on her heels.

"You, little ones!" she called out. "You remember me, don't you? You're Orla and Maeve."

The older girl's eyes lit up. "Oh, sure. You were the one with the fella from Kilkenny."

"Fella from Kilkenny?" Maggie asked.

"She means Harry," Ruthie answered quickly. "He's Irish."

"He's Irish?"

"Yes, now please hush." Ruthie turned to the girls. "Where's your mother?"

"We lost her a ways back," the older sister said, glancing over her shoulder. "The baby in her belly makes her slow."

"She's with child?"

The girl nodded. "She said it was our da's last gift to her be-

LOVE SPORT

fore going up to heaven."

"I'm not sure if I'd call it that," Maggie whispered, causing Ruthie to elbow her in the side.

"Why are you wanting our ma?" the younger sister asked. The way her little fingers held on to her sister's arm reminded Ruthie of Julia. So trusting. "We're not bothering ya, so don't be telling her we were."

Ruthie shook her head. "No, of course not. I just want to talk to her about a position I need filled and to inquire if she's found a suitable place to live."

The older sister eyed Ruthie cautiously as if this were all some trick. "We're doing just fine," she replied rather testily. "We're staying with our auntie and cousins and granda and granny. It's lovely."

"We're sure your home is very lovely," Maggie piped in, no doubt trying to make amends for her previous comment.

It didn't work. The girl stared at Maggie as if she were speaking Greek. "It's not a home," she spat. "We left our home in Ireland. It's a room. And it's a fine room. We get by, even though the landlord spits on the floor every time we open our mouths, and he threatens to increase the rent. He says the Irish are nothing but good-for-nothing mongrels. I think he's the mongrel. At least we don't spit on our own floor."

"Why do you stay there?" Maggie asked.

The girl's face screwed up like she was explaining something to a dim-witted child. "Not many people wanted to rent to us. They say the Irish are lazy and never pay on time. But that's not true. Ma spends every day looking for a position. All she wants to do is work, but no one will let her."

Ruthie put her arms around the girls, turning them around. Together they walked down the path until they spotted their mother catching her breath under the shade of a tall oak.

"You don't have to feel sorry for us," the oldest girl said. "As we said, we're doing fine. There's nothing for you to worry your pretty head about."

"I'm sure it is just fine," Ruthie replied, catching the mother's eye. "But let's see if we can come up with something better than fine."

⟫⟫⟫✦⟪⟪⟪

"MY GOD," MAGGIE whispered in her ear. "How many are there?"

Ruthie nudged her friend with her elbow once more, certain that Maggie was never going to spend the afternoon with her again. She probably had a bruise from all the prodding. But it was a rude question—although Ruthie had caught herself wondering the same thing.

When Ruthie had told the mother—Colleen—that she had suitable rooms to let in her house for her and her family, she had no idea that the woman was going to bring so many others. But here they stood in the corridor of the third floor of the Lucky Fish—all eleven of them, though seven were children.

At Ruthie's prodding, Ernest opened one of the vacant rooms, and they all clamored inside. "Oh, this is lovely," Colleen exclaimed. "Yes, this will do well. There's not a rat in sight!" She nodded at the other woman, her sister, Sinead. "We'll be most comfortable here. And we won't make a fuss or any trouble, will we, girls?"

Orla, the oldest daughter, nodded, while Maeve decided it was the appropriate time to curtsey. "We'll be as good and quiet as church mice."

Colleen couldn't contain her smile. "We promise. And we'll be out on our feet in no time."

"I'm not worried at all," Ruthie said, encouraged by how well the situation was turning out. "But don't you want to see the other room?"

Sinead looked puzzled. "Other room?"

Ernest stepped forward. "There's no reason to share, miss. Your family can have its own. Right next door." He lifted his arm to shepherd them out and showcase the next room, but Sinead refused to budge. Her hair was lighter than her sister's and already interspersed with wisps of white. Ruthie gathered she was Colleen's older and less trusting sister.

"I don't need to see it," she said, folding her arms. "I know what's going on now. I know what this place is. I've seen men come and go. I've heard stories."

"This is a gambling hall," Ruthie said. "My husband is the proprietor."

Sinead gave her sister a look before turning back on Ruthie. "And do you know what it is your husband *propriets*? What's he going to ask us to do for these nice, comfortable, separate rooms? Because I know. I know all too well."

Poor Ernest wobbled on his feet, close to fainting. "Mrs. Holmes is a l-lady," he stammered. "You mustn't speak to her like that. She...she—"

Ruthie cut him off. "*She* knows exactly what goes on at this club," she replied evenly. "I also know my husband would never force anyone to do anything. I brought you here because I am in need of a lady's maid. And I'm certain Ernest can find more work that's agreeable for the rest of you. But this is not a prison. This is not a workhouse. You are free to leave at any time." She looked at Colleen. "I just wanted to help. I'm asking you to trust me."

Sinead cocked her head. "I've lived in this cursed country for months now and no one has bothered to help us without making us feel like scum for receiving it. We don't know you. I'm sorry, missus, but why should we trust you? I just can't understand it."

Ruthie's shoulders slumped. "Do you really want to know?"

"I do."

She released an exasperated exhale. "Because my husband's Irish mother told him on her deathbed that he was going to die alone and go straight to hell unless he repented. And the foolish man believes her so much that he's taken to keeping a ledger of every benevolent thing he does so he can show the Almighty at the pearly gates. Now he's relying on me for his salvation. It is my job to spend his money for good to save his soul." Ruthie shrugged. "And I love the man. There's that. So will you help me?"

Sinead's expression slowly broke into a wide grin. "Oh, missus. Why didn't you say all that before? An Irish mother? A healthy stab of guilt? Now, *that* I understand perfectly."

Chapter Nineteen

L ATER THAT NIGHT, Ruthie studied her husband carefully. Harry always ate quickly, seeming to wish to get the act out of the way so he could move on to more fulfilling things. She didn't mind that those things now included her. In fact, she approved wholeheartedly. Only, now his bites were slow and measured, his gaze far off, as if he were contemplating a puzzle hidden in the air.

"Is something wrong? Are the carrots not to your liking?" she asked. "Ernest said the cook made them the way you like…"

"They're fine," Harry replied evenly. He took a small bite of one as if to make a point.

Ruthie played with the chicken on her plate. Harry's room, which usually seemed so large and exotic, shrank before her eyes like the couple was being forced into a very polite and quiet box. Her new corset felt entirely too tight. She would never call Harry a moody person, yet here he was, in a definite *mood*.

She tried again. "Holly came by today to see me," she said, keeping her tone light and conversational. "She said that Bennie took her to the Adelphi Theater last night to see a new bur-lesque."

Harry continued to chew.

Ruthie went on. "She said we would like it; it's not as racy as some of the others and made Bennie laugh so hard he almost fell out of his chair, which…which is something."

Harry nodded absent-mindedly and cut off another piece of chicken.

"Maybe you'd like to take me there sometime?" Ruthie asked hopefully. "It sounds like a fun thing for couples to do."

"I don't like the theater," Harry replied.

"Have you gone?"

"Yes. And it felt like being stuffed in a smelly shoe."

Ruthie huffed. "It couldn't be that bad."

He bobbed his shoulders. "If you want to go, then you should go."

"I'd want to go with you."

Harry placed his knife and fork on his plate and wiped his mouth with his napkin. When he stared at her, Ruthie felt like she'd been doused in freezing water. "And I want to know why it sounds like an entire fucking Irish clan is in the middle of a three-day wake a few doors down from my own."

Ruthie's expression froze on her face. "Oh! Did I forget to tell you?" she said breezily, stalling for time. "I thought I told you."

Harry's smile did nothing to thaw the freeze. If anything, it made it colder. "No, as a matter of fact, you didn't."

"Well, husband, remember when we had that talk about my starting a charity?" she said, sitting as high as she could in her seat, gathering her confidence. "I've decided on one."

Harry lifted his brow. "And?"

"Aaand I thought about you and me and the kind of good we want to do in the world, and about you… I *really* thought about you—"

"Ruthie," he groaned.

"Don't be upset," she said, her control slipping. "I didn't know where to put them. And I thought since this house is so large and Ernest said there are rooms not being used, I…" Ruthie cringed, waiting for Harry's reaction, but it was taking too long, and talking—a lot—seemed like the only thing to do. "And I know you don't like discussing Ireland, and you don't have many good memories from that part of your life—or *any* part of your life, really—but I just thought that it would be good to help them. Because no one is, Harry. No one. These poor people have nothing to eat. They've lost their land and their homes and their families, and all we do is blame them. Have you read the newspapers? The Irish are called lazy, and people say the famine is all their fault. I don't understand how it could be. And you have so much, and you want to give so much, and...and..."

"Stop, stop, darling. Come here." Harry reached across the table for Ruthie's hand and tugged her out of her seat and into his lap. She was as surprised as she was flattered. He'd never done something so casually demonstrative before. She found it difficult to think when the soft leather of his glove skated affectionately across her back.

"I didn't mean to make you so upset," Harry said, hugging her torso. He leaned Ruthie back until she was resting on his chest. "I just wanted to understand how your mind worked."

Ruthie smiled. She recalled saying something very similar to him not long ago. "So, you don't mind? They were getting taken advantage of in the old rooms they rented. Did I tell you it's the two little girls we met in the park?"

"Naturally." Harry grinned.

"And their aunts and cousins and grandparents."

"It certainly sounds like it," he said as thumping and laughter were heard behind the walls. "What the hell are they doing in there?"

"They're children," Ruthie said. "They're acting like children. But don't worry. They promised me they would be good and quiet and not interfere in the club."

Harry squinted playfully. "And you believed them, did you? You believed a whole gaggle of Irish children when they told you they would behave."

"A gaggle?" Ruthie laughed. "They're not geese."

"You're right. They're not as quiet as geese."

She fingered the buttons of his coat. "So, you're not mad?"

"No, I'm not mad."

"And this isn't too personal for you?"

"Of course it's too personal for me!" he grumbled. The emotion came straight from his chest and nearly jostled Ruthie to the floor. "I've spent most of my life scratching that country off my skin. But the marks are too deep. I was nothing there. A bastard son. A freak. Unwanted. Unloved. I want nothing to do with their church and their superstitions." He hesitated. "And yet...sometimes when I wake in the morning, I can smell the grass. I can smell the color green. It's unmistakable and clean, and alive. It has so much energy and vitality. And all I feel is grateful."

Ruthie wondered if anyone's hands could ever touch another as intimately as his words had just touched her. They shot straight to heart and soul.

Harry blinked and frowned once he saw the look Ruthie was giving him. He wiped a hand across his face, and the moment was gone. "But why didn't you think about the Belgravia house? It's empty and bigger and probably more suitable for a gaggle of curious children and whoever else comes along. Feed them, house them, buy them clothes, find them work. Do what you can."

"Really?" Ruthie asked in astonishment. "I can do that?"

"I don't see anyone stopping you."

"Oh, thank you, Harry!" She threw her arms around her husband's neck, placing wet kisses along his chin. "Thank you. Thank you."

She noticed the tension in his body as well as the effort he was using to hide it. Instantly, Ruthie pulled away, resting her hands against the safety of his chest instead. She didn't apologize. She knew he wouldn't want her to.

"I'll start organizing everything the moment I get home from the cricket exhibitions. I can't believe it's almost time to leave. Four whole weeks away from London." She whistled, winking cheekily. "You're going to miss me something fierce, aren't you?"

"Undoubtedly." Harry's smile was genuine, but Ruthie thought she recognized a dash of sadness at the periphery.

She went back to playing with his buttons. "You know…you could come with me. I hear that Bath and Exeter and Manchester aren't so different from London. Myfanwy says the houses we are staying in are very comfortable, plenty of your own space to be had. And the families are the very best—highly virtuous and commendable."

"Oh, I wouldn't say that." Harry chuckled. "They lost their ancestral homes to me, so they weren't that virtuous."

"What do you mean?"

"I mean, darling girl, that you and your teammates are staying in my homes—all of them. And yes, I hear they are very comfortable. I'm sure you will enjoy them."

Ruthie flinched. "But I… She said…" Her eyes widened. "You have estates in all those cities?"

"You know I do."

"Well, yes, you've told me, but…I don't think I ever believed you."

"Believe it, darling." Harry leaned in for a kiss that was over much too soon. "You're disgustingly rich now."

Ruthie slumped on his lap. "Well, that is something."

"I like to think so."

"So, you'll come?" Ruthie told herself not to be embarrassed by the hope in her voice. Or by the way it swiftly died when his expression turned serious.

"Ah, no," Harry said. "I told you. I don't travel outside the city."

"But that doesn't mean you can't. Or won't."

"It does for me. I told you, Ruthie, it's best for me to stay here. I like it here. I can be myself here."

Ruthie hopped out of his lap. "But you're not yourself here. You're always trying so hard to be the opposite of yourself. You just said so yourself. You play an Englishman, but you're not and never will be."

"That's hardly what I meant. Don't twist my words around on me," he said. The harshness in his tone shocked her. "I'm Harry *fucking* Holmes. I own most of the buildings and half of the men in this damn city. I've made it this way. Me. I did that. And now you're asking me to leave it?"

"I'm not!" Ruthie protested. "I'm not asking you to do that at all. I just thought it would be an adventure, something to do together. But let's not worry about it. If it makes you upset—"

"I'm not upset."

"Fine. You're not upset. Let's just change the subject."

Harry crossed his arms like a stubborn child, stretching out his legs. "Fine. What do you want to talk about? Seen any good theater lately?"

Ruthie groaned. Her neck lolled back until she was staring at the ceiling. "Now you're just being an ass."

Harry laughed. "I am, aren't I? I'm sorry. Christ, I seem to be apologizing a lot tonight," he said. Ruthie didn't have enough time to react. He reached out and caught her by the waist, returning her to his lap. "Truly. I'm sorry. I didn't mean to take my anger out on you. It's not your fault. I… Sometimes I worry that you'll grow tired of me, tired of this life. What's worse is that I wouldn't blame you if you did."

Ruthie swiveled in his lap until she was facing him. She maneuvered her legs until one rested on either side of his hips. She could feel him growing beneath her and couldn't hide her own building excitement. This could be the night. She would ask him to take her again, to place his bare hands on her naked flesh. Somewhere in the back of her mind she knew Harry wasn't ready, but she would ask anyway. He wouldn't take her to the theater; he wouldn't take a train. He could do this.

"Harry," she said slowly, bracketing his face with her hands. She held him there for a moment, allowing his body to acclimate. A hot flush came over her as he stared at her lips and worked on undoing his necktie. "How many times do I have to tell you that you're enough? This place is enough." She held her mouth inches from his, toying with the idea of kissing him. His breath was sultry and warm. His jaw was tight and unyielding beneath her hands. "I just ask that you keep trying. Please?"

Harry nodded, nipping her lips with his teeth. He reached around for her arse and grabbed a handful of flesh. Then he pushed her hips down, grinding them into his shaft. "I'll always try for you," he said, moving his pelvis along with the motions. "Always. Always. Always."

"Shh," Ruthie purred, placing her fingers over his mouth. Instantly, he was soothed. "I know, dearest. I know."

His eyes darted back and forth between her own, wide, child-like, lost in wonder. "My God, you're so fucking beautiful," he whispered. "So fucking beautiful."

Ruthie shook her head. "Please don't—"

"Be quiet," he said gruffly. "You're the most beautiful woman I've ever seen. Sometimes I can't look at you, you're so beautiful. I thought so the moment I first saw you, dressed up like a man. I couldn't stop staring at this arse."

Even as Harry was growing more and more aroused, he was dousing her mood. Ruthie squirmed under his gaze.

"Stop it," he ordered her. "Let me look at you. You're all I've ever wanted, Ruthie Waitrose. From the freckles that are determined to never leave to the smile that is always so mysterious to me. To your hair that reminds me of the day"—Harry ran his nose along her neck—"to your smell that reminds me of our nights." He placed a gentle kiss on her jumping pulse. "You do more than make me feel safe. You are my safe haven. My refuge. You are where I belong."

She was so mesmerized by his words that Ruthie didn't notice her dress sliding up until the cold air hit her thighs. Harry had it pooled around her waist before he moved to his trousers. With a kiss, he lifted her to her knees as he shifted underneath.

He kept her there, poised on the tip of his shaft, waiting until she met his gaze. Only when she had did he continue. His expression was brutal and intense, savage in its intensity. "I've tried and tried for you, and I will keep trying," he declared. "But tonight, I'm going to ask you to do something for me. Tonight, I want you to try to see yourself through my eyes. Try to feel as beautiful as I know you are, as courageous and strong. Tonight, I want you to take everything I have to give and only want more. Because that is what you deserve, my love. Everything."

When Harry surged into her, Ruthie was ready. She took him wholly and completely, with a freeing wantonness she'd never experienced before. When they came together, she hugged his face to her breasts, keening into his hair. The cataclysmic exchange was heavenly and divine.

Harry released inside her, giving her his heart and his future, and Ruthie took it greedily.

And in the end, she did as he said. She only wanted more.

Chapter Twenty

H ARRY RESTED ON his side. He couldn't sleep even though
they'd been in bed for hours. The club vibrated through
the floors below him, still operating merrily through the night—
not that it ever stopped. Ordinarily, the noise didn't bother him.
Harry was used to the ambiance.

The occasional yelp and song still came from the Irish family
next door, but they'd settled into a listless quiet. Harry had no
doubt they'd become immune to the Lucky Fish's nighttime
harmonies as well. People were amazing creatures. They could
acclimate to just about anything, given enough time and
patience…and understanding.

Harry fixed on his wife, who had a tendency to start sleeping
on her back but roll onto her stomach soon after. Her face was
smashed against the pillow's edge, and a tiny line of drool trailed
from her gaping mouth.

Harry smiled at the sight. And, oddly enough, he slid closer to
her. He had the sneaking suspicion that no matter how hard he
tried, he would never be able to get close enough. It was a strange
feeling, both unnerving and tantalizing, especially since, when
he'd made love to her that night, he still hadn't been able to take
off his gloves.

Ruthie didn't ask him to. She never did. And later, languid

and content on the bed, she'd been so proud when she pointed out that he hadn't worn the necktie over his eyes. Harry was changing, she said.

But would it be enough to keep her? Harry tried to believe Ruthie when she said that she would never want to leave him; however, something stopped him from taking her words to heart.

Everyone always left him. Just as the world could be too much for Harry, he had been too much for all the people in his life who were supposed to love him. From the father who'd never held his hand to the mother who'd released it too eagerly, Harry had always been the person left behind.

The years with his gang and running the Lucky Fish had been no different. People dealt with Harry because he made them money, or tricked them into thinking he could. That Harry Holmes was an illusion of his own design. He was the tiger who disguised himself in the environment in order to fool his prey. But he couldn't do that with Ruthie. She peered through the layers of stripes and muted colors and saw the real him.

And the real Harry Holmes had always been found lacking. Earlier he'd asked Ruthie to try something for him. To try to see herself the way that he saw her. Could he be as brave? Could he ever look at himself and see anything other than an aberration?

Ruthie snored, interrupting his thoughts. Yet another thing she did when she reached the deepest part of her sleep. Harry chuckled at the ungodly, adorable sound and tugged the cover higher to her chin. His hands were bare. For a moment, he paused near her face. He tried to count the freckles dotting her nose, but the shadows of the room made it too difficult. His fingers hovered there, just over her bridge, as if he were waiting to slide down to the tip.

One day he would do it, he told himself, dropping his hand back to the bed. One day he would surprise his wife with that little touch. He just needed her to keep wanting him in the meantime. Because he would never stop trying.

>>>><<<<

THE SOUND OF rustling pages nagged at his consciousness. He opened his eyes to find his wife across the room seated on the couch, a small lantern lit beside her.

Harry rubbed at his eyelids. "What are you doing?"

Her head jerked up. Slowly, she lifted a book out of her lap. "I couldn't sleep," she replied stiffly.

Her strange tone made him regard the book more closely.

It wasn't a book. It was his ledger.

"You shouldn't be reading that," he snapped, jumping out of the bed. In two steps he was on her, and he swiped the item from her hands.

Ruthie folded them in her lap, her expression opaque, which only fueled Harry's annoyance.

"This is mine. You had no right to read it."

She lowered her gaze, nodding her head. "I'm sorry," she said, her tone as expressionless as her face.

Harry released a breath, his irritation lifting at her immediate apology. He sighed, tossing the journal on the couch next to her. Ruthie didn't look at it. "No...I overreacted. I didn't need to yell like that. It's just..." He found his robe on the chair next to his bed and put it on before returning to her. "It's personal."

Ruthie's laugh was short and acerbic. "Oh, I'm aware." Her gaze lifted to him slowly. "Don't you want to know why I'm sorry?"

Harry shrugged, unable to hide the frustration. "Because you invaded my privacy without asking me?"

"Yes, there's that. But I'm also sorry that I didn't read it sooner."

Harry yanked the belt around his waist, not recognizing the woman in front of him. "Explain yourself, Ruthie. How could you say something like that?" He paused, fear gripping like a vise. *What did you read?*

Finally, Ruthie's calm veneer cracked, and Harry watched the sadness pour into her.

"You wrote about me. In your do-good journal. I was an entry."

Fuck. Harry had forgotten all about that. He tried to recall what he wrote, but nothing came to him. It had been so long ago, and done on a whim. It had meant nothing to him.

But he could tell it meant something to her. Ruthie's stare was too damning and heartbroken. Harry panicked under the strain.

"It's not what you think," he said, hoping to stanch the wound quickly.

But it ran too deep and was flowing too fast. "Was I just another good deed, Harry?" she asked, her voice catching when she said his name. "Just another way to buy yourself into heaven? Convince your creator by telling him how you married a poor, helpless, plain wallflower with no hopes or prospects?"

"You know that's not it," Harry said. He took a step toward her, but Ruthie flinched.

She stared at his bare, outstretched hands. "Don't touch me," she said quietly. "I don't want that right."

Harry dropped his hands to his sides as an inner alarm banged between his ears. This was it. He was losing her. He could feel her slipping through his fingers.

So he squeezed harder. "Goddammit, Ruthie," he said. "Stop behaving this way. You know that journal means nothing. It's just a place for my thoughts. It's…it's meaningless."

"No," she replied evenly. She'd recaptured her coolness, and it threatened to destroy him more than her animosity. "It's your soul. It's what you believe. It's your hope. I know you, Harry. It means everything. And it means I was a fool."

Harry fell to his knees in front of his wife, once more causing her to jerk back into the cushions. "You are not a fool. *You* are my everything. Why can't you believe me? Don't listen to that stupid book. I married you because I wanted you."

"You married me because you were afraid of being alone."

"So what?" he shouted. "That was then. It's not now. You've seen me change. You know what I'm capable of. I need you to trust me. I care for you. You have no idea how much. You've saved me."

Ruthie let out a sardonic laugh, her blue eyes boring into him. She reached for the book, lifting it, only to let it drop again. "That was my job, wasn't it? That was my purpose for you. And it looks like I'm doing it."

"Stop it, Ruthie," Harry growled. The desperation made it impossible to control the anger in his voice. "You're more than that. You always were."

"Was I?" she asked softly. "I wanted to believe that. A few days ago"—she blushed—"a few *hours* ago, I might have—"

Harry clutched the ends of the couch on both sides of her, caging her in. Ruthie, who was undeniably compassionate and perceptive, always so generous and sympathetic to his deficiencies, was not understanding what he was trying to tell her.

Or not willing to this time.

Harry was jumping out of his skin. He needed to touch something. This disastrous situation was dragging him out to sea, leaving him alone and untethered. He needed something. He needed to hold Ruthie. "My love, you have to believe that. Let me explain. Just listen."

She shook her head. "I'm tired of words, Harry. Just let it be." She cast another doleful glance at the ledger. "I don't want to talk any more tonight."

"But—"

Footsteps pounded through the corridor, cutting off his plea. As one, Ruthie and Harry twisted toward the sound. They had no time to question it. Mason Waitrose's crazed voice shook through the door.

Harry fell back to his ankles. "I'm going to fucking kill your brother."

"You won't have a chance," Ruthie retorted, scrambling to

her feet, "because I'm going to do it first."

Mason's voice intensified. "If you don't get out of my way, old man, you're going to regret it!" he barked.

Ernest.

Harry launched himself at the door. Just as he was about to reach for the handle, it flew open and Mason exploded in, leaving Ernest behind, shaking in the corridor.

Ruthie screamed, "Mason! What on earth are you doing?"

Her brother instantly commanded the atmosphere, waving a pistol in front of him as if it were a sword. He was drunk again, which, to Harry's estimation, made the man more dangerous than he'd ever been.

"Be quiet, Ruthie. This is none of your concern!" her brother barked.

"Are you mad?" she replied, flopping her hands at her sides. "Of course this is my concern! Put that down at once. You'll hurt yourself."

Harry cast his wife an incredulous look. "Hurt *himself?*" His laughter tasted sour in his mouth. "He's pointing the damn thing at me! And since he's wobbling around so much, also at you!"

Ruthie lowered her head irritably. "He doesn't even know how to use it."

"Stop talking about me like I'm not here!" Mason fumed. "I've been taking lessons, and I'm a pretty good shot, if I do say so myself." He took two steps toward Harry. "And you don't have to be an expert marksman at this range, sister."

Harry stared at the pistol, thinking it familiar. Where had he seen it before?

"Do as your sister says," he advised darkly. "This will not end well for you."

"Oh, shut your mouth, Holmes," Mason said. "From my end, I'd say otherwise."

Harry scowled. "You can shoot me, but there's a whole house of men that won't let you leave here in one piece. Think this through, *Lord* Mason."

Mason scoffed, continuing to wave his pistol all about the room. "Do you really think your men care about you? Do you really think they'd kill a baron for you? You are delusional. And you are so, so wrong."

Sweat dripped off the baron's forehead. His face was red, his eyes bloodshot. Harry would bet that the fool hadn't slept in days.

"You thought you could embarrass me," Mason went on. "You thought you could make me a laughingstock in front of my friends. *My* friends—not yours!"

"Mason, they're not your friends," Ruthie cried.

"Shut up! Shut up, Ruthie. You've done quite enough, ruining your reputation, whoring yourself to this"—he sneered at Harry—"*bogtrotter*."

Harry lunged forward. "I'm going to smash your face in!"

Mason threw his arm out toward Harry once more, the tip of the gun mere inches from his nose. "Oh, I completely forgot! I'm sorry, sister. You're not a whore because your husband doesn't touch you." He laughed wildly. "Isn't that what you told Mother? He's one of *those* men. Ha! That's my only regret in all of this, Holmes. You'll be dead and won't be able to hear me telling all of London about your little...*quirks*. Isn't that what you called them, sister? How adorable." Mason's eyes darted to Harry's pants. "Is that one of them now? Tap, tap, tapping?"

Harry's jaw clenched. He hadn't even known he was doing it. He stretched out his fingers, but that weakness made Mason laugh louder.

"How did you do it, Holmes?" he asked. "I really want to know. How did you convince this whole city that you're normal, that you're not a freak?"

"Mason! That's enough," Ruthie said, sobbing.

Harry could feel Ruthie look at him, feel the way she implored him to turn his face to her. But he couldn't. His control was slipping. He had no idea which Harry she would see—the crime boss who didn't care what anyone thought of him, or the

MARGAUX THORNE

husband who was demonstrably hurt by what she'd done. Her betrayal.

"You've had your fun, brother. Now go home. Mother will be upset when she hears about this. You know it."

Mason made a nasty noise in the back of his throat. "Mother? Who do you think I'm doing this for? She'll be so fucking proud of me. Besides"—he shrugged, for the first time showing a semblance of doubt—"we need the money. This will ensure our future."

"Money?" Ruthie stepped lightly in his direction. "What money? What are you talking about?"

Mason lolled his head dramatically to the side, using the gun like a conductor uses his baton. "You didn't honestly believe I was going to give up and move to Uncle's home in Berkshire once you ruined your chances with Lord Dawkins? Christ! How could Mother ever think that I would rent out the townhome? That's my home! That's my birthright. That's my destiny! I couldn't just give it up without a fight, so when an opportunity presented itself to me, I took it."

"Mason," Ruthie said, lengthening the word in a terrifying warning. "What presented itself? Who?"

The baron's jaw wobbled. He blinked at his sister as if trying to break through the prison of alcohol that he'd built around himself. She took another step toward him, and his elbow bent slightly.

It was what Harry had been waiting for. Lowering his head, he charged, hitting Mason straight in the gut. The men flopped to the floor, sending the gun flying across the room. It went off with a terrible *bang!* but Harry wouldn't be distracted. Once he unleashed his first punch, the others followed of their own accord. His skin stretched and tore as it connected with Mason's jaw; his knuckles bled and cracked as he continued to rain down blows.

Blood and tears, spit and snot mixed and whirled between the men as Harry released his vengeance on this enemy. His stomach roiled and lurched the more he swung; his vision blurred; his head pounded as blood caked his fist.

Someone touched him. A hand clung to his arm. A voice begged him to stop. Ultimately, it was his own, ever-failing body that did it. Acid burned at the base of his throat, and Harry leapt off the inert man and ran to the distant corner. He was sick at once. He heaved and gagged until he thought he heard a rib break. And then he did it again.

Through the hell, he heard his wife's voice. "Harry? Harry, look at me. It's over. Are you all right?"

She reached for his shoulder.

"Don't touch me!" he screamed. He rounded on her. Ruthie's eyes widened, her fear palpable. "Stay away from me!"

Harry's heart beat erratically. The room spread out before him, and everything was coming at him at once.

Except his wife. Ruthie backed away from him slowly, until she was at her brother's side.

She knelt down and shrieked. "Mason," she sobbed, clutching her brother's bloody face in her hands. "Mason, wake up. Wake up, brother."

Wiping his mouth with his robe, Harry heard a commotion at the doorway. He saw Ernest squeeze through a crowd of people. Softly, the butler walked to Ruthie and placed his arms around her quivering shoulders. "He's alive, miss," he said over her cries. "But just barely. We have to get him some help." He lifted his head to Harry. "What should we do?"

Harry went to rub a hand over his face but froze when he saw all the blood. He couldn't drag his eyes away when it began to shake uncontrollably.

"Harry?" Ruthie called out. "Please help him. Please. He didn't mean it. He doesn't know what he does. Please."

Harry shook himself awake. He marched to the door, throwing all the curious onlookers out of his way. "Vine! Vine!" he screamed down the corridor, looking for his man to clean up this mess.

Helplessly, Harry watched Ruthie collapse further into Ernest's arms. "Vine!" he shouted again, but no one came. Harry was alone.

"It's all right, Miss Ruthie," Ernest said, patting her shoulder. "Everything will be fine. I'll make sure of it. Don't you worry. This will right itself. I promise. We promise."

The butler stared up at his employer, but Harry was gone. His face was white; his expression dazed. He was lost in the moment; lost in the violence of what he'd done.

And he stood there much later, still immobile and speechless, as he lost his wife.

Chapter Twenty-One

"You have to drink, Mason," Ruthie urged, holding the cup to her brother's swollen mouth. As before, she only managed to get him to take a couple of sips before he nudged her hand away.

"Please, no more. I can't. It hurts."

Ruthie leaned away from the bed and sat back in her seat. It had been two days since the terrible scene at the Lucky Fish, and her brother's face was still swollen and bruised. His mouth could barely move, and one eye still hadn't opened. Dr. Cameron had informed him that it might never work the same.

"The doctor gave you orders. He said you need to drink water and rest."

"He should have given me laudanum."

Ruthie frowned. "He said you didn't need it." What she really wanted to say was that the doctor wouldn't give him any because he thought Mason deserved the pain.

Mason groaned. "Oh, God," he said, muffled through his mangled lips. "I'll never drink alcohol again. As God as my witness, I won't. This is torture."

Their cousin Reggie appeared in the doorway, leaning lazily on the frame. Ruthie knew his easy demeanor was an act for Mason's benefit. He was just as worried as she was. "You're lucky you're still alive, mate," he announced jovially. "And every day you get luckier that Harry *bleeding* Holmes doesn't storm through my doors and finish what *you* started."

The mention of her husband caused Ruthie to flinch. She hadn't returned to the club since Ernest and a few of Harry's men had dragged Mason into a carriage and sent him off to Reggie's home. She'd followed her brother, wanting to be certain he lived, and also because she didn't have any clue what to say to Harry. He'd told her to leave, so she'd left.

Would he even want to see her now? That night had been confusing even before her brother barged in. Ruthie didn't know where they stood and lacked the courage to find out.

For now, administering to Mason was easier than dealing with her marriage.

"What were you even thinking?" Reggie asked, entering the room. He draped himself on one of the bedposts, glaring at his suffering cousin. "You could have been killed, or worse, *you* could have killed someone!"

"I know. I know!" Mason cried. "Please, stop. I don't want to think about it."

"Well, I'm sorry, but you're going to have to," Reggie mercilessly went on. "Just because you're alive doesn't mean you're out of the woods. Holmes can have you arrested for attempted murder. All of London knows what you were doing at the club. It's all anyone is talking about."

Mason jerked to Ruthie. It was difficult for her to meet his gaze. His one eye might work, but it was red and ghastly from all the broken blood vessels. "Do you think he'll do it? Would he accuse me in court?"

Ruthie lifted her shoulders. "I honestly don't know what he'll do. I don't know him that well."

"That's bullshit," Mason blustered. "Of course you know him. You love the bastard."

"Just stop, Mason."

"Don't tell him to stop," Reggie said. "It's obvious. It's been obvious from the beginning."

Ruthie glared at him. "Hardly."

"There's no use denying it," Mason said. "Why else did you marry him? Especially when you could have had the immensely popular and handsome Lord Dawkins."

Ruthie sighed through a smile. "Mason…" she drawled. "How can you laugh at a time like this?"

Mason chuckled and then groaned, lifting a hand to his ribs. "Christ that hurts. I laugh, dear sister, because that's the only thing you can do when your life is over. I'm done. I've ruined everything. I have nobody and nothing. I'm a grown man without a penny to his name who is afraid of his own mother."

"Can't fault you there, cousin," Reggie said. "She's terrifying."

Mason's lips curled into a dismal smile. "She is, isn't she? And she always has been."

"What are you talking about?" Ruthie said, picking up Mason's water glass again. She brought it to his lips. "You are her favorite, her darling boy. She's always pampered you and let you get away with everything."

Her brother sobered, pushing the water away. "You don't know the half of it."

"It's you who don't know," Ruthie countered. She placed the water back on the table and sat on her hands. She was close to throttling the spoiled imbecile. "She never hounded you like she did me. She controlled everything from my weight to my clothes to my calendar to my suitors. All while you got to go off on your whim, drinking and acting like an idiot with your friends."

"Because that's what she wanted," Mason replied. "Do you know how many times I heard that I would never be the man that my father was? Hundreds. Thousands. I was force-fed stories of his wild and crazy adventures, encouraged to make a name for myself like he'd done. Do you know how horrible it feels to have to live up to the man you hated most?"

His words struck her. Ruthie paused. "You…you didn't hate

Father."

"I *loathed* him," Mason said. The words were low and deep, as if they'd come from the deepest reaches of him—the parts Ruthie never saw. "Do you want to know what the worst day of my life was? And no, it wasn't when your husband almost beat the life out of me. It was the day I watched Father sell our horses. I stood next to him and cried and cried as these foul men came and tugged them away, bucking and kicking. Then he smacked me over the head, said that I was a disappointment, that I wasn't behaving like a man." Tears wobbled in Mason's eye before they flooded down his bruised cheek. "But he was the one who disappointed me! I loved those horses. I would sit in the barn with them whenever Mother and Father had their rows. They were my friends. I took care of them. And then they were gone. And then Father was gone…before I could tell him how much I hated him."

Fresh tears dropped in Ruthie's lap. She was so much younger than Mason, but she remembered the horses, remembered how he would have to be dragged inside at the end of the night smelling like dirt and leather. "Then why do you act exactly like him? Why do you do such foolish things?"

Mason sniffed, blinking up at the ceiling. "I thought that was my destiny. I never had a choice. I was never as brave as you, Ruthie. I'm sorry I always let you down."

"Oh, Mason," Ruthie sobbed. "I'm not brave—"

"Of course you are," he said sharply. "You're the bravest person I know. Reggie told me all about the times he took you to the club. It was stupid and dangerous and so very, very brave."

Ruthie let her brother's words sink in, let them hug her heart. "Thank you," she said quietly. "I think I needed to hear that." She squeezed his hand, which was the only unbruised part of his body. "You have choices now. You can make a new plan for yourself. I'll help you." She wiped her eyes and looked at Reggie. "We all will."

Her cousin nodded. "Of course. Just tell us about that night, mate. Why did you do it? It doesn't sound like you. You can be rather thick at times, but I never thought you were suicidal. Where did you even get the blasted pistol?"

Mason covered his face with his palm. "I don't want to think about it right now. The last week has been so hazy. It makes my head hurt."

"Please try, brother," Ruthie urged. "It's important that you tell us. You mentioned money that night. What did you mean?"

Mason sighed, and Ruthie could see exhaustion creeping in. He needed to sleep, but Reggie was right—Mason had to tell them everything before his memory became even hazier.

"It's not me. I would never think to shoot anyone. You were right," he began, nodding at Ruthie. "I'm shit with guns. But there was this man. I can't remember his name. Why can't I remember his name? He's at the club. He's always at the club. He said he'd help me get my revenge, even pay me to shoot Harry. He said no one would blame me after what he'd done to Ruthie."

"He didn't do anything to me," Ruthie said.

Mason shrugged. "It didn't matter. I was drinking too much, not thinking straight. And I was embarrassed about everything that had happened. A man's ego is a fragile thing, sister."

"Think, mate," Reggie pressed. "Who was he?"

"Was it one of Dugan's men?" Ruthie asked.

Mason frowned. "What? Who's Dugan? No, I told you. He was one of the Harry's men at the club."

"That doesn't make sense. You're not remembering right," Ruthie snapped. "Try harder."

"I am trying hard, dammit!" Mason bellowed. "But I don't know his name. He never told me. He just had an eye."

"We all have eyes," Ruthie said.

"No…" Mason waved his hand over his damaged face. "He had a weird eye. One that never looks straight. I don't know. At least, it seemed that way. Maybe *I* was the one too drunk to see straight. Who knows anymore?"

USING REGGIE'S CARRIAGE, Ruthie went straight to the Lucky Fish. It was still early; the regulars hadn't begun to fill the main rooms yet, and Ruthie had no trouble entering through the kitchens unnoticed. Not that it mattered. For better or worse, the club had become her unlikely home for the last few weeks, and no one would question her. But Ruthie didn't have time for pleasantries, nor did she desire unwanted attention. No doubt the gossip had made much of her absence; she didn't want to give them any more.

True to his nature, Harry was exactly where she'd hoped he would be. She opened the door to their bedroom just as he was putting on his dark coat. Water from his afternoon bath still clung to the ends of his black hair, and his face was freshly shaved for the second time that day. If he'd been a wreck since she left, it certainly didn't show.

Ruthie would be lying to herself if she said she was happy about that sign.

Harry continued to study his reflection in the mirror as she stepped to the center of the room. The line of swords along the wall caught the waning sun. He straightened his necktie, scowling when he couldn't get it to sit right against his throat. His disregard stung her. The behavior was aloof and cold, something he'd never been with her before.

"You might not want to see me," Ruthie began softly, "but I need you to hear what I have to say. Regardless of how you feel about me right now, it's important that you listen."

Harry grunted and ripped the thin fabric off his neck, starting the process again.

The floor felt like it was wobbling underneath her feet, but Ruthie remembered what Mason had told her—especially the part about her being brave—and went on. "It was Vine. He was the one who put the pistol in my brother's hand," she said firmly.

"I suspect it was Vine who was behind the other shooting as well. Your friend wants you dead."

Harry waited until he finished with his necktie and then turned to face her. His blank expression threatened to bring her to her knees. He was a stranger to her. But he was alive. Ruthie hadn't got to him too late. "I know that. The pistol your brother pointed in my face and threatened me with looked familiar." His words were perfunctory, his tone amiable and bereft of any knowing. "I stayed up the entire night thinking about it. I didn't put two and two together right away. But when Vine continued to stay away from the club, I began to understand why. Once he discovered your brother was still alive, he knew it was only a matter of time before I found out."

Ruthie placed her hands around her face. "But why would he want you dead? You've known him since you were children."

Harry shrugged, not nearly as upset as Ruthie had expected him to be. "Hazard of the trade, remember? Besides, there's no honor among thieves. I should have suspected, really. It was my only fault for being so…preoccupied. Vine had told me that the men were upset with the way I was running things, focusing more on legitimate ventures. But it seems that *he* was the one upset. *He* wanted to run things. Bring everything back to how it was. What can I say?" He lifted his arms at his sides. "I suppose some men just aren't made for change."

Ruthie wasn't ready to tackle that comment. "Did you find him? Did you…deal with him?"

Harry's arms fell and his expression darkened, almost as if he were disappointed that she avoided the real topic—them. "Not yet, but I will. I heard that he ran out of town. But I'll find him. I always do."

"And then what?"

He cocked his head. "What do you mean? And then life goes back to the way it was."

Ruthie stepped forward, and Harry stared at her slippers. "Am I a part of that normal?"

His voice was gentle. "I didn't think you wanted to be."

"You told me to leave, so I left."

Weariness lined his features. Harry sighed and walked back to his bureau. He reached for the tiaras, grazing the emerald one at the top of the pyramid with his fingers. "I suppose it's for the best."

Ruthie was shocked that she couldn't hear her heart crack. The pain felt worse than Mason's face. "The best for whom?"

"You. Me. What does it matter?" He turned to face her. "The fact is that I was selfish when I married you. I knew you deserved better. I knew I was using you and I still did it. But I think it's clear now that it was a mistake. I'll never change. This life will never let me."

"What are you saying, Harry?"

He shoved his hands in his pockets. "I'm saying you tried your best, darling, but even you can't save my soul. There's no use trying. You saw me that night. You believe I'm one man, a good man, but I'm not. And no scribbles in a journal will change that."

Ruthie's knees shook. She was finding it harder and harder to stand her ground. But her legs were strong, and her determination even stronger. "I know you. You're better than this."

"Really?" Harry asked bitterly. "Even though you believe I only married you for charity? Even though you honestly think I wanted you because you made me feel safe?"

Ruthie bit her lip, staring at the floor. "I don't believe that. You lie to yourself because you're afraid. You're afraid to see who you really are. I know you care for me. I know your affections have grown since we married—"

"My affections haven't grown!" Harry slammed his hand to his chest and balled his lapel up into his fist. "They were always this size, so fucking big I worry that any second my fucking heart might beat out of my chest. But it doesn't matter now. I don't need you anymore. I'm a lost cause and I'm never going to be the man you deserve."

"You're not even trying," Ruthie cried. "You promised me you would never stop."

Harry sighed haggardly. "I'm too old and too tired, darling. Besides, I'm giving you your ultimate freedom, Ruthie. You don't have to stay here anymore, in the same room, in the same club, with the same people. Go out and experience the world. Go out and be the person you want to be. Isn't that what you always wanted?"

He strode to the door and held it open for her. Ruthie couldn't look at him as she walked by. But she couldn't leave without saying one more thing. "I don't know what I want anymore."

Chapter Twenty-Two

THE WALLS WERE too goddamn thin.

They'd been singing all afternoon. Harry had to give them credit—those two little Irish girls knew a wide variety of songs, and he'd managed to block them out for the better part of the day. But when he left the club early that night and retreated to his room, frustrated and annoyed by everyone who'd crossed his path, he found he couldn't ignore the tiny voices anymore. The song wafting through the walls hit him with something tragically familiar, and he was too exhausted to stop it.

Soft and terribly mournful, the sound was like a melody from one of Harry's dreams. And it woke something deep inside him, a hopeful memory, a sparkling memory that tickled just at the border of his mind. It was the smell of green that sometimes struck him in the morning, the image of life and possibility.

Harry's feet moved before he could stop them. He left his room and walked down the corridor to stand outside the door. The singing was louder there, the words clearer. He rested his head on the wood and closed his eyes as the strong, high voice carried the song into the night.

"*...your offer, sir, is very good, and I thank you, said I. But I cannot be your son-in-law, and I'll tell you the reason why...*"

Emotions swelled as the words were called up inside Harry.

Like a gift from a fairy at his birth, they felt like they'd been a part of him from his very beginning. They leapt off his tongue as he opened his mouth to sing along. *"Although we at a distance are, and the seas between us roar, yet I'll be constant, Peggy Bawn, to thee forever more."*

The door flew open, and Harry stopped himself from falling on his face just in time. Two little girls with matching dresses and distrustful expressions stared back at him.

"We weren't being too loud," the younger one said firmly. "Mam told us not to be too loud, so don't you be telling her that we were."

Harry found his first real smile in days. "You weren't too loud." He shoved his hands in his pockets, telling himself to leave, but, fool that he was, he didn't listen.

"You're the man who owns this place," the older sister said. "The one with the pretty wife."

"That's right."

"I'm Orla. This is my sister, Maeve. Our mother will be back soon, but you won't be telling her that we were too loud."

Harry couldn't tell if it was a question or a statement, but by the way Orla raised her little eyebrow at him, he guessed the latter. "No, I won't."

Orla's mouth screwed up to the side of her face. She gave her sister a look before returning to him. "Are you here to kick us out?"

Harry shook his head. "No. I just wanted to hear your singing. You have a beautiful voice."

"She knows," Maeve said, causing her older sister to hit her with an elbow.

"I like to sing," Orla told Harry. "You have a good voice too."

"Thank you. You sing a lot. I like it."

Orla hugged her chest, shy at the compliment. "Mam knows so many songs. Do you know any songs from home?"

Harry shook his head. "I didn't think so, but I remember that one. My mother used to sing it to me when I was much younger than you."

Maeve cocked her head to the side, squinting up at him. "Are you really from Kilkenny? Sometimes you sound like it, and sometimes you don't."

"I don't know where I'm from anymore. Or who I am," he replied hoarsely.

"Have you forgotten, then?"

Harry shrugged.

For some reason, that seemed to make sense to the girls, who nodded like wise old women. "Mam says one day we're probably going to forget Wexford," Maeve said. "That's why she makes us sing all her songs. She says we have to try to remember so it always stays with us. Mam worries about that a lot."

"Your mam is right," Harry said sadly. "You probably will forget one day."

"And then will we be sad like you?"

"No," he said. "You don't have to worry about that. You'll never be sad like me." He nodded at the girls. "You have each other. You have your ma and your auntie and your granny and granda. They love you, so you don't have to be sad."

"You have your wife," Maeve pointed out. "Where is Miss Ruthie? We miss her. She plays with us sometimes and braids our hair. She tells us stories about her little sister."

The reminder of his wife brought back a fresh round of pain. Why hadn't he done more to bring her sister to visit her? Why hadn't he noticed that she missed her? Because he was a selfish bastard who only thought of himself. Well, he'd remedied that. She could spend as much time with her loved ones as she wished now. In fact, at the moment she was on her way to Bath to play in her cricket exhibitions.

He'd done the right thing, letting her go. Harry hated living with himself; how could anyone else think any different?

"She's gone now. You won't be seeing her anymore."

"Why not?" Orla asked, standing on her tiptoes in alarm. "Is she dead? Did she go up to heaven like our pa?"

"No, she's not dead. Just gone."

Orla's eyes narrowed. "She left you, then? What did you do? Do you take to the bottle too much? Was she tired of you chasing other women?"

A rusty laugh escaped his chest. "No, none of those things."

"What was it, then?"

Harry bobbed a shoulder helplessly. "I'm just different."

"Different?"

"Too different," he said.

"Sometimes I cry because the other kids say we're different," Maeve replied. "But then Mam dries my eyes and tells me to yell back, 'I'm not different, I'm Irish!'"

Harry laughed again. It was easier this time. "Your mam is a very smart woman. You're lucky to have her."

Maeve perked up. "You can marry her now. Be our pa. We don't mind that you're different."

"I'm sorry, little one," he said, pulling the girl's braid gently. "I'm still married, remember?"

"But she left you."

"She didn't leave me. I let her go. I lost her, really."

Orla planted her hands on her hips. "Then go find her."

"Is it really that easy?" Why did everything sound so reasonable coming from a child's lips?

They nodded in unison.

"And what if she doesn't want to be found?"

Orla shrugged. "You won't know unless your try. And it doesn't look like you're trying to me."

Harry scowled. "It's harder than you think."

She cocked her head. "Because you're different?"

"No," he answered slowly. "Because I'm not a good man."

Maeve shook her head. "Well, there's no helping that. But as Granda says, even black hens lay white eggs."

"And what does that mean?"

Orla started to close the door. "It means, man from Kilkenny, even bad men do good sometimes, like marrying Miss Ruthie. So go fetch your wife. It's obvious you miss her. You look like shite."

Harry stuck his hand out to stop her from shutting the door in his face. "Aren't you at least going to wish me luck? What would your granda say about that?"

Orla thought for a moment, scratching her head. Finally, she looked Harry straight in the eye, somber as a poet. "He'd probably say that you're a damn fool for taking advice from us. And then...good luck to you, sir. May you be in heaven a half an hour before the devil knows you're dead."

Chapter Twenty-Three

RUTHIE NODDED TO the crowd of spectators as she walked off the field. She painted a smile on her face and tried to enjoy the attention the cricket players were receiving. Her teammates didn't seem to have that problem. Lady Everly took the adulation and applause like a queen accepting her due, and Maggie was practically flying with all the waving her arms were doing.

The first exhibition game had been a resounding success. The people of Bath had come out in their thousands to watch the London Ladies Cricket Club take on their local girls. Ruthie had thought the townspeople would be against them, wanting their local team to put the Londoners in their places, but once the match began and both teams exhibited strength and talent, the crowd split its admiration equally, relishing an afternoon of sun and sport. It didn't matter that women were on the pitch, only that good cricket was being played.

Lady Everly graciously shook yet another insistent young girl's hand before catching up to Ruthie's side. "I hope you don't mind my saying, Mrs. Holmes," she began in her serene tone, "but you played marvelously today. I don't know what came over you."

Ruthie flushed. She'd hit for thirty-six runs and didn't make one error in the field. Her lungs still stung from all the effort. "I'm sorry about that one wicket," Ruthie said, not sounding as guilty as she would have liked.

"Yes." The lines around Mrs. Everly's mouth tightened. "The ball was coming right toward me. I called to everyone that I would catch it. Did you hear me?"

"Yes," Ruthie admitted, "but I couldn't stop myself. I just knew I was going to catch it. I wanted the ball."

Lady Everly's mouth relaxed. "It's quite all right. Assertiveness is needed, and we all lose our head sometimes in the rush of the game." Her voice sharpened. "Just don't make a habit of it."

"I won't," Ruthie said quickly.

Together, the ladies made their way to the edge of the field, where a tent had been set up with refreshment tables for the players and spectators. The local team didn't have a pitch of their own yet, so Samuel had suggested the match take place on the grounds of the Earl of Warren's estate, where they were staying.

The sprawling country pile sat high against rich, rolling green fields and abundant, ripe farmland. An elegant, manicured park and imaginative, exotic gardens surrounded the great Baroque house, along with two idyllic ponds and countless meandering walking paths. It was a nature lover's dream, and Ruthie regretted that the team wouldn't have more time to explore it—especially since Harry had informed her that it was technically his...and hers. Her team only been in Bath for five days and were set to move on to Exeter in the morning for the next round of matches. Ruthie knew that this was most likely the only time she would ever spend in this gorgeous home and couldn't help but mourn it like a small death. Much like she was mourning her short marriage.

Lady Everly handed Ruthie a glass of punch from one of the tables. The tent seemed even louder than the field, since all the players gathered around one another, talking at once. Ruthie noticed how different the atmosphere was from a ball or other formal gatherings that ladies were used to spending time together at. Conversations ran the gamut from preferred batting stances to sore muscles—topics that mothers usually frowned upon when eligible bachelors were nearby, searching for dance partners.

Lady Everly surveyed the charming scene and took a sip of her punch. A few years older than Ruthie, the widow had always been friendly toward her, but vaguely aloof. Ruthie could never scrape past the surface of the austere woman, nor did she believe Mrs. Everly wanted her to.

"How did you find Bath?" the lady asked. "This was your first time, wasn't it?"

"It was," Ruthie replied, irritated by the stabbing sensation that pricked at her heart. Would it ever stop? "I enjoyed it immensely. The architecture…the pace… I can't wait to come again, take more time exploring."

The lady nodded in approval. "I thought the same when I first came here. Perhaps your husband will bring you back for a longer trip."

Ruthie's smile was weak. She'd only told Anna about that horrible night with Harry and her brother and wasn't ready to inform the rest of the group yet. What would she say to them, anyway? *She* hardly knew where she stood with her husband. Their relationship seemed irrevocably broken, but that didn't necessarily mean their marriage was over. Most couples lived together for years in polite disdain. But Ruthie couldn't imagine that tepid future. She wouldn't spend her years tiptoeing around the Lucky Fish avoiding Harry's ambivalence. And there was no reason to think he wanted that either. As he'd told her, his life was small. He didn't have room for people he couldn't tolerate. Perhaps Ruthie would end up in the Belgravia house after all.

"Yes," she said. Her forced smile was beginning to hurt. "Maybe we'll come back. That would be nice."

Lady Everly took another sip of her punch and gazed out toward the gardens. As usual, her expression was placid. Ruthie had only ever seen her ruffled or vexed when she spoke of her ex-teammates from the matrons club, who had forced her to leave after her husband had died. But Ruthie thought she saw something in the lady's expression, a restless heartache that Ruthie could only understand now that she'd experienced her own.

"Does it ever get easier?" she asked softly. Her arm grazed the lady's as they stood shoulder to shoulder away from the others. "Being alone, I mean."

The young widow shook her head wistfully. "I'm not alone."

"No, I meant—"

"I know what you meant," Lady Everly replied. Her eyes narrowed against the retiring orange sun. She reached for her necklace and rubbed the small heart pendant between her finger and thumb as if conjuring a vision.

"I'm sorry," Ruthie said. "I overstepped." She ducked her head, ready to give the woman her peace, but Lady Everly spoke again.

"My husband was a good man, my oldest friend. He's always with me even though it hurts sometimes to think of him. So I'm afraid my answer isn't very helpful. Some days are hard, and some days are...less hard. You simply must endure."

Ruthie nodded. A month before, she never would have approached the woman in this way, but something had changed in her. She valued Lady Everly not just as a teammate, but as an equal, which made it easier to create this intimacy and ultimately accept it. "Thank you," she said, "for being honest with me. It sounds like you had a lovely marriage."

Lady Everly laughed. "It wasn't always so. At times, I found our marriage to be very...*trying*. But as I've grown older and had time to think about it, I've come to learn that marriage is difficult because people are difficult. And my husband was a complicated man. There were so many layers to him that I wish I could have asked him about, tried harder to understand. But I suppose that's life. It's only human for people to hide parts of themselves away, create disguises to protect their hearts. I do. You do. Everyone in that tent does, even if they don't want to admit it. I think the key is to find someone who isn't afraid to get to the very heart of you. If you do that, you won't regret anything."

"Do you have regrets, Lady Everly?"

The widow's smile was wan. She reminded Ruthie of her mother, beautiful and statuesque, regal, with a hint of the coldness that only life could create. "Oh, my dear Mrs. Holmes, what do you think?" she asked.

RUTHIE COULDN'T SIT idly by any longer. She'd once declared to her husband that she refused to have anything less than a real marriage. Then why had she been so quick to accept defeat? Why had she allowed him to make that decision for her?

Unfortunately, Ruthie knew the answer. She'd fallen into an old, nasty habit. For years she had stepped aside, letting her mother control her life, too meek and afraid to face her. But Harry wasn't Lady Celeste, nor had he done anything to make her fear him. Harry was her partner. He was her companion. And he was her love.

If Ruthie had learned anything from her cricket match that morning, it was that she *wanted* the ball. And she could withstand the pressure and weight of it.

Harry Holmes could tell himself he didn't need his wife until he was blue in the face. It didn't matter. Because Ruthie knew the truth. He loved her. He wanted her. Just as she wanted him.

And she wasn't giving up on them without a fight.

As her teammates clustered together in the drawing room, putting their feet up and relaxing before they had to dress for dinner, Ruthie made a beeline upstairs. She wanted nothing more than to hop on the first train back to London to surprise Harry and force him to speak to her, force him to understand that she would never stop trying, but she couldn't desert her team. They were already dangerously short on players as it was, with Myfanwy, Jennifer, and Anna stuck on the sidelines due to their delicate conditions.

Leaving was not an option. But Ruthie couldn't wait either. A letter would have to do. With a single-minded focus, she burned a path to her room and dashed toward the little writing desk looking out to the pond. She found a pencil and paper in the drawer and flopped into the chair, ready to pour her heart onto the page.

"I've never seen you move so fast in your life. Where's the fire, darling?"

Ruthie hopped off the chair at the voice, barely saving herself from falling on the floor. She twirled to the bed, where Harry Holmes was lying back like he owned it, comfortable and relaxed with his ankles crossed and his hands tucked behind his head.

"Harry?" she exclaimed. "What... What are you... Here! You're here!"

His eyes twinkled at her inarticulateness, and Ruthie shot to the bed. Without a second's pause, she jumped on the surprised man and landed kiss after kiss on his face. "You're here. You're here," she kept repeating in between kisses. "I can't believe it. How did you do it?"

Harry raised his hands gently, trying to create enough space to speak. "Well, I certainly didn't fly."

Ruthie laughed and sat back on her ankles. Harry looked like Harry. His black hair was combed neatly off his forehead and his chin sparkled from a fresh shave. But on closer inspection, the bags under his eyes were prominent and his cheeks had sunk deeper in the days since she'd been away. "You took the train?"

"Of course I did."

"And how was it?"

"How do you think?" he said, shifting as if he was still in the distressing confines. "It was like being stuffed in a fast-moving, smelly shoe. I hated every second of it. Well, not every second. It became tolerable once the scenery changed. It was actually quite fun after that."

Ruthie wanted to leave the next question unsaid, but she'd always wonder if she didn't get it out of her. "And you did it for me? You left the city…for me?"

Harry scowled. "I certainly didn't do it for my health. This horrid man sitting behind me was coughing so hard I'm surprised he didn't lose a lung in my lap. It was revolting. But I…I couldn't stay away." He reached up and tucked a piece of her loose hair behind her ear.

He wasn't wearing his gloves.

Ruthie cocked her head, her lips forming a sly smile. "What's different about you?" she asked, remembering the day he'd found her in the park without her bonnet. "You look…incomplete, for some reason."

Harry's arms wrapped around her, and he hauled her into his lap. "I am incomplete. I've been living half a life since you left. I've come to beg for it back. And, according to two little girls, I look like shite." His expression sobered, and Ruthie could feel his fight for composure and calm as she straddled him. She placed her palm on his chest, hoping to curb his anxiety.

Slowly, with great intention, he held her hands to his lips and kissed the inside of her wrist.

Ruthie was touched.

"But I won't allow you to forgive me this easily, Ruthie," he said. "I came here perfectly prepared to fight for you. Make me beg. Ask me for anything. Tea with queen, remember? I'll feed, clothe, and house every Irishman who lands on these shores hoping for a better life. And it will have nothing to do with my eternal soul. I'll only do it for you. I love you."

Ruthie couldn't see her husband anymore. Her eyes were filled with tears. Harry reached for her face. He held her cheek in his palm, stroking his thumb back and forth over her jaw.

"This isn't hard for me, Ruthie. In fact, it's easy. You make it easy. I realized that don't need to hide from you. I don't need to try so hard not to react. With you, I can just be."

"I know," she said, leaning into his chest, capturing his lips and his words, drinking them into her body where they would forever be a part of her. "I love everything about you. There's nothing to be ashamed of, nothing to ever worry about when we're together. I'll keep you safe, my love. I'll keep you safe from everyone."

Harry took a lock of her hair and caressed its ends with his fingertips. His face was raw and open, like he were a child noticing all the colors of the sunset for the first time. "I'm not afraid of dying alone, darling," he said softly before bringing his gaze back to hers. "I'm afraid of living alone without you. It terrifies me more than death ever could. I wrote about our marriage in my ledger not because I thought I was doing *you* good. You were a gift that I gave to myself. I won't allow you to think any differently. Can you accept that? Can you accept how dear you are to me? How important?"

Ruthie nodded, too choked up to form an answer. She searched for the handkerchief Harry always kept in his pocket and blew her nose into it before wiping the tears from her face. She was a mess, but her reflection was so bright and perfect in his happy eyes. And it was there that she finally saw the Ruthie that she wanted to be—*his*.

And she was beautiful.

Harry accepted the handkerchief back and returned it to his coat pocket. They gave each other the space and time to stare at one another. There were no anxious looks or darting, embarrassed glances. Ruthie allowed her husband to take in the memory, and hoped that it would be the first of many more for him to cherish as they grew old together.

Then he lifted his hand and did something she'd wanted him to do from the first time she'd met him. Harry imprinted himself on his skin as he traced the contours of his face. His fingers didn't shake as they rode the pointy ridge of her jaw, the long, straight slope of her nose. She opened herself completely and could feel him color in the shades of gray under her eyes and fill the lines bracketing her mouth. His touch made her whole again. His touch made her alive.

But, as ever, Ruthie wanted more.

She slid his jacket off his shoulders and undid the five buttons of his waistcoat. She nudged Harry to lift his arms, and she lifted his shirt off, so he was bare to the waist.

Pink and white scars slashed his chest, though the black, curly hair managed to disguise most of them. However, Ruthie wouldn't let them hide from her. She swept her fingers over all the places that had caused him pain in his life, giving ample attention to his side, where the *almost*-straight line from her stitches stood out from the others, still a deeper shade of red, in need of time and patience to truly heal. Solemnly, she kissed it. Harry's stomach jumped and flexed beneath her lips, and his hands latched on to her arms.

Ruthie giggled, raising a brow. "You're ticklish?" she asked, not having seen that coming.

Harry's cheekbones were apple-tinted; his forehead was slick with a thin layer of sweat. He was trying so hard for her. He'd told her it would be easy, but Ruthie knew it couldn't be. A person couldn't change their core overnight, no matter how much they wanted to.

But whatever Harry was willing to give would always be enough, because it would always be everything he could.

He seized her mouth while she giggled. The heat of the moment took over, and Harry leaned Ruthie back, giving her his weight. She tried to wrap her legs around his hips, desperate to feel all of him, but his busy hands waylaid her. He stripped her of her clothing, and only then, when she was naked and free underneath him, did he rise from the bed and rid himself of his trousers.

Ruthie grinned at this lovely man who was finally giving her this gift. He was thick and strong, tall and confident before her, with muscles that traveled in sleek, roping lines down his body.

He lifted one pointed brow and matched her grin. "Have you seen enough, wife?"

She shook her head, blushing at her blatant hunger. "If I say no? What if I told you that I like to watch?"

"Do ya?" he asked softly, his accent coming through. "Do ya like to watch?"

Nerves gathered in the pit of her stomach. Ruthie had only been joking, but her husband wasn't. She worried where this might take her, and if she'd be brave enough to follow.

She mustered her courage, coming up on her elbows, crossing one leg over the other. "I don't know. I've never been given the chance before. I should take it," she decided. "I'm going to ask you to do things, things that give you pleasure. Can you do that for me?"

"Lass, you know the answer to that," Harry replied instantly. His voice was deep and hoarse, and it made Ruthie's toes curl in the air.

She ran her tongue over her bottom lip. "Then touch yourself, Harry. Show me how you do it when I'm not with you. Show me what feels good."

A shudder ran through him as his hand lowered to his shaft, already hard and swollen. He rubbed it lazily with his palm while he stared at Ruthie, his sinful green eyes daring her to go on.

When she didn't say more, Harry's movements came faster as his fist pumped the length of his shaft. Velvety sounds erupted from his chest, and the tendons of his neck strained.

Ruthie uncrossed her legs and scooted to the edge of the bed. Harry slowed as she came closer, completely stopping when she reached out and took him in her hand. She mimicked his hold, and when she squeezed, Harry groaned, dropping his head back in ecstasy.

"I can't take this any more, wife," he rasped, cupping Ruthie's face and forcing it to look at him. Naked desire reflected back to her. *Her* naked desire. "I want you."

Without releasing him, Ruthie settled back on the bed, guiding him inside the apex of her thighs. Their lips skimmed as he entered her, slowly and reverently. Harry filled her body. He filled her heart and her soul.

And she did the same to him.

Their passion soon took over, and their bodies rocked as one. Their hands weren't as tame. Harry left no space on her body untended to. He worshipped the ridge of her collarbone with his tongue and kissed the skin behind her ears. When he took her breast in his mouth, he massaged the other with his palm. He couldn't get enough.

He was knowing his wife.

And when the moment came upon them, when their senses screamed and their spines curved and every ounce of energy felt used and depleted in the holy quest for fulfillment, Ruthie heard music in her heart. Her husband had sung an ancient song that her body had always known.

She still didn't believe in destiny, but at that thrilling moment, she knew it must have always been written in the stars.

Chapter Twenty-Four

THE HOUSE STIRRED the following morning, forcing the exhausted couple awake. Harry stretched his legs and arms out in the small bed, his feet easily peeking out over the edge of the frame.

Ruthie yawned next to him and curled into his side. Harry laid his arm around her shoulder, relieved that the magic hadn't disappeared through the night. Touching others would always be a challenge for him, but as long as he could hold Ruthie, he didn't care.

He kissed the top of her head, filling his lungs with the rosemary smell he'd missed. He would never allow the herb on his food; however, he couldn't get enough of it on his wife. "I demand we take the master suite in the next house," he said casually. "Just because I'm away from the city doesn't mean my comfort has to suffer."

Ruthie's head popped up and she rested it in her hand. "Do you mean to say you're traveling with the team? You'll stay with us until the end?"

Harry shrugged, nearly upsetting her head from its perch. "They're my homes. I should be the one to enjoy them, dammit. Besides," he said, sneaking in for a swift kiss, "I heard my wife played the game of her life yesterday. I'd hate to miss a star on the rise."

Ruthie toyed with the hair on his chest, twisting it around her finger. "But what about the club? You're always so busy. And Vine? Isn't there something we can do? I can't stand the fact that he's still out there. It's unnerving."

Harry placed two fingers over her lips. "Ernest can handle the club, and I've told Holly and Colleen exactly where we're going to be and when so they can keep me informed. Hiring Colleen was the best decision. The woman is terribly efficient. Not to mention her children are...insightful. And as for Vine..." He shook his head, refusing to let his anger and disappointment over that situation ruin their morning. "He'll emerge eventually. I've got most of London searching for him. He can't stay hidden for long."

With a frown, Ruthie laid her head back on Harry's chest, though her fingers increased their fidgeting, tickling him something fierce.

"Wife," Harry said, "stop that. If your hands are desperate to move this morning, I can think of a much better place for them."

Ruthie's lips curled, and she placed a wet kiss on his chest. And then she continued to move lower down his body. "Show me," she said.

THE FOLLOWING WEEKS flew by in ways that Harry could never have imagined. He and Ruthie were like carefree children as they toured with the club, eating up the new experiences and scenery like—in Harry's case—a fresh bowl of plain carrots. Try as she might, by the time they'd reached their last stop in Manchester, his wife still couldn't get him to finish his meal with a dessert. Gelatinous goops of any flavor and creams, however cloudlike, would always be off the menu.

Despite his obstinate eating habits, Harry was proud of himself. He'd been an excellent travel partner. Yes, he still took longer than anyone else to relax on the train, and yes, there was that bumpy, frightful stint when he spent a half-hour repeating "we're going to die" under his breath, but besides that, he'd been a wonderful success.

Especially as he continued to surprise his wife, who boldly liked to announce that she knew him so well. Harry Holmes might enjoy his habits and routines, but that didn't mean life with him was boring.

He was on a mission to prove to his wife that it was anything but.

He would never forget her face when her younger sister, Julia, showed up at his estate in Manchester, three days before the cricket club's last match. Nor would he ever forget the wild and imaginative way she'd chosen to thank him for the gesture.

That night, as they'd lain together in the former master suite of Viscount Harrington (a degenerate gambler, to say the least) and Harry had finally caught his breath, he recounted how he'd been able to navigate around Lady Celeste's spite.

"Mother never let me leave London," Ruthie said, luxuriously draped over her husband. "She used to say that nothing exciting ever happened outside the city." He yelped as the minx bit his neck. "She was wrong."

Harry took her hand and held it against his heart. "It wasn't that difficult to persuade her. I merely told her that if she didn't let me help her financially and allow you to see Julia, then I would take her son to court for attempted murder. And I would win."

"That was it?"

"That was it," he said. "I have to admit, getting her to take the money took some coaxing, but she came around in the end, and I actually think she was relieved to have the matter out of her control."

"I have no doubt," Ruthie said quietly. "She held such control over all of us for so long. I used to think she enjoyed it, but maybe

I was wrong. Maybe it was exhausting and terrifying for her, too."

"I'm sure it was," Harry replied, kissing the top of her head. "And she also told me to tell you to pay her a visit when we are back in town."

"She did?" Ruthe laughed bitterly, but she couldn't fool Harry. He could hear the sadness she was trying to mask. "What did you have to give her for that? I suppose she took you up on your offer of tea with the queen?"

"No," he said. "She didn't ask for anything. The lady said she only wanted you."

"Only wanted me?" Hope replaced the hurt in her voice.

"Yes, my love," Harry said. He turned to his side and hugged her. "It's the one thing we have in common."

THE ONLY DOWNSIDE of the trip was that Julia was not allowed to travel alone. Harry had recommended Reggie to chaperone the young girl to Manchester, but Lady Celeste wouldn't budge on her dreadful son. It seemed that the lady still believed nothing exciting happened outside the city, and that that mundane environment was just the place for Lord Mason.

Harry did his best to avoid him, still firmly concluding that if hell existed, it was most certainly a place of never-ending awkward encounters. And the last thing that Harry wanted was to feel sorry for the lazy bastard. However, when he stumbled upon his mopey brother-in-law in the stables the afternoon after his arrival, Harry couldn't help but shudder. Mason Waitrose's face looked like it'd been run over by a four-horse carriage.

Harry almost got away with it. When he strode into the stables and spotted Mason petting a speckled mare in her stall, he stopped in his tracks, hoping to backtrack without being noticed. But just like in London, everyone noticed Harry Holmes when he entered a room.

Mason turned to him, and his face grew red, or at least Harry thought it did; it was hard to tell with the bruising that still marred the baron. One eye was better off than the other, but Harry was relieved to see that Mason could open the other as well, although only slightly. He still believed that Mason had got what he deserved, but his wife had voiced her worries over it.

The baron cleared his throat. "I'll leave," he said in a tone that still wasn't as humble as Harry would have liked, but marginally better than before.

Harry waved a hand. "It's fine. I was just cutting through. I was told there was a chapel in this direction; however, I can't seem to find the damn thing."

"In need of some forgiveness?" Mason chuckled, but it died quickly. "I apologize. That was rude of me."

Harry shook his head. "It's fine. I know you're an ass, and I'm also aware a man can't change overnight, however much he might want to."

Mason snorted, turning back to the mare. "What makes you think I want to?" Despite his harsh tone, he had a soft touch, and the horse responded in kind, allowing Mason to stroke the velvety pink middle of her nose.

"I can spot hate. I can also spot when a man is disappointed in himself. All too well."

"What do I have to be disappointed about?" Mason asked. "My sister married a rich man, and now the family is saved. All our money problems are over." He arched a brow at Harry, though the act made him grimace. "I assume my debts will be cleared at the club?"

"I suppose they have to be."

Mason nodded, his expression grim. He rifled inside his pocket, took out a few small carrots, and offered them to the delighted horse.

"You're good with them," Harry said, gesturing to the animal. "I barely know how to ride. I've never liked horses much—the smell always got to me."

Mason threw him a confused look. "I thought the Irish were mad for their horses."

Harry shrugged. "I'm a different sort of Irishman, I guess." His own words struck him. He couldn't remember ever referring to himself that way…Irish. It felt odd, but not wrong. Like most things in his life lately, he would have to give it time, acclimate to it.

Mason finished feeding the mare and gave her one last pat before dusting off his hands. "I've always loved them. You know, I used to think I could talk to them. Before my father sold ours, I would spend hours with them having entire conversations, knowing in my bones that they understood me. I might be insane, but I think they were the only things that ever did." He lifted his shoulder sheepishly, embarrassed that he'd offered that part of himself to Harry. "Well, I'll leave you to it. You're very lucky, Mr. Holmes. These are fine stables. Viscount Harrington had a good eye for horses. Some of the best thoroughbreds in the country are now in your hands."

"Luck had nothing to do with it."

Mason bowed his head. "As you say."

He was just about to make his escape from the uncomfortable meeting when Harry stopped him.

"What if I told you that your debts at the club weren't paid off?" he said.

Mason spun around. "What are you talking about? My sister would never allow that."

"She will," Harry countered firmly, "if I give her a good enough reason."

"And what's that?" Mason asked, crossing his arms. "You want to watch me dangle from your hook a little while longer? Well, go ahead. I deserve it. I know it, but I'll warn you, I'm tired of being the clown. I'm sure my misery won't be half as entertaining as it used to be."

Harry threw up his hands. "My God, man, you tried to *kill* me. Don't play the victim now."

"I apologized for that!"

"No, you didn't!"

Mason's head jerked straight. "Oh... Well, you know..." His voice dropped. "I'm sorry for pointing a gun in your direction."

"You mean for almost shooting me?"

Mason rolled his eyes. "I never would have shot you. I lacked the courage."

"Well, don't sound sorry about it!" Harry said. He raked a hand through his hair and reminded himself to tell Ruthie again how much he loved her. He had to, to put up with her idiot brother. "I accept your apology," he grumbled. "Now, are you too depressed to work?"

"*Work?*" Mason spat out the word like Harry would spit out souffle.

"Yes, work," Harry said, nodding to the stalls. "I had no idea the horses were so valuable. It seems a waste for them to sit here not doing what they were bred to do."

Mason crept further into the stables, his expression wary but hopeful. "What are you saying?"

"I'm saying I need a good man to manage my horses. I don't just have these. I must have plenty of others getting fat and bored at my other estates. Find them, train them, or hire people who will. Or go back to your worthless existence in London living under your mother's thumb. I don't care."

Harry had him. He could see it in the man's good eye—and his bad one.

"You'd let me do it?" Mason asked. "You'd really let me run your stables? You don't even know me. I could have no idea what I'm doing."

"If you're shite, I'll tell you to fuck off. I can promise you that."

Mason laughed, and it was the first time that Harry had seen him look genuinely happy and sober. Because it turned out that the man didn't need a destiny—he needed a purpose.

"But wait a second," Mason went on just as Harry was about

to look for that blasted chapel. "You never gamble on horses. I've heard you say that only fools who want to lose everything bet on them."

"I'm not betting on them," Harry returned. "I'm betting on you. Now, don't make me regret it."

Chapter Twenty-Five

H ARRY SAVED HIS best surprise for the end.

On the last day of the trip, after the London Ladies Cricket Club had successfully played (and soundly trounced) the local team in Manchester and then celebrated with them, Harry held his wife's hand and guided her down the garden path on the grounds of their estate.

Ruthie followed him blindly—literally, because Harry had tied one of his old neckties around her eyes before they set out.

He ordered her to keep it on even after they'd reached the outside of the chapel. He left her there alone while he ran inside to check that everything was just right. He'd screwed up one wedding to the woman of his dreams; he wouldn't be doing it twice.

His bare hands trembled when they touched Ruthie, removing the cloth from her head, but this time for reasons very different than before.

She rubbed her face, dashing her wheat-colored hair off her freckles. "Why do you look so nervous?" she teased. "Should I be worried?"

Harry kissed her smile, lingering on her lips because he'd learned they were the safest place in his world. "You never have to worry with me. You know that."

She twisted her neck and looked around them. "Then why are we here? Oh, this is lovely, isn't it?"

It was, Harry had to admit. He'd been lucky. The chapel was as quaint and charming as the rest of the ground, reminding him of the gingerbread house from the fairytale he'd heard Orla and Maeve reading through the walls one night. Ivy covered most of the gray stone, but each rectangular window at its side was filled with dazzling, jewel-toned stained glass.

Without answering, Harry towed Ruthie toward the entrance. He stopped to kiss her one more time before he opened the door and ushered her inside.

And then he realized he would have to push her down the aisle, because her feet had decided to stop working. Ruthie froze when everyone in the chapel turned to welcome them, all wearing grins as wide as Harry's.

Not taking her eyes off her teammates and her siblings that Harry had gathered for the event, she reached for him. "Why are they… What is everyone… Why are they all looking at me that way?" she stammered.

Harry squeezed her hand proudly. "They're looking at us, darling," he said, leading her down the aisle, where a very somber and very *sober* priest was waiting for them. "We're getting married. Again. But the right way this time."

She stopped him before they made it to the end. "But we were married the right way."

Harry managed to keep his voice down, but he couldn't hold back the curse. "Dammit, Ruthie, you deserved so much better than that blasted farce. Like a priest who wasn't sick all over, and one who actually got your name right. Did you ever think about that? I'm not even married to you. I'm pretty sure that I'm married to someone named Ruby Winrose!"

Ruthie didn't laugh, but the blue of her eyes sparkled brighter than the ruby ring she wore on her finger. The ring that Harry had given her. He'd done just about everything wrong that day, but at least he'd got that part right.

Her smile was gentle. "I love you, Harry," she said.

"I love you," Harry said, tugging her once more. "But now no more talking, because I want to get this over and done with."

"Over and down with?" she squawked as she stumbled after him. "Whatever happened to getting married the right way?"

Harry settled Ruthie in front of the priest and leaned toward her ear. "There's a lot to do, my love. Because I also have to make up for our wedding night, and I have a feeling that's going to take a while."

Ruthie's blush covered her face. "You don't have to make up for that," she whispered, darting a nervous glance to everyone watching them. "That was wonderful."

"Yes, but this day is about making everything better, and I'm determined, wife. I'm very determined not to disappoint you."

"You've never disappointed me, and you never will."

"Tell me that again in fifty years when we're old and gray."

"I will," Ruthie said.

The priest waved his hands in front of the couple. "We're not there yet, Miss Waitrose," he said with an impish wink. "But we'll get there soon enough. Can everyone stand so we can get started?"

The ceremony wasn't as quick as Harry would have liked. That was the problem with sober priests, he realized. They tended to have more to say on the subject of marriage and had no issue standing for long periods of time. Despite that, Harry found himself moved by the experience and let himself get lost in it. Holding Ruthie's hands, he repeated his vows from the very bottom of his heart, knowing that he would never forsake this woman. Equally, as Ruthie did the same to him, his gratitude was almost too much to bear.

Harry Holmes was a lucky man. He'd found a woman who could go toe to toe with him. Maybe Ruthie's youth was the answer to her madness. As he'd concluded the first night they'd met, only the incredibly young were foolish enough to believe they could do what they wanted, have what they wanted—that they could bend the world to their whim.

And Ruthie Waitrose had wanted him.

These were the thoughts that filled his head when he watched her repeat the priest's solemn words.

Which was why Harry didn't pay attention to a short man entering the chapel. And why Harry didn't register that, although the man had one lazy eye, the good one was squarely on him. And that was why Harry's instincts didn't kick in when the man lifted his pistol.

But this time, Harry wasn't too late.

When the shot was fired, Harry acted instantly, throwing Ruthie to the ground. As he turned to run for Vine, a searing pain knifed through the top of his arm, and he stumbled back. He knocked into the priest, who followed him to the floor, taking the brunt of the fall against the two steps leading to the altar.

People were screaming, but Harry couldn't hear anything. His mind was a whirlwind of sensations and tumbling thoughts threatening to drag him under until Ruthie came into his view. At once, the madness stilled as she reached for him. She pulled him off the priest, not relenting until he was resting in her lap.

"Are you hurt? Oh, Harry! Please tell me this isn't happening again." Ruthie sobbed, checking his body for the wound. She followed the blood to his arm, poking and prodding until he commanded her to stop.

"I'm fine. I'm fine… I think," Harry said, trying to ascertain if that was true or not. He forced himself to move the arm that vibrated with pain. He took it as a good sign that it wasn't numb. The wound smarted like a bastard, which usually told him that it wasn't as bad as it looked.

The priest confirmed it. "He missed. The bullet just grazed you." He pointed to the altar, which had a sizeable chunk taken off the corner. "It was a miracle."

Harry shook his head, craning his neck to check the wound. "It wasn't a miracle."

"It was," the priest argued. "The Lord was watching out for

me today. You saved me, sir. That bullet was coming straight at me, and you stepped in its way. You saved my life."

Harry didn't have the heart to tell the priest that he hadn't done it on purpose. He must have stepped in front of the man when he'd moved to throw Ruthie to the floor. It was a happy accident.

It was luck, not a miracle.

Ruthie helped him to his feet, and across the chapel, Harry could see Samuel Everett holding Vine's hands behind his back. Vine's face was bloody and battered, and the man could hardly stand without Samuel holding him up. Harry didn't have to check Samuel's fists to know they were covered in blood. He nodded at his friend, and Samuel nodded back before letting Vine drop to the floor with a demonstrative *thump*.

Later they would find out that Vine had followed Harry after he left London, keeping his distance, waiting for the right moment to strike. As Ruthie had guessed, he had been behind Harry's original shooting. With Harry dead, Vine planned to take over the old gang, returning to a full-time life of crime, battling Dugan and his boys for supremacy of London's streets. Some men just didn't respond well to change, and Thomas Vine was one of them.

When the commotion died down, Ruthie and Harry were the last to leave the chapel. As she helped him down the aisle, Harry regarded the detritus of the ceremony—roses broken and stomped flat on the ground, bloodstains from where he'd fallen, a reticule left behind by a startled woman—and unleashed a filthy curse.

Ruthie's eyes latched on to his. "Harry! What's wrong? Is it your arm?"

"It's not my fucking arm," he muttered.

"Then what?"

His head fell. "Why do all our weddings have to be such fucking disasters?"

Ruthie laughed and patted him lovingly on the chest. "This

wasn't a disaster. Yes, it was a bit dramatic, but Vine is caught and can't harm you anymore, and no one was hurt. You should be happy."

"Well, I'm not fucking happy," he grumbled. "I'm upset. I wanted something better for you."

"Harry." Ruthie stopped to look at him. "You're the best thing for me. I want nothing more."

"I suppose that helps," he said.

"Good," she said with a decisive nod. "And let's not forget about the most important thing to come from this day."

Harry arched a brow in question.

She smiled. "You saved a priest's life. Don't you see? Now you never have to worry. You're certainly going to heaven now."

Harry laughed and kissed the top of his wife's head. "I told you, darling, I don't worry about that anymore. Because I've been in heaven since the day I met you."

Epilogue

Dublin Port, Ireland 1855

THE LITTLE GIRL tilted her head up to Harry and wrinkled her nose. "I thought it would look different," she declared pensively, squeezing her father's hand to punctuate her disappointment. "I thought ..." Her sentence trailed off as she scrutinized the squat, rough-hewn buildings and jutting piers that meandered closer as their steamship waded cautiously into Dublin Bay Port.

Harry pulled his gaze away from the unassuming site, smiling at the five-year-old. "And just what did you think, Cara?"

His eldest daughter scrunched her brow, inspecting the landscape shrewdly, her jet-black hair whipping against her pale pink cheeks. "I'm not sure," she replied with a forlorn exhale. "I suppose I thought it would be grander, more exciting. But it looks just like Liverpool's port...only smaller."

Harry nodded. "Most ports look the same," he said, "and everything is a little smaller in Ireland. Not worse, mind you, just smaller."

Cara glanced at her father once more, her mischievous smile displaying a missing front tooth. Harry could look at the empty space now without shuddering, even find it adorable, but he hadn't initially thought so when the girl had tripped over the edge of their carpet and flew headfirst into the drawing room's marble fireplace three weeks before. Harry had never expected to have children—let alone at his age—and his three girls were hellbent on shaving years off his life.

"But you're from Ireland, Papa," Cara pointed out with a chuckle. "And you're not small."

Harry's smile faded, his expression turning winsome. "Oh, but I left Ireland a long time ago. I was barely older than yourself."

"But you always tell people you're Irish."

The wind picked up, surrounding Harry with the telltale aroma of rosemary. He hadn't noticed how tense his shoulder had been until the anticipation of his wife's presence instantly soothed him. "That's because he couldn't bear anyone thinking he's English," Ruthie said, coming up beside him with four-year-old Hannah's hand clasped in her own and Eva on her hip.

Harry kissed her cheek and took the one-year-old out of her arms, settling her against his chest. He would still rather cut off his hand rather than touch another person, but that didn't apply to his wife and children. Holding their hands, tucking them into bed at night, grazing their cheeks with his palms—they felt like the most natural things in the world.

Eva sucked on her fist greedily, her green eyes lighting up the moment she saw him. Harry and Ruthie laughed about it, but there was something wildly odd about all of his daughters sharing his black hair and green eyes. Ruthie often teased that if she hadn't carried the babies in her belly she wouldn't even know they were hers. But Harry knew all too well. Their personalities, their cleverness, their quickness to laugh, and their steely determination were all from their mother, and Harry couldn't be more grateful or prouder.

"Is it so bad to be English?" Hannah asked, nudging Cara out of the way so she could hug her father's leg. "We're English."

"You're *half* English," he replied, caressing his middle child's silky hair on the top of her head. "And that's enough."

"But what about Mama?" she returned, a hint of panic in her sweet voice. Of the three, Hannah was his worrier—which she also got from her mother.

Harry met his wife's eyes. Countless conversations had been spoken this way, with just a look and a wink, a purse of lips or an arched brow saying everything.

When Ruthie's mouth widened in amusement, Harry remembered that his daughter had asked him a question. "Your mother isn't English or Irish," he replied, speaking to his wife. "She's mine. Always was and always will be."

Harry caught Cara rolling her eyes with a silly grin, and he followed her attention back to the shoreline. It *was* a dismal sight. All weather-worn, faded wood and meandering rock walls. And yet something still struck Harry in his chest, making it tight and fluttery, apprehension and excitement sparking like lint on stone. He rubbed his lips against the baby's head, back and forth, inhaling the heavenly, powdery scent of her newness.

Ruthie leaned against the side of the ship. She wore a bonnet today, but it was small, barely there. Her freckles popped off her creamy skin. A mother of three, she still had the look of a girl he'd first met in her, up for anything, ready to conquer whatever she wanted.

"Is it how you remembered?" she asked, her gaze forward. A rush of activity heightened on the docks as workers readied for the steamship to glide into its berth.

Harry shrugged, causing Eva to gurgle and drool even more on his black jacket. "I'm not sure," he replied. "To be honest, I don't remember much, only…what I felt." He hugged his daughter, and she pushed against his chest, insisting on more space. "I remember being scared. So scared." He cocked his head to his wife, forcing a self-deprecating grin. "I'd never been on a ship before. And it felt like the journey took days—months, even."

Cara *hmphed*. "That's how *this* journey felt!"

"Oh, my little love." Harry laughed. "You have no idea. At least you got to ride on a steamship. This trip was only seven hours! My mother and I had to rely on the wind, and it took twice that time to get to Liverpool." Harry shivered at the memory. "You girls don't know how lucky you are."

Ruthie snorted. "And whose fault is that?"

Harry didn't bother to respond. He was a smart man and knew when to keep silent. Besides, his wife wasn't wrong. He did spoil his daughters. He spared no expense. They had the best of everything, and they always would. The best tutors, the best food, the best opportunities in life. They would have everything they ever wanted—even tea with the queen. He would make it happen. All they had to do was say the words. Ruthie allowed his indulgences, though she didn't always approve. For instance, she wasn't too happy about Harry buying Cara five horses for her fifth birthday. Looking back, he conceded that might have been a little too eccentric. What five-year-old needed more than four?

Ruthie lifted an eyebrow at his taciturn response and stifled a smile. "Will we go directly to the hotel, or do you want to stop at the house first? I'm sure you're as anxious to see it as I am. And it would be nice to be there when all the supplies are delivered."

Harry nodded thoughtfully. The house she referred to was Holmes House, the charity they'd begun two years before. They'd planned to purchase a small building to provide the soup kitchen and sleeping quarters for those left suffering from the famine, but in the end, Harry bought an entire warehouse. The space was needed. Contributions were coming in from all over the world to help the Irish, but it still wasn't enough. In his more pessimistic moments, Harry wondered if anything ever would be.

At first, he'd dismissed the idea of putting his name on the charity. Harry had given up believing he wouldn't be accepted into heaven anymore—his wife was going to be there, and he wouldn't spend eternity apart from her—so having his name on the charity seemed needless and sounded a bit too pretentious; however, his wife would not be swayed. Holmes House it would be, she'd declared, and her reasoning shook him. "I want people to see your name and immediately think of hope," she'd told him one night while they drifted off into each other's arms in bed. "No more fear."

Harry had made love to her then because he didn't want her to know he was incapable of speech. His wife continued to surprise him, and, he figured, she would probably never stop.

He leaned in and kissed his wife. It was hungry and sweet, and he caught the spice of her shock in his mouth, savoring the taste that was forever Ruthie. He could hear the girls *tsking* and giggling from his impulsiveness, and, again, Eva pushed at his chest to create more space for her arms to wave.

Harry pulled away slowly, enjoying Ruthie's eyelids hanging heavily over her clear, loving eyes. "Let's go to the hotel," he said firmly. "It's been a long day, and we all need a good sleep."

Ruthie's gaze narrowed. "Sleep?"

Harry winked at his wife. "Well... The girls need a good sleep. We'll sleep when we're dead."

⟫⟪

HARRY REMEMBERED THE roads, especially how bumpy and uncomfortable they made traveling all distances, long and short.

"Are we almost there?" Hannah asked the following morning, her black curls bobbing every time the carriage hit a divot in the road. She hugged her tiny stomach. "I think I'm going to be sick."

Harry pushed the curtain out of the way and looked out the window. Kilkenny had felt like a metropolis when he was a child, but with its medieval architecture and Norman roots, he considered it quaint now, even magical.

"We're almost there," he assured her, reaching across the carriage to pat her hand. "Only a few more minutes...I think."

Harry couldn't recall exactly how long the drive had been from the town center. It had felt like ages when he was younger;

however, that couldn't be the case. His mother would walk him from the cottage to the River Nore on occasion when she was in one of her better moods.

"Are you sure you want to do this?" Ruthie asked him softly. She entwined their fingers tightly, as if trying to imbue him with all her strength. "It's been so long."

Harry's jaw clenched, and he merely nodded. It *had* been a long time. Over forty years. And that was long enough. Besides, it was the whole reason for the family trip. Sure, he'd said he wanted to visit Holmes House, witness all the good it was hopefully providing, but that had only been an excuse. This day was what he'd been waiting for. This was his moment.

Ruthie sighed. "I can't believe he's still alive. I'm sorry your grandmother isn't. Are you sure he received the letter? He didn't respond. Is it right to just show up?"

"I'm sure," he said. Of course his grandfather had received the letter. Harry had paid the messenger to come back and tell him that he'd delivered it right into his old, wrinkled hands. But the sullen bastard naturally didn't respond. Fine. Good. Harry hadn't expected him to. He was going to show up anyway and knock as hard as he could on that damn door. The one that Harry hadn't been allowed to cross while his mother cried and pleaded for help so long ago.

Ruthie's voice was gentle, breaking Harry from his thoughts. "Do you know what you're going to say?"

"Yes."

He'd always known. He'd played the conversation over and over in his head his entire life. The only thing that would be missing from the picture was his grandmother, who, he'd learned, had died two years before. Harry would miss not seeing her astonished face as he stood outside the house, but he would settle for the old man's. That would be enough.

He wiped his palms on the front of his thighs. The urge to tap overwhelmed him, and his fingers started to move. Harry could sense Ruthie watching them, though she didn't say anything. It so rarely happened anymore. He hadn't outgrown the twitches and tics, but it was like he'd outgrown obsessing over them. Once he'd stopped giving them so much attention, so much power, they'd all but disappeared. Or maybe Harry just stopped noticing them now that he spent so much worrying about more important things, like his girls.

Ruthie leaned into his side. "It's going to be all right," she whispered, her breath brushing along his cheeks, forcing his eyes to shut as he let out an audible exhale.

"I know that," he said gruffly, perhaps with a little too much force.

Harry had to contain himself. It would be all right. Everything would be all right after this was done. He just had to see the old man and then this would finally be done.

But that wasn't completely true. Harry didn't just want the old man to see him—see the successful, confident, rich man he'd become—he wanted him to listen to every blistering word he said. Harry needed this closure. He needed this part of his life to die along with all the animosity and regret he'd held for his mother. Now, he saw her as a tragic figure, one whose life hadn't turned out the way she'd planned. A woman who shouldn't have been a mother; a girl who shouldn't have been deserted by her man and forgotten by her parents.

Harry would look his grandfather in the eye and ask him how he'd done it, left his only daughter to fend for herself with a bastard in tow. Now that Harry had children of his own, he couldn't fathom such callousness, such blatant disregard. He'd ask the old man how it felt to live alone in his miserable cottage with no family or joy. He'd ask the old man if he was proud that he would die alone with his misery and stubbornness.

He'd ask if it was worth it. Was it worth losing your child just because the church declared her wicked and her bastard child an oddity? Harry hadn't been an oddity; he hadn't been an abomination. He'd been a little boy who deserved love. Every child did.

The carriage stumbled to a halt. The girls all clapped even as

Hannah's complexion had turned a dismal green. Harry opened the door, fanning it to get the poor girl some air. "I want you all to stay by the carriage," he said pointedly. "I won't be long."

"You promise?" Cara asked.

He held her gaze. "I promise."

"And then we can visit the castle?"

"And then we can visit the castle."

Cara nodded. Hannah smiled as she craned her neck out the door to suck in more air.

"Good luck," Ruthie said. She squeezed his hand one more time before letting it go. "I'll—we'll—be right here if you need us."

Harry forced a smile, trying for nonchalance. "This won't take more than a second. I'll be back before you know it."

Ruthie's lips slid into a tight line, but she said nothing. What more was there to say?

Leaving the carriage door open, Harry turned toward the cottage. Small and efficient, it looked exactly as he'd remember it—almost. The whitewash on the bricks had dulled with dirt and age, and the thatch of the roof was thin near the top. Flowers that his grandmother had once tended were overgrown and meandering, and the smell of lavender clung heavily, drowning out everything else. Harry's steps were measured and purposeful. He only allowed himself a small moment of pause to let his fingers trace along a clump of blue flax growing wildly along the path.

He couldn't hear anything inside, but the chimney smoke meant someone was there. His grandfather must have seen the carriage. Whether the old man answered the door or not was up to him. Harry hadn't taken him for a coward—a bastard, but never a coward.

Harry knocked on the door. Five times. He tried to stop at three, but it couldn't be helped.

A rustling sounded through the thick wooden door. Feet shuffling. "Who the hell is it?"

Harry waited patiently, bringing his shoulders back, lifting his chin. He allowed himself to acknowledge he was nervous. He was forty-eight years old years and had been transported to being five again.

Harry had lifted his fist to knock once more when the door cracked open. A rheumy eye peeked out from the sliver with an avalanche of white eyebrows almost blocking its view.

The eye grew rounder, and slowly, very slowly, the man opened the door. Was it the shortness of his grandfather that made Harry stretch his spine even more? He'd once thought the man a giant, but the years had warped him, shriveling his body into a curved shape, with his eyesight square to Harry's chest. He had to be close to ninety. How had he survived so long? Out of spite, no doubt.

The pathetic creature appeared like a sad caricature of his former self. His skin was chalky and hung loose on his face, and his hair—once so black it carried shades of purple—was gone, with only white wisps shooting up like skinny seedlings. He wore only a shirt and pants, both tattered and old, badly in need of a wash.

Nevertheless, when his grandfather lifted his face, Harry could find the man he once was, the shrew, confident man who'd probably thought that age and dying would happen to everyone but him. Didn't we all?

"Yes?" the old man said, almost resigned, as if he were ready for Harry's speech.

Harry cleared his throat, searching for the words he'd practiced more times than he could count. He raised his chin higher. It was the same chin as his grandfather's. "Do you know who I am?"

The words came out soft—not weak, but non-threatening. Harry searched for his anger. He attempted to pull it up, not understanding why it had sunk to the deepest parts of him. It had always been right there in his reach, right on the surface of his very being. It resisted him now, evading his hold, spilling out from between his long fingers like water.

Maybe it was the way the old man looked at him. The recognition in his eye, the flash of…embarrassment, or was it shame? Guilt? His grandfather blinked quickly, and his shoulders slunk lower down his withered body.

"Do you?" Harry asked with more force, but that force took effort, and his voice broke. He ran a hand through his hair, exasperated at the childishness that was overtaking him, the desperation.

But Harry wasn't the only one affected. The old man's mouth began to quiver, his throat wobbling like he was trying to suppress a sob. His glassy eyes filled and glinted against the late morning sun. He inhaled and then let it all out in one long breath. "I know…who you…are," he said finally, his tone thin, his words skipping like a rock along a pond.

A sob lodged itself in Harry's throat. All his control and anger were slipping away in front of this feeble man. It felt like his tics. Like them, the obsession Harry held with his family was unnecessary, unhelpful. He'd given it too much power over his life.

He turned to look over his shoulder. Cara and Hannah were out of the carriage now, chasing one another around it while Ruthie and Eva watched with amusement. They were his family. They were all he needed. Why had he brought them here? What was the point of all of this?

Harry shook his head, coming back to his grandfather, who continued to watch him with curiosity and a little fear. "I'm sorry to bother you," Harry said. He nodded one last time and spun to rejoin his family.

But the words stopped him. "You're Harry Holmes," his grandfather announced, louder than he'd spoken before, as loud as his frail body would allow him. Harry paused, looking at the ground for a beat before eventually raising his gaze back to the old man.

His grandfather clutched the edge of the door, using it to stand straighter. "You're my grandson. My grandson…Harry."

The sentence struck Harry like a bolt to the chest. And yet he didn't feel any different. He was the same. Nothing had changed. And nothing would ever change if he continued to stand in front of that cottage wishing his grandfather would have been a different man. Because then, maybe, Harry would have been a different man, with a different life, with a different woman and different children to share his love.

And a reaction finally came from that thought, a visceral reaction that almost brought Harry to his knees.

He could go now. He *had* to go now.

"Thank you. Thank you for answering me," he said. And Harry returned to his family. He kissed his wife soundly on the lips and tickled his two oldest daughters back in the carriage. Harry didn't need his grandfather to tell him who he was. Harry knew who he was. He was fucking Harry Holmes. A father. A husband. Nothing more. Nothing less.

The old man's hearing wasn't as good as it used to be, but he could hear laughing and chatter as the carriage rolled away. And for the first time in a long time, he felt a weight lift. And when he closed the door, he rested his head against it and smiled.

About the Author

I'm a lifelong reader of romance novels. Some of my earliest memories are of sneaking into my mom's room at night and stealing any books I could find.

After moving around quite a bit, I've finally put down roots in New England with my two sons and husband. I've always been a writer, starting out in newspapers, but it wasn't until my sons began going to school full-time that I began working toward my dream of becoming a romance author.

I enjoy crocheting toys for my kids, hiking with my Saint Bernard, and watching Real Housewives on the couch with my very old and very fat pugs.

Milton Keynes UK
Ingram Content Group UK Ltd.
UKHW021002241024
450188UK00012B/552